# RAPTUROUS

## QUANTUM SERIES, BOOK 4

### BY: M.S. FORCE

Rapturous
A Quantum Novel
By: M.S. Force

Published by HTJB, Inc.
Copyright 2016. HTJB, Inc.
Cover Design by the Designing Women: Courtney Lopes and Ashley Lopez
Interior Layout by Isabel Sullivan, E-book Formatting Fairies
ISBN: 978-1-942295-39-6

All characters in this book are fiction and figments of the author's imagination.

*www.marieforce.com*

**The Quantum Series**

Book 1: Virtuous
Book 2: Valorous
Book 3: Victorious
Book 4: Rapturous

# CHAPTER 1

*Addie*

*Camouflage* cleaned up at the Oscars, and Hayden Roth kissed me. I'm not sure which is a bigger deal. We're surrounded by Oscar gold. Hayden won for Best Director, Flynn for Best Actor, Jasper for cinematography and all the Quantum principals for producing the year's Best Picture. They're euphoric as they celebrate at one party after another. But all I can think about is that when Hayden won, he kissed me—and he kissed me like he meant it.

He kissed me the way I've wanted him to for almost as long as I've known him, which is going on ten years now. That's how long I've wanted him. At times, and never more so than when he kissed me earlier, I've suspected he wants me, too, but neither of us has ever given in to the attraction that simmers between us.

It could be because I work for Flynn, Hayden's best friend and business partner, as well as Hayden and the other Quantum principals. Or maybe he thinks I'm too young for him, although six years isn't that big of a deal. It's not like I'm seventeen. I'm twenty-seven and fully grown, but I fear he thinks of me as the little girl I once was and not the woman I've become.

Flynn's wife, Natalie, puts her arm around my shoulders and gives me a squeeze. "Having fun?"

"Absolutely. You?"

"Best night ever. They're so happy."

"Flynn is flying high because you're here, not because of the Oscars." The two of them are wildly in love, and though I'm thrilled for my friend and boss, I'm envious, too. I want that. I want the connection they have, and I want it with a man who is perpetually unavailable to me.

"I'm so glad he won," Natalie says. "He deserves it."

"Yes, he does." Flynn's fearless, gutsy performance as a severely injured veteran has been the talk of the award season this year, with a clean sweep at the Golden Globes, SAGs, BAFTAs and now the Oscars.

Hayden deserves a big chunk of the credit as the director who'd coaxed that gutsy performance from his best friend. The two of them are gold together, as evidenced tonight and over the last couple of months.

We're crammed into a booth at the Vanity Fair party. Hayden is on one side of me, Natalie on the other. The heat of his leg pressed against mine has my full attention, whereas Natalie's leg on the other side doesn't do a thing for me, as much as I adore her.

No, Hayden is the one I want, in all his complicated, maddening, sexy, frustrating glory. It has occurred to me often during the years I've nursed this impossible crush that I could've chosen a far simpler man to worship from afar. I could've chosen a man who isn't my boss's best friend and business partner, two things that put me more or less off-limits to him. I could've chosen a man with fewer sharp angles and rough edges.

I'm a smart woman, and I'm well aware this fixation I have on such a difficult man isn't healthy for me. Tell that to the heart that does backflips and handsprings any time he's in the room, let alone wedged up against me, radiating the kind of heat that has me fantasizing about being naked in a bed with him.

I don't care if it's not in my best interest to want him. I don't care that Flynn probably wouldn't approve or that Hayden is more secretive than the CIA when it comes to his private life. I don't care that my dad can't stand him or that many of the people who work for him live in fear of his unpredictable rages. I don't care that his family is one of Hollywood's most dysfunctional—and that's saying something in this town.

None of that matters. I want him, and after the way he kissed me tonight, I'm on fire with desire and determination. Tonight is the night. When he takes me home later, I'm going to make my move and to hell with the fallout. I'm sick and tired of wishing for something and not doing a damned thing to get what I want. It's time to put up or shut up.

I groan at my own cliché-ridden thoughts, but this situation has become one giant, ridiculous cliché. If he doesn't want me the way I want him, then why would he kiss me like a lover when he won the Oscar?

As if he can read my thoughts, Hayden turns away from the conversation he's been having with Jasper to smile at me. Although, to call the subtle movement of his lips a smile is giving it far too much credit. It's more like a cocky smirk than an actual smile.

"You okay?" he asks, his usually cold blue eyes gone warm with what might be affection.

I have to resist the urge to sigh with the pleasure of having his undivided attention. "I am. You?"

"Never better," he says with an honest, genuine smile, so rare and so fleeting that I wish I could get a photo of it before it disappears.

"I'm so thrilled for you guys. I know how hard you worked on *Camouflage*. You deserve all the awards and accolades."

"Thank you. I'm rather thrilled myself."

Hayden is a complicated mix of brilliant and moody, driven and ambitious, ruthless and loyal. To see euphoria creep into that mix of intense qualities fills me with an unreasonable amount of happiness on his behalf. He works so hard and rarely takes the time to enjoy his success.

In the tight confines of the booth, he somehow manages to raise his arm and lay it across the back of the banquette. One small move, and that arm could be around me.

I squirm slightly, enough to press against him, jarring his arm. It falls to my shoulders, and I venture a glance at him, surprised to see heat and desire in his eyes that only add to my determination.

The poor bastard has no idea what he's in for.

*Hayden*

I'm dying a slow, miserable, painful death jammed into this fucking booth with Addie's sweet body squeezed against me, my cock as hard as a freaking rock for her and not a goddamned thing I can do about it. I can't believe I kissed her when my name was called earlier. I didn't plan to do that. In fact, I actively planned *not* to do anything inappropriate where she's concerned tonight.

Flynn asked me to bring her as my date so she could share in the celebration we expected for *Camouflage*. I agreed because he's right—she deserves to be here after the way she supported our entire team during the grueling shoot.

If I'm being honest, I wanted her here for me, too. I like to look at her. I love to breathe in her sexy, alluring scent and fantasize about burying my face in her thick blond hair while I fuck her. I want to lose myself in her and never come up for air.

But I won't. I won't lay a finger on her, as much as it kills me to resist an urge that seems to multiply exponentially every time I'm around her.

I avoid complications the way some people avoid germs. Everything about my obsession with Addison York is complicated. Other than the fact that Flynn would fucking kill me if I so much as look at her cross-eyed—and that's not an insignificant *other than*—she deserves much better than me.

She should be cherished, not tied in my web of ropes and fucked to within an inch of her life, which is exactly what would happen if I ever let my inner beast run free with her. That's *not* going to happen.

Now if only my fucking cock would get the message and stand the hell down, I might actually be able to enjoy this incredible night. It's not happening with her, no matter how badly I might wish otherwise. I repeat this refrain to myself over and over again, but when she snuggles into my embrace, laying her head on my chest, my cock tells me to fuck off.

I look to my left to find Flynn eyeing me with an astute look that tells me I'm not fooling him by trying to act like I don't care that Addie is lying all over me. I care. I fucking care way more than I should, and Flynn knows it, even if I've never fully owned up to his suspicions about my feelings for her.

He called me out on it recently, going so far as to insinuate that I'm in love with her. I did what I always do when my name and Addie's are mentioned in the same sentence—I denied it. What else can I do? Everyone loves Addie, and the last thing I need is my closest friends and business partners turning against me when I fuck things up and hurt her.

Because I would fuck it up—and I would hurt her. I have no doubt at all about that, which is one of the many reasons I keep my distance. Or I usually keep my distance. With her body pressed against mine, I allow my hand to curl around her shoulder, enjoying the rare lack of distance.

I instantly realize I've made a huge mistake by touching her.

Holy fuck. Her skin is like silk, soft and smooth. One touch will never be enough. And was that… Fucking hell, she *moaned*. I have to get out of here. I have to get away from her and the wicked temptation she represents. Except I can't move a fucking muscle with our whole crew crammed into this goddamned booth.

Not to mention, I'm so hard there's no way to escape without giving myself away to Addie and everyone else in the room. FUCK! I break out in a cold sweat. Then her hand lands on my abdomen, and I nearly lose my shit.

"Move," I growl to Jasper, who's next to me.

"What?" he yells over the loud music and voices.

"I need to take a leak."

"Oh, okay. Let Hayden out, you guys," he says to Kristian and Marlowe.

"Be right back," I mutter to Addie. Jarred by my sudden movement, she sits up, a stunned expression on her face—as if she just realized she was lying on me. Not that I minded. I didn't mind. In fact, I loved it a little too much. As I slide out of the booth, I remove my tuxedo jacket and fold it over my arm, hoping it will hide my raging "problem."

I'm reminded of eighth-grade science class, when I popped a boner for my lab partner, Jamie, when we were presenting our findings in front of the class. She had the best rack of any girl in our grade, and I was hard for her for a solid year. I thought everyone must've noticed, but no one ever said anything—and they would have if they'd seen it. I've never forgotten how humiliating it was to discover that I had absolutely no control over what—or who—my dick chose to get hard over.

As an adult, I've devoted a lot of time and energy to the concept of control. So it's galling, to say the least, to lose control the way I have twice tonight.

I can't remember the last time any woman made me sweat just by sitting next to me. I'm a fucking Dom, for Christ's sake. My control is legendary. Except, apparently, when Addison York is pressed against me.

With my jacket still strategically positioned, I make my way through the crowded room, accepting handshakes and congratulations from colleagues on the way to the men's room. Once there, I lock myself in a stall, hang the jacket from the hook on the back of the door and lean my head against the cool tile on the wall.

*Get it together, will you?*

I want to pound the shit out of something. Anything to rid myself of the frustration and desire that possess me like a demon I can't shake no matter how hard I try. What the *fuck* was I thinking when I kissed her? I wasn't thinking. I just acted. In the biggest moment of my career, I took what I've wanted for as long as I can remember. I took *her*. I took Addie.

I fumble with my belt and the irritating buttons and hooks on my tuxedo pants, nearly swearing out loud at how cumbersome the process is. Then my cock springs free, hot and hard. I take myself in hand, looking for relief from the most painful desire I've ever experienced.

I *cannot* have her. I *will not* have her. I *cannot* have her. I *will not* have her.

The thoughts parade through my mind as I relive that kiss, that one fleeting, magical moment in which I had absolutely everything I ever wanted—the ultimate career success and the woman I love. *Fuck.*

Hearing voices outside the stall, I bite back a moan. I've never admitted to anyone—even myself—that I love her. Motherfucking hell, I *can't love her*. I *cannot*. I *will not*. I grip my cock so hard that it hurts. Part of me can't believe I'm actually doing this here, a heartbeat away from colleagues and paparazzi, but I can't stop what she started in that booth.

I can't control that which cannot be controlled. I love her. I want her. I need her. *I can't have her.* From deep within my sex-addled brain, I have the foresight to reach for my handkerchief in the seconds before I come. Every muscle in my body participates in the soul-cleansing release. The relief is immediate and overwhelming.

Breathing hard, I close my eyes and stay perfectly still, letting the oxygen feed my starving muscles. I stand there until my cock begins to finally retreat, satisfied for now. With shaking hands, I clean myself up and knot the soiled cloth into a tight wad that I store in the pocket of my jacket.

I know better than to dispose of a cloth full of my DNA that also bears my initials in a public restroom at a Hollywood event. Such is the life of a celebrity. "Leave nothing behind" is one of our mottos.

I give myself another five minutes to calm down before I take the leak I came in here for. I restore my clothes and inhale a series of deep breaths, determined to get through the rest of this night, to get her home and then head for Club Quantum, where I'll find someone who can help slake the need she stirs in me.

I emerge from the stall to a room that's empty except for an attendant. Thank God for small favors. I wash my hands and splash cold water on my face, mopping it up with the towel the attendant hands me. I suspect he knows exactly what I just did.

Whatever. With the evidence tucked away in my pocket, let him try to prove it.

I'm heading for the door when Flynn comes in, placing a hand on my chest to move me backward into the room.

"We need to talk."

"No, we don't."

"Yes, we do!" Thankfully, he keeps his voice down. "So this thing with Addie… It's happening?"

"No, it's not happening."

"We all saw you kiss her. We saw her eyes light up with surprise and joy that you finally did *something*."

"It was just a kiss." I keep my tone intentionally nonchalant, even though I feel anything but. "Nothing to go crazy over."

"Except *she* is going crazy because you gave her hope! I swear to God, Hayden, if you hurt her, I'll kill you."

Flynn is one of the few people in this world who I genuinely love. But right now, I want to pummel his movie-star face. "Thanks for the warning. Can I go now?"

"Hayden... If you aren't in this, really *in* it, you can't. You absolutely *cannot.*"

I keep my voice down, lest Flynn and I be all over the tabloids tomorrow for "fighting" at the Vanity Fair party. "Do you think I need you to tell me that?"

"Either go all in or hands off," he says through gritted teeth. "I mean it."

"You're a fucking hypocrite, you know that?"

"What the hell is that supposed to mean?"

"Remember when I told you that you had no business getting involved with Natalie?"

"That's not the same thing."

"Isn't it? Isn't it exactly the same thing? A nice girl who deserves better than us?"

With industry people and press in and out of the room, we can't afford to let this get out of hand. So as much as we might like to let loose and go at it, we know better.

"It's not the same. Addie is—"

I raise a brow in inquiry. "*Special?* Is that what you were going to say? And Natalie isn't?" It's never a good idea to drag a man's wife into an argument, but I need Flynn to acknowledge his own double standard. Before he can pounce, I do. "Leave me alone, Flynn. I'm not going to touch her—and I'm certainly not going to hurt her. Why do you think I've kept my distance all this time? I don't *want* to hurt her."

I start to walk away, but he grabs my arm, spinning me around to face him. "Give me your word."

I look into the eyes of my oldest and closest friend, my business partner, one of those few people I truly love. "Fuck you." I rip my arm free of his hold and leave the room before I make the huge mistake of punching him.

# CHAPTER 2

*Addie*

Since his sudden trip to the men's room, Hayden has completely ignored me. I can't even get him to make eye contact. I saw Flynn take off after Hayden, and when they returned to the table, they both seemed tense and pissed.

"What do you suppose is going on with them?" Natalie asks.

I suspect I know exactly what's going on, but I can't say it—not even to her. If I say it out loud, it becomes real, and I've never acknowledged my feelings for Hayden to anyone. I'm sure our mutual friends have their suspicions, as we've both done a piss-poor job of hiding our attraction. But feeling it and saying it are two very different things.

"I don't know," I reply to Natalie. "You know how they are—best friends one minute and about to kill each other the next." My hands are shaking, as is my earlier resolve to take what I want from him. I'm wavering. If I can't even get him to look at me, how will I pull off a seduction?

It's not like I haven't had lovers before. I have. Quite a few, in fact. But I've never felt this bone-deep sense of fear at the thought of what might happen if I blatantly come on to a guy. I don't mean to be arrogant or anything, but I know I'm considered pretty by most people. My dad says I'm the most beautiful girl in the world, but he sort of has to say that.

Guys look at me when I walk down the street. They have since high school, once my boobs showed up—better late than never—and my body filled out in other areas that men tend to notice. Okay, I'll say it. I have a killer ass. Years of squats and lunges and Rollerblading have resulted in an ass that one ex-boyfriend called magnificent.

I like that word. I have a *magnificent* ass, and fantastic boobs that are *all* mine, and real boobs in Hollywood are the exception rather than the rule. I work for the biggest movie star in the world. I have amazing friends, a fabulous condo at the Santa Monica Pier thanks to my awesome boss, who is also the big brother I never had, and tons of famous friends. I'm on a first-name basis with all the most important stylists in Hollywood. Not to mention, I'm smart, savvy and the most organized human being on this or any other planet.

I'm a *catch*. I could have any guy I want, so why is it that the only guy I want is currently ignoring me? "It's total *bullshit*," I say as I glare at the man in question. Oh crap. Did I say that out loud? A glance in Natalie's direction confirms my worst fears.

"Um, what's total bullshit?" she asks.

Have I mentioned that I *adore* Flynn's new wife? If I could've handpicked the perfect woman for him, I would've chosen Natalie. She's lovely and sweet and sincere, and she loves him for him, not his fame. We hit it off the day we met and have become friends in the short time she's been in his life. I want so badly to tell her what I'm thinking and feeling, but I'm afraid to cross the line that Flynn and I walk between our close friendship and our work relationship. I love Natalie, but she's my boss's *wife*.

"Talk to me, Addie. Whatever's wrong, let me help."

She says exactly what I need to hear, and suddenly I don't care that she's my boss's wife. Right now she's the girlfriend I desperately need, which is why I take her up on the generous offer. "I'm about to make a huge mistake."

"What do you mean?"

I fix my gaze on Hayden, who's standing a few feet away from our table, talking with actors whose names you'd recognize. Everyone wants a piece of him tonight. With his big win, he's officially the hottest director in Hollywood. I could've told them that long before tonight.

"Addie…"

"I'm going to seduce him."

"Oh. Well. What's your plan?"

"When he brings me home later, I'm going to take him by the hand and pull him into my place. I'm not going to take no for an answer." I tear my gaze off Hayden and glance at Natalie, who's looking at me with big eyes. "You're horrified, right?"

"No, of course not."

"He kissed me, Nat. You saw it."

"The whole world saw it."

"That means something. I'm going for it. I don't care anymore about all the reasons why I shouldn't. I'm sick of wanting someone I can't have—and knowing he wants me, too. We're fucking adults. It's time we started acting like it."

"I, um…"

"What?"

She starts to say something but stops herself. "Good luck."

"Do you think I'm crazy for acting this way?"

"No. I understand it, actually. I just… Be careful, Addie. He…" She shakes her head. "You know him better than I do."

Something that looks an awful lot like guilt skitters across her face and is gone before I can be certain of what it was. Why in the world would Natalie feel *guilty* about anything where Hayden is concerned? I'm so amped up, I'm seeing things that aren't there.

Flynn slides back into the booth and puts his arm around Natalie. "You ready to go home for some private celebrating, baby?"

"Whenever you are."

"Can we give you a lift, Addie?" he asks.

"Oh, um, no, thanks. I'll go with Hayden."

Flynn glowers at Hayden, who has a fresh drink in his hand and a whole new group of actors surrounding him. "You'd be better off coming with us. He's just getting started."

How can I begin to compete against the beautiful women he works with every day? The women who throw themselves at him, hoping he'll want them in one of his films? Some of them would do *anything*, give him *anything*, to get what they want.

*Stop, Addison. You're worth a thousand of them, and you've never sacrificed your morals for a job.* I realize Flynn is staring at me, probably wondering what level of meltdown I'm having.

"I'll keep an eye on him and make sure he gets home okay." I get up to hug them both. "Congratulations again. I'm so happy for you."

"Thanks, Addie." He kisses my cheek. "Couldn't have done it without you."

"We both know that's not true, but it's nice to hear anyway."

"It's entirely true. I'm sure I'll talk to you tomorrow."

"I'm sure you will."

When Natalie hugs me, she whispers, "Be careful" in my ear. I'm not sure what she's telling me to be careful about. Is she warning me off Hayden? Why would she do that? Does she know something I don't? Of course she doesn't. She's known him a couple of months. I've known him for ten years. What could she possibly know that I don't?

I give her a reassuring smile and send her on her way. I try not to notice the way she looks back at me over her shoulder, her brows knitted with obvious concern. Does she think I can't take care of myself? I love her, but she's worrying needlessly. And why do I feel like the younger of the two of us when I've got four years on her?

Summoning courage and resolve and determination to get what I want, I approach him and place my hand on his back.

He startles when he realizes it's me. "Oh, hey," he says, still managing to avoid eye contact. Is he really that much of a coward?

"What do you say we get out of here?" My heart beats wildly while I wait to hear what he'll say.

He finally looks directly at me, and the heat I see in those usually frosty blue eyes tells me everything I need to know. He wants me, but he doesn't *want* to want me. I can work with that.

"Um, okay. Sure."

After we say good-bye to Jasper, Kristian and Marlowe, I curl my hand around his arm, because of my four-inch heels and my legs feel rather unsteady all of a sudden. Despite my earlier bravado, I'm a nervous wreck about taking this particular bull by the horns, and Natalie's odd reaction to my plans has put me further on edge than I already was.

But that kiss… That damned kiss. Whatever happens next is his own fault. He started it. I intend to finish it once and for all. It's about damned time.

*Natalie*

I'm gripped with indecision. Do I tell Flynn about Addie's plan, or do I keep it to myself? Addie has no idea that Hayden, Flynn and the rest of the Quantum principals are Doms. She doesn't know about Club Quantum or the playroom in Hayden's Malibu house that tipped me off to his preferences even before I knew that Flynn shares them.

My stomach hurts when I think about Addie getting way more than she bargained for with Hayden. But then I tell myself Hayden loves Addie. He'd never hurt her or push her too far or… God, I don't know that for sure. Yes, I've gotten to know Hayden much better since our inauspicious first meeting when I messed up his shot in a Greenwich Village park and was subjected to a tirade. But I don't really *know* him all that well. I certainly don't have the first clue how he treats a woman in bed outside the Dom/sub relationship. Does he even have what they call "vanilla" sex?

I don't know, and the fact that Addie could be walking into something she's woefully unprepared for has my nerves on full alert. My dilemma is not something I can easily hide from my incredibly attentive husband.

"Why are you fidgeting?" he asks when we're settled in the backseat of the car he hired to get us around on Oscar night.

"No reason." Addie has been a good friend to me from the first day we met, through the storm of my past being made public, to my marriage to Flynn and everything in between. She's made me feel welcome in my new life, and I want our friendship to flourish. How can that happen, though, if I betray her confidence?

Flynn snuggles up to me, and I end up on his lap with his arms around me and his lips doing wondrous things to my neck that have me on the verge of forgetting all about Addie and her plan.

"Tell me what's wrong. Did someone say something nasty to you? Who do I need to have killed?"

"Don't even say that. We've had enough murder mysteries tied to your name to last us a lifetime." I'm still getting my head around the fact that my father killed the lawyer who ratted me out to the press. My father didn't do it to avenge me, though. No, he did it because the lawyer besmirched my dad's precious friend— the same friend who attacked and raped me when I was fifteen. My father has always chosen Oren over me—and he always will.

"The girls had a good time tonight," he says of my sisters, who've gone home to spend the night with his parents.

"Thanks for including them."

"Of course they're included. They're our family."

"Yes," I say with a happy sigh, "they are." I love having my sisters back in my life, which has been the best thing to come out of the recent uproar over my past. Well, Flynn is the very best thing, but my sisters are right up there, too. Candace and Olivia grew into lovely young women during the eight years we spent apart, and I'm so proud of them.

"Someone asked Jasper about Olivia," Flynn says.

I'm immediately on alert. "What about her?"

"Whether she might be interested in modeling."

"Seriously?"

"Jasper wouldn't have told me if it wasn't serious interest."

"I don't know what to say to that. She's got school and work and... Wow."

"I know, right?" His smile stretches across his handsome face. He's had a lot to smile about lately after sweeping the award season for his amazing performance in *Camouflage*, not to mention getting married. "Will you tell her?" he asks.

"I suppose I'll have to. It should be her choice."

"I agree." He kisses my cheek and then my lips. "Now will you please tell *me* what's got you stressed out?"

"You won't like it."

"Tell me anyway."

"You know how Hayden kissed Addie and they were awfully cozy earlier?"

Because I'm sitting on his lap, I'm instantly aware of his body tightening with tension. "What about it?"

"She's planning to seduce him. Tonight."

His brown eyes go wide with surprise. "She told you that?"

Nodding, I say, "And please, you can't make a big thing of it with her. She confided in me, and I don't want her to think I run to you with everything she tells me."

"I understand, sweetheart. She's become a friend, and I get that. You don't have anything to worry about. Hayden won't touch her."

"How do you know that?"

"Because he knows I'd kill him if he touches her without being willing to commit to her. In fact, we had words about it in the men's room tonight."

"What kind of words?"

"The kind where I told him to leave her the hell alone if he's not fully invested. He has no desire for a committed relationship, and she's too important to me and everyone else in our group for him to play his games with her."

"From what she said, I don't think she plans to take no for an answer."

"He won't let it happen."

Hearing that, my heart aches for poor Addie.

Flynn traces his finger over my lips. "Why is my wife sad?"

"I'm worried about her. She really cares about him. I understand why it might not be a good idea for them to get together, but I hate the thought of her being disappointed."

"I do, too, but it's for the best. She wants love and marriage and babies and a life with someone. After the way he was raised, he wants nothing to do with any of that."

"How was he raised?"

"Ah, jeez," Flynn says with a deep sigh, "his family life was a disaster. His parents split before he was born. His mom, who has chronic drug and alcohol issues, has been married and divorced three times, but Hayden is her only child, so all her problems fall on his shoulders. He just paid for another trip to rehab for her, and now he's in that fragile, hopeful period of waiting to see if it'll work this time, and the rest of us are waiting to prop him up when it doesn't. His dad is on wife number four—she's three years younger than we are—and Hayden has a bunch of half siblings from his dad who he barely knows. Both his parents had some early success as actors, but they faded out pretty quickly, and now they're has-beens. His dad hits him up for money on the rare occasions Hayden actually hears from him."

"I knew his family was messed up, but I didn't know *how* messed up." Hearing his story softens me to Hayden ever so slightly. He isn't my favorite of Flynn's friends, even if he did step up for me during the firestorm of my painful past becoming public, but I know how important he is to Flynn, so I try to respect that.

"It's been really embarrassing for him. He keeps his distance from the whole catastrophe, but he has no desire to ever get married after the hell his parents' various marriages put him through. He thinks marriage is for idiots."

"We know better, don't we?"

"We certainly do."

"You changed your mind. Maybe he'll change his under the right circumstances."

"I suppose anything is possible, but his scars run pretty deep on that subject, even deeper than mine did after the horror show with Valerie." He scowls at the mention of his ex-wife. "The shit with his parents made for a very unhappy childhood for him, and when they ask him for money..." Flynn shakes his head, his disgust apparent. "It's hard on him."

"Maybe someone like Addie is exactly what he needs."

"You've seen him at the club, Nat. Can you picture her wrapped up in his ropes, while he spends hours torturing her every way he can think of?"

"Not really, but you couldn't picture me there either, and we know how that turned out."

His grunt of laughter makes me smile. "You think you're quite clever, don't you, Mrs. G?"

"I know I'm clever, and you know I'm right. She might take to the lifestyle the same way I did."

He cringes. "I can't even..."

"Don't think of her as Addie, your adored assistant and the little sister you never had. Think of her as a woman with a mind and heart of her own."

"I'm happy to think of her that way, as long as I'm not thinking of her as a woman with Hayden."

"He's your best friend, Flynn."

"And I love him. He's a great friend and business partner, a talented filmmaker and a better son than his parents deserve."

"But?"

"I worry that he'll hurt her."

"So you'd stand in the way of her happiness? It'll matter to her if you don't approve."

"She's all light and love and joy. He's dark and broody and broken. As much as I want them both to be happy, I fear it would turn into a match made in hell for her." He curves a hand around my ass. "And now I don't want to talk about them. I want to talk about us and how we're going to celebrate my big win."

"How do you want to celebrate?"

His hand slides down my leg to dip under the hem of my red Givenchy gown. With his palm flat against my inner leg, he drags it up to find I followed his earlier directions and left my panties at home.

"Ahhh, fuck," he whispers. "How is it possible that I have you four times a day, and it's still not enough?"

I spread my legs to encourage him, but he isn't in any rush. "It's not enough for me either, but we can't keep this up forever. Can we?"

"I can if you can."

I laugh nervously. I've learned not to challenge him on these things. "Touch me, Flynn."

"Are you giving the orders now?"

"*Please?*"

"Mmm, you know just what to say to me, don't you?"

Before I can come up with a witty reply, he renders me speechless when he pushes his fingers into me. No preliminaries, no playful teasing... *Oh God.* "Flynn."

"What, baby?"

"I—" He curls his fingers and finds my G-spot, and as if he's flipped a switch inside me, he makes me come hard. Like always, he plays my body like a maestro. "I forgot what I was going to say."

Laughing softly, he continues to stroke me with his fingers. "Whose idea was it to go home tonight?"

"Yours. We could've been in a hotel room by now."

"Who needs a hotel room?" Punch drunk from the champagne and the powerful orgasm, I'm unprepared for him to abruptly withdraw his fingers. He deals with his clothes and arranges me on top of him, bringing me down onto his hard cock, making me moan from the incredibly tight fit. It's always like this with him, so hot and so tight. I'm never sure whether to scream or sigh from the pleasure. Usually I scream, but with the driver behind a thin screen, I contain that urge tonight.

With his hands tightly gripping my bottom, I drop my head to his shoulder, adrift in a sea of sensation. I shift ever so slightly, and he gets bigger and harder, making me groan from the tight squeeze. "That's *enough*."

His low chuckle draws a smile from me. We have this "argument" frequently. Just when I think he can't get any bigger, he does. Every time.

"It's your fault," he says. "It's all you."

"From my perspective, it's all *you*."

"It's all *us*. We're perfection together."

I can't deny that, so I don't bother to try.

"I wish you could feel what it's like to be inside you, the way your muscles ripple and squeeze me. It's all I can do not to come the second I feel the first squeeze."

His gruff words, spoken directly into my ear, make me tremble.

"Ride me, sweetheart. Make me come."

Next to him on the seat, his two Oscar statues lie abandoned, almost an afterthought to what's happening now. That makes me giggle.

"What's so funny?" he asks, his teeth gritted from the effort it takes not to come when I'm riding him. I know this is a challenge for him because he's told me so many times before.

"Poor Oscar one and Oscar two, discarded in the heat of passion."

"Who the fuck cares about Oscar when I'm fucking my sweet Natalie?"

Part of me wants to be appalled by his language, but I can't deny that his blunt words turn me on.

He throws his head back and groans. "I love how you get wetter when I say things like that. I fucking *love* it."

And I love him. Desperately. I'm so proud of those two gold statuettes that validate my belief that he's the most talented actor of our generation, and he's all mine. Tonight he deserves to be worshipped, and I can tell I shock him when I lift myself up and off him, dropping to my knees in front of him.

"Nat... What the *fuck?*"

"Shhh. Just enjoy." He's taught me how to do this the way he likes it best. I tightly grasp the thick base and suck the wide tip into my mouth, flicking him with my tongue as I ease him into the back of my throat.

"*Fucking hell,*" he says on a hiss. The tight pull of his fingers in my hair and the surge of heat in his hard cock let me know I've got his full attention. I take him up, nearly to the point of climax before backing off and doing it again and again until he's all but begging me to end the torment.

"Nat. *Christ*, Nat. *Baby.*"

He's warning me as he always does, giving me the choice as to where and how he comes. I want him in my mouth, so I tuck my finger in tight against the spot under his balls that sets him off every time, and he comes with a fierce growl, thrusting into my throat with wild abandon. I love him this way. I love him every way, but watching my controlled, dominant husband lose control because of something I did to him is an incredible high.

I bring him down the same way I took him up—slowly. And then I venture a glance at his face and find him watching me with fire in his gorgeous eyes. "Congratulations," I whisper as I smile at him.

"I need to win a couple of Oscars every day if that's how you congratulate me." He's slumped in the seat, but the casual pose is deceiving. I know him well enough by now to surmise that I'm witnessing the calm before the storm that will strike when we get home. I can't wait. His outstretched arms draw me up and back into his lap. He holds me close, stroking my hair and kissing my swollen lips. "My wife is the sexiest, most incredible wife in the whole world."

"I don't know about the whole world."

"She's my whole world."

And that's way more than enough for me.

# CHAPTER 3

*Addie*

I'm not the only one who wants a piece of Hayden tonight, and it takes nearly an hour to break free of the party. Men and women alike fawn over him, hoping he'll remember their platitudes when casting his next film. However, I can tell that most of their insincerity goes in one ear and out the other with him. He's never been one to play the Hollywood game, and he isn't about to start now that he's scored directing and producing Oscars.

When he reaches his breaking point, he grabs my hand and half walks, half drags me to the main entrance where our driver is waiting along with at least half the Hollywood press corps. Exploding flashes blind me as he sees me into the car ahead of him and then joins me, muttering curse words under his breath.

"How anyone can make a living stalking celebrities is beyond me." He cracks open the bottle of bourbon that's waiting for him in the minibar. Filling a glass, he offers it to me, and I take it, needing additional liquid courage to see my plan through to fruition.

The first sip burns me from the inside, stealing my breath and bringing tears to my eyes. I look out the window so he won't see my reaction to the potent liquor. I want him to find me sophisticated, not untried with things that are commonplace to him. And bourbon is an everyday presence in his life. I've never seen him completely wasted, but he does love his Pappy Van Winkle's Family Reserve. The twenty-year-old whiskey sells for fifteen hundred bucks a bottle, and I know this because I order it in bulk for him. Keeping Hayden Roth in bourbon—and making sure the car is stocked with his favorite brand tonight—is one of my duties at Quantum, but I've never actually tried it until now.

"You don't like it, do you?"

I realize he's been watching me far more closely than I thought he would after refusing to make eye contact for the last three hours. "It's okay." I bravely take another sip, though I honestly don't want it.

His bark of laughter surprises me. "Don't waste my Pappy if you don't like it. The stuff is like liquid gold." He takes my glass and pours the remaining liquid into his glass. "What would you rather have?"

"There should be champagne."

"It's Oscar night in Hollywood. Of course there's champagne." He uncorks a bottle of Cristal, pours it for me and hands me the glass, stashing the bottle in an ice bucket.

I take a sip of the cool, refreshing wine that's much more my pace than the bourbon will ever be.

"Better?"

"Much. Thank you."

"No, thank you for coming with me tonight and for seeing to things like having Pappy in the car for me."

"Just doing my job."

"You're very good at your job."

"That's nice to hear." I'm on fire from the inside, glowing with pleasure at the rare compliment from him. I would've guessed he had no idea how Pappy found his way into every chauffeured vehicle Hayden steps foot into. To know he pays attention is the kind of validation that assistants to the rich and famous dream about.

The traffic is hideous, and for once, I'm thankful for that. It buys me some time to calm my nerves and flesh out my plan. The number-one secret to my success as the assistant to the biggest movie star in the world is that I have backup plans for my backup plans. That's what I need now—plans on top of plans. When we get to my place, he'll walk me to the door because he's too much of a gentleman not to.

That's when I'll make my move.

Unaware of my impending attack, he makes himself comfortable for the ride to Santa Monica, his feet up on the other seat and his tuxedo jacket discarded. I watch as he tugs at his bow tie until the knot gives way. The shirt buttons are next. I'm riveted watching the movements of his big hands. His moan of relief at having the top button released travels directly to my clit. I cross my legs against the painful surge of desire.

What would he do if I straddled his lap and kissed him?

I wish I had the guts to find out. But the thought of him rejecting me or pushing me away has me rooted to my seat. No, I'll wait until I'm on my turf to put Operation Nail Hayden Roth into motion. In the meantime, he's a foot from me, but that foot may as well be a mile. He keeps his hands and every other part of him to himself, as much as I wish he wouldn't.

How can he be so calm, cool and collected when I'm about to spontaneously combust over here? I've never been so uncertain around a man before. Why, when it's never been more important, am I unable to get a read on *this* man? *What* does he want? *Who* does he want? Until tonight, I would've said I had no idea. But when he kissed me, spontaneously and very, very publicly, well, that made a statement, didn't it?

Except it was followed by… nothing. After what felt like forever waiting for *something*, no way am I going to let him off the hook without something *more*. I keep telling myself that on the interminable ride to Santa Monica.

"What did you think of your first Oscar ceremony?"

"I loved it. Especially the part where all my friends won."

"I liked that part, too." Leaning forward, he grabs the Pappy bottle by the neck and refills his glass. I begin to worry about him being too drunk for what I have planned for him, but then this is Hayden, and he doesn't get drunk. Buzzed, yes. Drunk, no. Flynn once told me that Hayden never gets drunk or stoned because he doesn't ever want to be out of control like his mother often was during his childhood—and much of his adulthood.

"I'm so happy for you guys. The film deserves every accolade and then some."

"It'll be a tough act to follow," he says, his brows knitting.

"What do you mean?"

"*Camo* was a once-in-a-career confluence of events that led to pure perfection. How do I top that? How do any of us top it?"

"You and Flynn and Quantum are just getting started. We've only begun to see the full extent of what you're capable of."

He turns to look at me—really look at me—and the vulnerability I see in his eyes goes straight to my overcommitted heart. "You really think so?"

"I know so. You guys are magic together—and on your own. I predict you'll top yourselves many times over."

"I hope you're right."

"I usually am. Just ask Flynn."

My comment draws a lusty laugh from him that makes my mouth go dry and my heart pound. God, even my palms are sweaty, and that never happens. I have never, *ever* wanted a man the way I want Hayden. Nothing I've experienced with any other man can compare to the way I feel just sitting next to him.

It's this last thought that cements my resolve. If I don't do this, if I don't take advantage of the opening he gave me with that kiss, I'll never forgive myself. I simply can't live the rest of my life wondering what if I'd been gutsy enough to go for what I wanted? So he's my boss's best friend. Who cares? I'm not on Flynn's time right now, and he's not the boss of my personal life, even if he sometimes thinks he is.

Fifteen minutes later, the car comes to a halt outside my building, and I'm hit with another unsettling thought—what about the driver? Hayden will expect him to wait, but he doesn't know he's going to be here awhile. What do we do about the driver? I don't have a backup plan for that plan, and my stomach knots with nerves as Hayden extends his hand to help me out of the car.

I take hold of it and don't let go. I hold his hand into the lobby of my building and in the elevator to my fifth-floor condo. I keep a tight grip on that lifeline to him as we approach my door.

"I'm really glad you were there tonight, Addie."

"Thanks for inviting me." New dilemma: how to produce my key without letting go of his hand? That can't be done, so I reluctantly release him, and he jams his now-free hand into his pants pocket. I unlock my door and take a deep, cleansing breath.

*Go time.*

Turning to him, I look up to find his hungry gaze fixed on me, and I take that as the sign I need to proceed.

"Come in."

"Oh, um…"

I take a firm hold of his arm and draw him into my home. He doesn't resist in any way. Closing the door behind us, I make the snap decision to leave the lights off when I place my hands on his chest and look up at him again. He's so much taller than me, even with my four-inch heels. I love that he towers over me. I love the idea of being overtaken by him, surrounded by him.

"Addie—"

Before he can protest or tell me why this is a bad idea, I curl my hand around the back of his neck and rise up, brushing my body against his as I bring his lips down to meet mine. At first, he doesn't resist. In fact, he actively participates, kissing me back with the same sense of urgency that I'm feeling. I want to shout *hallelujah.* I'm finally kissing Hayden! But that would require me to stop kissing him, and now that I have him—

He turns away, breaking the kiss abruptly. "*Addie.*"

"Don't stop. Please don't stop."

His hands frame my face, his thumbs caressing my skin. "I can't do this. It wouldn't be fair."

"How would it not be fair when I'm telling you it's what I want, too?" I use the word "too" intentionally because I can feel the hard length of his cock pressing against my belly.

"I can't."

"*Why?*"

"Addie, we're friends. We can't—"

I drop my hands from his shoulders to his waist, suddenly thankful for all the time I've spent with stylists choosing tuxedos for Flynn. I know exactly how to quickly gain access to what I want. And dear sweet baby Jesus, he's commando under there, and the cock that falls into my hand is long and thick and hard, the biggest I've ever felt. My mouth waters at the thought of taking it inside me.

I tighten my grip and stroke him, learning how he likes it by the way he reacts.

He keeps his hands on my face, as if he's afraid to touch any other part of me, but his forehead lands on mine. His breathing is rough and choppy, and his lips hover close to mine. "What're you doing?" he asks, sounding desperate and needy, just the way I want him.

"I'm doing what I've wanted to do for so long. Tell me you want me, too."

"Addison…"

I drag my thumb over the tip of his cock, letting it slide through the moisture that's gathered there. "Tell me, Hayden."

His lips come down on mine, hard and demanding.

I open my mouth to his tongue. This, this, *this* is what I want. *He* is what I want. My eyes are wide open to his many faults. He's a difficult, moody bastard when he wants to be, but I'm crazy about him anyway.

Because I'm paying such close attention, I'm aware of the exact second his control snaps. His hands fall from my face to my shoulders to tear at the straps holding up my designer gown. The kiss turns savage as he pulls at the fabric until it gives way, the seams popping. My breasts spring free of the tight confines of the bodice, and I want to cry from the sweet relief and the wild excitement of his reaction to me.

The heat of his hands on my sensitive flesh sears me. His cock gets harder and longer in my hand, feeding the fire that burns between my legs. I have never wanted anything more than I want him inside me. Right now.

I keep my lips pressed against his when I say, "Bed. Now."

He hesitates, and I worry my two little words took him out of the moment long enough to remember why he thinks this is a bad idea. How could anything that feels this good be a bad idea? I believe this will turn out to be the best idea I've ever had. He rallies, turning me toward the bedroom, which is when I remember that he lived here for a short time, while his place in town was being renovated, before he bought the Malibu house.

Keeping his hands on my hips, he steers me through the dark space to the master bedroom at the end of the hallway. I turn on the bedside lamp because I've waited too long for this to do it in the dark. In the soft glow of the light, he zeroes in on my bare breasts. Before we pick up where we left off, I want him naked. I unbutton the black vest he wears over a crisp white shirt. Still afraid he might change his mind, I work quickly to uncover his broad, muscular chest and abdomen.

Silently, he turns me to unzip my dress. That's when I begin to believe this is actually going to happen. He's not going to change his mind. Laying his hands on my back, he slides them down to my waist, leaving a trail of fire and taking the dress with him. I help him along by shimmying out of the tight dress and look up in time to see his cool blue eyes go hot when he sees the thong I'm wearing.

I push his pants over his hips, and he kicks them off along with his shoes and socks.

Dear God, he's beautiful. I always knew he would be, but the reality takes my breath away. Taking him by the hand, I sit on the edge of the bed and lie back, hoping he'll accept my engraved invitation to take whatever he wants from me. For a brief, paralyzing second, he seems uncertain and torn.

We can't have that. "Hayden." I give his hand a little tug, and he comes down on top of me, resting that magnificent cock on my pubic bone. Holy shit, this is happening. I want to take a minute to celebrate, to do a squealing happy dance, but I can't stop now when I'm so close to getting exactly what I've wanted for so long.

Wrapping my legs around his hips and my arms around his neck, I ensure that he can't easily get away.

"Addie…"

"Yes, Hayden?"

"You won't hate me for this, will you?"

I stroke his hair, his face and his back. "No, I won't hate you." It hurts me that he feels the need to ask.

"Do you promise?"

"Yes, I promise."

"In case I forget to tell you… You're beautiful. I've always thought so, but seeing you, all of you… You're stunning."

Okay, I can now officially die happy. "So are you."

"I'm not. I'm a heartless bastard, and you deserve better."

Before he can head down that road, I draw him into a kiss intended to make him forget everything other than what we're about to do. I give him all I have, without reservation or worry about what tomorrow will bring. Who has time to care about tomorrow when Hayden Roth is naked and aroused in my bed?

His desperation matches mine. His hands are everywhere, his lips ravenous, as if he's been starving for me the way I've been for him. Every one of my senses is on full alert to his taste, his scent, the texture of his skin and the rub of his chest hair against my painfully sensitive nipples. I wonder if I have an actual fever or if I just feel as if I do.

My body is on fire for him, and he knows how to fuel the flames like no one else ever has. Breaking the kiss, he moves down to focus on my breasts, which he holds in his big hands. He ventures a glance at my face, and I see uncertainty mixed in with hunger and desperation. I don't want him uncertain. I want him to want this as much as I do.

If I give him too much time to think, he'll talk himself out of it. I can't let that happen. I'll never survive having gone this far only to stop now.

I sink my fingers into his hair and pull gently. "Turn over, Hayden."

He draws my nipple into his mouth, tugging and sucking so hard that tears fill my eyes. It's the most exquisite thing I've ever felt, and I want more. I want everything, but not before I'm sure he's with me. I push on his shoulder. "Hayden."

Groaning, he lets my nipple pop free of his mouth and turns onto his back.

I let my gaze take a full, perusing journey from broad shoulders to well-defined pectoral muscles to washboard abs and thick, ropy hip muscles. The incredible, gigantic penis that lies hard and hot on his abdomen makes my mouth water. Leaning over him, I run my tongue from the base to the tip, focusing on the slit at the top that's leaking pre-cum. I lap him up, and he groans, grasping handfuls of my hair.

I love making him groan, and I want to hear that sound again and again. Taking him in hand, I draw the head into my mouth, licking and sucking until his hips come up off the bed and his fingers tighten in my hair to the point of pain before he seems to realize what he's doing and lets up.

Opening my mouth as wide as I can, I slide him in over my tongue until I feel the head nudging my throat. I can't possibly take all of him, but I can take enough to make this really good for him. Squeezing the part I can't take, I stroke him while I lick and suck until he's panting and groaning.

"Addie… Addie stop. *Stop*."

Wondering if I've done something wrong, I release him slowly, almost afraid to look at his face. He sits up and reaches for me, bringing me onto his lap so I'm straddling him. I curl my fingers around his cock and watch the pulse of tension that jumps in his cheek. "You didn't like it?"

His wry smile goes a long way toward calming my nerves. "I liked it too much."

For a second, I'm left off-kilter by the potent impact of that smile and the fact that I'm actually sitting naked on Hayden's lap while I stroke the biggest penis I've ever seen—or felt. It's surreal, to say the least, and I want that big penis inside me in the worst possible way.

"Are you safe?" I ask him.

A quizzical look passes through those cool blue eyes. "How do you mean?"

"I'm not going to catch anything if we do this without a condom, am I?"

"No, you're not."

Because he's been my friend for a long time, I believe him.

"Are you protected?"

I notice he doesn't ask if I'm safe, and I'm strangely complimented. "Yes."

"Addie, before we do this, we should talk."

"No, we really shouldn't." I have all the information I need to take what I want, and I've waited long enough to have him. How many days in the office, nights on the town, getaway weekends with our mutual friends and other events have I withstood wishing for what I have in my hand right now? Far too many to count. But there is one thing I have to know before I seal the deal. "Is this what you want, too?"

He glances at the proof of his arousal, which stands tall and hard, stretching well above his navel. "You really have to ask?"

"I'm not naïve, Hayden. I know what happens to men when they get their hands on a naked woman."

"So you think any naked woman will do?" He cups my breasts and tweaks my nipples, drawing a sharp gasp from me.

"How am I supposed to know?"

"I want this, Addie. You know I want it as much as you do, if not more. But—"

I don't want to hear how that sentence is going to end. I don't want to hear any "buts," so I kiss him as I rise up to take him in. I'm so wet that the head slips in easily, but that's the only part of him I take easily. The rest is a battle. I begin to fear that I've taken on an impossible task.

His hands grasp my ass, squeezing tightly, which gives me something to think about besides the *other* tight squeeze.

"Relax, babe," he says in the gruff, sexy voice that made my panties damp long before I decided it would be a good idea to seduce him. "Breathe."

I try to relax. I try to breathe. I try to let myself go and enjoy this moment that's been a very long time coming, but nothing seems to help. I can't make my body relax to admit him. I want to cry from the frustration.

Hayden lifts me up and off him, easing me onto my back. "Relax," he says again as he kisses my breast and draws my nipple into his mouth, rolling it between his teeth. The sensation zings from my nipple to my clit. "Stop thinking so much. This is supposed to be fun."

Fun… It's the most insane thing I've ever done. Seducing my boss's best friend, my longtime friend and one of my employers isn't exactly the smartest career move I'll ever make.

"You're still thinking."

I feel like a failure. I've finally got exactly what I've always wanted, and I can't seem to figure out what to do with him. But he has his own ideas. He kisses a path to my core, lifting my legs up and onto his shoulders. *Dear God.* I've done this before—or had it done to me, I should say—but something about the way *he* does it is all new and totally consuming. It should come as no surprise to me that he knows his way around the female anatomy, including just where to touch and lick and suck to gain ultimate results. And the results are, indeed, *ultimate*. His fingers are inside me, his tongue is insistent, and when he sucks on my clit, I come so hard, I see stars.

I've barely begun to process the mind-altering orgasm when he is pushing into me, pressing in and retreating and then repeating the process until he's fully seated, and I'm having constant orgasms from the struggle it took to get there. I can't seem to be still for even a second.

"*Hayden.*" I grasp his ass as he hammers into me. His pace is relentless, his eyes are closed, and his jaw is clenched. It's a relief to know he's equally affected by what's happening between us. I feel a connection to him that I've never experienced during sex, maybe because I love him. I've never had sex with a man I'm in love with before, and the love makes all the difference.

Curling my arms around his neck, I hold on tight to him. I have no choice but to hold on, because he's ruthless in his fierce possession. I'll be sore tomorrow. Hell, I'm already sore, but no way will I stop this. Not when an orgasm of epic proportions is growing with every deep stroke of that amazing cock.

"Addison," he says in that low growl that's such a huge turn-on.

"Yes, Hayden. *Yes.*"

"Tightest pussy I've ever fucked. So hot and wet. You feel so good. Tell me it's good for you, too. Tell me."

"It's so good. Don't stop."

"No, never stop." Amazingly, he begins to move even faster, slamming into me harder, deeper, triggering an orgasm that makes me scream from the power of it. I come down from the incredible high to realize I'm the only one who came. God, not only is he hung, he's got incredible stamina, too. He's like an Olympic gold medalist at making it last.

I open my eyes to find him watching me intently. "You okay?"

"Yeah," I say between breaths. I can't seem to get enough air to my starved lungs.

"Had enough?" he asks with a challenging smirk.

"Not even kind of."

He slides his hands under my ass and presses into me so far, I swear he touches my heart. His fingers delve between my cheeks, pressing against my anus, which has never been touched before. Oh God, I'm going to come again if he keeps that up, which of course he does, because he seems to know me better than I know myself.

Then he's withdrawing, and I'm left reeling from the sudden change of plan.

Hayden turns me over, props pillows under my hips and enters me from behind before I've had even a second to process what's happening. One stroke at a time, he's changing my life and my expectations. Nothing and no one will ever be able to live up to the standard he's setting with each deep thrust, with each push of his finger against my anus, with every squeeze of my nipple and every mind-altering orgasm. They come from my soul, searing me with their heat and power. One orgasm rolls into another and still he doesn't let up on me.

He fucks me, literally, to within an inch of my life. If it were possible to die from an overabundance of pleasure, I'd be dead many times over by now. His fingers are everywhere, stroking, touching, penetrating. If he'd asked me first, I would've said no. Not there. But I find myself pushing back, looking for more. He delivers, adding a second finger, and I cry out from the shock of the painful pleasure.

I begin to wonder how long he can keep this up.

His teeth clamp down on my shoulder, and I come again, my internal muscles tightening around his cock and fingers.

"*Fuck*," he mutters in the second before he comes, too. He withdraws his fingers first and then his cock, which is still hard.

Wincing from the burn of his withdrawal, I release a deep breath when I feel him get up and leave the room. I hear water running in the bathroom before he returns with a towel that he uses to clean me up. I can't move. Every muscle in my body has gone liquid, and it's quite possible I may never move again.

His lips are soft against my shoulder, his tongue soothing the spot where he bit me. He kisses his way down my back. When he nips my ass, I cry out from the shock as well as the bolt of heat between my legs. Then I feel his hard cock against my ass, and I can't believe he's already ready to go again. I want to sleep for a week, and he's hard again?

"Are you wimping out on me?" he asks.

Oh, he knows just what to say to me! I find a source of energy I didn't think I had and turn to face him, hoping to find that he's joking.

He isn't. His gaze is as hungry as it was before we had the hottest sex of my life, and he's zeroed in on my breasts. My nipples tighten painfully as he drops his head to run his tongue over one of them.

Moaning, I reach for him, curling my hand around his head.

His tongue is soft and gentle, in sharp contrast to the intense desire he demonstrated earlier. My body reawakens with every stroke of his tongue, and the tight throb of desire begins anew. He moves from one nipple to the other, continuing with the soft and gentle theme, until I'm squirming from the sensations that spiral through me.

His hand on my back draws me toward him as he rolls onto his back, taking me with him. He arranges me so I'm straddling his cock. "Now," he says, "let's try this again, shall we?"

He's returned me to our original position and is looking up at me expectantly. Based on the way he absolutely possessed me the first time, something tells me he doesn't cede control to his partner very often. That he's willing to do so for me does weird things to my insides. I'm breathless but determined to try. Grasping his cock, I angle him toward my tender flesh, wincing from the sharp burn of his entry.

Biting my lip, I manage to contain a cry of pain. God, it hurts, and I almost stop. But then I remember that challenging look in his cool blue eyes, and I force myself to keep going, to try harder, to give him what he wants.

His fingers press deep into my hips, and I'm sure there'll be bruises there tomorrow. That'll be the least of my concerns tomorrow. There's a very good chance I'll never walk properly again. Right when I'm sure that this is never going to happen, my body yields to him, and I take him to the root.

When I begin to ride him, he throws his head back and lets out a growl that rates as the single sexiest thing I've ever heard, to know that I've affected him so profoundly. I can only hope that the connection we've managed to find in this bed will stay with us long after this night is history. With him buried thick and hard inside me, his fingers gripping my hips, I've finally got exactly what I've wanted for so long. If I die tomorrow, I'll die happy.

# CHAPTER 4

*Addie*

My happiness is short-lived.

I wake up alone with every muscle in my body on fire from the most amazing, aggressive, all-consuming sex I've ever had. I make the huge mistake of moving my legs and moan from the pain that travels from my core to every nerve ending I own. Here I thought I was in such good shape, but no workout that I know of could've prepared me for a sexual marathon with Hayden.

Holy God, the man has stamina on top of stamina. I've never been with a guy who could make it last as long as he did. It was amazing, but the aftermath is painful. Thank God the office is closed today, because I fear I'd have to call in sick, which would tip Hayden off to the fact that he fucked me into a sick day. The whole night is a blur, from the moment he first kissed me to the fifth time he took me, after which I must've finally passed out from sheer exhaustion. Had he left right away or had he slept some first? I hate that I don't know. I hate that I have no idea what happens now that we've finally taken this huge step.

I force myself up and out of bed, groaning from the agony that radiates from between my legs. My first time was a lot of years ago, but I don't remember feeling this sore the next day. Then again, I've never met a penis quite like Hayden's. That thought makes me giggle as I limp into the bathroom to pee—ouch—and start the tub. I need a hot bath to soothe my aches and pains. As achy as I am today, I wonder how long I'll have to wait for another encounter with that exceptional penis and the man who owns it. How will I ever look him in the eye again at work after having experienced him and his magic penis?

A tingle of sensation between my legs makes me grimace from the realization that even though I had more than I've ever had before with him, it wasn't enough. I begin to suspect that I'll never have enough of Hayden Roth.

Settling into the blissfully hot water, I close my eyes and try to relax so the heat can do its thing. Images from the sensually decadent hours I spent in his arms run through my mind like a porn movie. Me on top, him on top, him behind me, him touching me where no one else ever has and me liking it way more than I expected to. I pick over every minute, every detail and every expression that crossed his incredibly handsome face as we finally surrendered to years of simmering desire.

I shiver from the memories that are already seared onto my mental hard drive, permanent reminders of a night that will never be forgotten. What is he thinking about today? Does he want more of me the way I want more of him? Was our encounter as life changing for him as it was for me?

I sink deeper into the tub, submerged to my chin. When I close my eyes, sexy, sensual images of the man I love are all I can see. I can't wait to be with him again, to touch him and kiss him and make love to him. I wonder how long it'll be before we can do it all again.

*Hayden*

Sleeping with Addie is the biggest mistake I've ever made, and it will not happen again.

Sleeping… That's the least of what I did with her after promising Flynn I wouldn't touch her. Sleep was the last thing on my mind when she took me by the hand and tugged me into her apartment to have her wicked way with me.

Toothpaste, mouthwash and two coffees later, I can't get the taste of her off my tongue. Her taste haunts me, as do the images that flood my brain regardless of my desire never to think again about what we did. If I go there, if I allow myself to wallow in the thoughts of her, it'll ruin everything.

She and I are friends. We're business associates. We have many friends in common, people who are important to both of us. People such as Flynn, who would have me killed if he knew what I did with his Addie and how I snuck out in the wee hours of the morning without a word to her, like she was just another random hookup.

I'm a heartless douche to have touched her in the first place, knowing I have nothing at all to give her. I shouldn't have kissed her at the Oscars, let alone everything I did with her later.

I've never been more thankful for my work than I am this morning as I sit in the quiet of the editing room, doing what I do best while trying not to think about how massively I fucked up with Addie. Nothing will ever be the same again now that I've touched her and tasted her and fucked her, now that I know how she sounds when she comes and how hot and tight her pussy is. How will I look at her now that I know those things about her?

I won't. I won't look at her or talk to her or do anything with her unless I have to. I'll keep my distance until she gets the message that last night—or this morning, I guess it was—was a one-time event never to be repeated, no matter how badly I might wish otherwise. There's simply no point to pursuing a relationship with Addie when I want none of the things she does.

She's the kind of woman a man settles down with. She wants a husband and babies and a white picket fence. I want my work and my friends and my ropes and Club Quantum and a life unencumbered by the sort of promises a man would have to make to have a woman like her.

Of course, I knew all this before I kissed her, before I fucked her, before I fucked up with her. I knew it, and I did it anyway, and that's what makes me a world-class asshole for letting things get so out of hand. But when she touched me and kissed me and let me know what she wanted from me... I'm not made of fucking stone, despite how it might seem sometimes.

I'm known for being cold and ruthless and relentlessly ambitious when it comes to my work, but I do have a heart, and that heart beats for her. It has for a long time. If my chaotic upbringing taught me anything, it's that we don't always get what we want out of life. So I want her. That doesn't mean dick when stacked up against all the reasons why I never should've touched her in the first place.

Why am I thinking about this shit when I've got a film to finish? A fucking film that still needs a fucking name. One-word titles are my signature. I love the way the right word can sum up so many things. Take *Camouflage*, for example. That's the perfect title for a film about a man trying to find out who he is without the uniform that has defined him. In this new film, Flynn plays an addict who hits rock bottom before scraping his way back to life where he discovers that everyone he loves has turned their back on him. We wanted to call it *Addict* because that summed up the story in a way that would be relatable to audiences around the world.

But the studio rejected it as too simplistic. Like that's not the whole fucking point. I fought for our title to no avail, and we've spent weeks trying to come up with something better. Flynn and I are so married to our original title that we can't see our way to considering anything else. Just what we need so late in the production, and now we're under tremendous pressure from the studio to name the fucker so marketing can do their thing.

Name the fucker. As if it's that easy. Snap my fingers and solve a problem they caused by rejecting the perfect title for no good reason.

I scroll through images on one of three massive screens that I use to do postproduction work, usually in close collaboration with Jasper, my cinematographer, and a team of editors and sound technicians who add polish to what I give them. I've still got a lot to do, but I can't find my usual zone. I do my best work after filming is completed, and a lot of people are counting on me to get it right. Yet all I can think about is the taste of Addie's sweet pussy and the way it gripped my dick in a tight, hot fist of pleasure.

My cock hardens as these thoughts pass through my mind, one on top of the other until I've checked out completely from what I was doing. As much as I might want to forget it ever happened, my brain refuses to go along with my plan, torturing me with images and memories and sounds I'll never forget. I'm already picturing her in the playrooms in both of my homes. Oh, the things we could do…

No. Stop. Not happening.

I'm sorely tempted to whip out my cock and take the edge off. Only the possibility that I might not be completely alone in the Quantum building stops me from acting on the sharp pang of desire. I had her five times, and it wasn't enough, not nearly enough.

But it has to be. I can't do this to her, to our friends, to myself, not when I can never be what she wants, and she can never be what I need. It's pointless and fruitless to have let this happen in the first place, but to continue it would be a recipe for disaster. I've had enough disasters in my life. The last thing I need is another one.

My phone chimes with a text that I glance at, double-taking when I realize it's from her.

*Where'd you go?*

Such a simple question with no simple answer. I stare at those three innocuous words on my screen for far longer than I should with everything else I need to do. Where *did* I go? I came to work, one of two places in my life where everything makes sense. The other being Club Quantum, where I'm allowed to be my authentic self, the man the rest of the world has never seen—the man Addison York has never seen and will never see, if I have my way. And I always have my way. I lead my life by my own rules, and no one, not even precious, beautiful Addie, is going to change that.

It's better to put a stop to this before it gets started. It would be better still to have put a stop to it before I fucked her, but that ship has sailed now. There's no going back to who we were to each other only yesterday.

Ignoring her text, I put the phone on my desk, telling myself it's better this way.

*Addie*

I don't hear from him at all on Monday, even though I know he received and read my text. I get up for work on Tuesday still aching and more than a little heartsick that he's blowing me off. I'm disappointed in my friend Hayden. At least, I think we're friends. If so, my definition of friendship and his differ wildly.

This, right here, is why smart people keep business and pleasure separate. Clearly, I'm not as smart as I think, because today I have to go to the office we share. I'll have to see him and possibly talk to him and act like nothing happened, when *everything* happened. I'll have to pretend in front of Flynn and the others that I'm fine when I'm not fine. I'm not fine at all. I feel broken inside, permanently changed in ways I've yet to fully process.

I finally got what I've wanted more than anything. I didn't expect to feel so hollow afterward, but then again, I didn't expect him to leave without a word either.

"What *did* you expect, Addison? Hearts and flowers and sonnets?"

Now he's got me talking to myself. I didn't expect any of those things, but is it crazy to wish that he'd at least said good-bye before he left? Was it too much to hope for that he might check on me yesterday after turning my world upside down in the course of a few sensually charged hours?

Or maybe what we did is so commonplace for him that it didn't occur to him that he needed to check on me. Maybe silence afterward *is* his routine. If so, his routine sucks donkey balls.

I turn the key to engage the dead bolt on my front door and take the elevator down to the parking garage to the sleek Audi R8 that my wonderful boss surprised me with for my birthday last year. Working for a total "car whore" has its advantages, and I still can't believe that this amazing car is all mine. Flynn being Flynn went all-out with a top-of-the-line V10 in a gorgeous metallic blue with black wheels and features I'm still discovering months later.

The biggest issue I have with the car is keeping an eye on the speed limit when I'm on the highway. I've already been stopped once for speeding and given a warning. Thank goodness, because that ticket would've been beastly.

I slip into the black leather seat, wincing at the dull pain that still resonates from between my legs. Closing the door, I breathe in that new-car scent that still lingers. That scent reminds me to count my blessings. I have a great home, a hot car and a job that make my high school and college friends green with envy. I'm friends with or acquainted with most of Hollywood's A-list thanks to my connection to Flynn, Hayden, Marlow, Jasper and Kristian.

My internal pep talk, while a nice reminder of how blessed I am, doesn't do a damned thing to assuage my wounded pride or aching heart. How can he do this to me? I'm not just any random hookup. It's me. Addie, his friend, his colleague, his...

The biggest mistake I've made is thinking that I matter more to him than I do. I thought there was something special between us. I thought what we did the other night was special. It was to me, anyway. I guess it wasn't to him. I have the time it takes to drive from home to the office to convince myself that I'm okay with that. So what if it didn't mean anything to him? It meant something to me, and I can hold on to that while I try to put my infatuation with him in the past.

Thank God I managed to contain those three little words that were on the tip of my tongue during every cataclysmic orgasm the other night. I cringe at how close I came to saying them more than once. But I didn't, and now he'll never know how I really feel about him. His loss.

My chest tightens and my eyes fill with tears I refuse to indulge. No matter how heartbroken I might feel, I'm not going to cry over Hayden Roth. I wanted him, I had him and now my feelings for him are in the past, or so I tell myself. Through rush-hour traffic, I focus on driving and the day ahead that will include a board meeting for Flynn and Natalie's new childhood hunger foundation, as well as training Marlowe's new assistant, Leah.

Everyone is excited to welcome Natalie's former roommate from New York, who recently relocated to LA to work for Marlowe. As soon as Marlowe offered Leah the job—and offered to buy her out of her contract—Leah resigned from her teaching position at the Emerson School.

Flynn asked me to help train Leah to be Marlowe's "Addie." I know it's a huge compliment that Flynn and the other Quantum principals think I set the gold standard for Hollywood assistants, but today I can't seem to muster my usual enthusiasm for my job.

In the thirty minutes it takes me to travel four miles to the office, I have myself convinced I can handle being in the same building with him today. I can pretend everything is fine, that I'm not shattered by his callous disregard after life-altering sex. I want to call it lovemaking, but that's not what it was for him. If he loved me, if he cared about me at all, he wouldn't have left without saying good-bye. He wouldn't have let more than a day go by without a word.

So screw him. Screw him every which way to next Tuesday. He can go fuck himself, because he is never going to get another chance to fuck me if this is how he handles the aftermath. No wonder he can't seem to maintain a relationship. He's an emotionally stunted fucked-up disaster area, and I'm better off without him.

Having moved from devastated to furious in the time it takes me to get to work, I pull into the parking lot and into my space next to Hayden's black Range Rover with the HAR license plate. Hayden Anthony Roth, named after both his grandfathers, and I hate that I know that, because I hate him, and I don't want to know every little thing there is to know about him.

I don't want to know the details of his hideous childhood or remember the photos of him with every hot young actress to come through the Hollywood mill in the last ten years. I don't want to think about him anymore. I'm done.

Grabbing my messenger bag and purse, I head into the building and use the palm scanner to gain access to the elevator. During the ride to the fifth floor, I go over the plan for the day—act normal, pretend like nothing is wrong, smile and under no circumstances show him that you give the first shit about him. Got it. I can do that.

The elevator doors open and who do you think is standing at the reception desk, chatting with our receptionist, Mackenzie, and laughing like he doesn't have the first care in the word? Yep, you guessed it, the man himself. And isn't it just my luck that he's wearing sexy faded jeans that hug his perfect ass, the same ass I clutched two nights ago as he slammed into me with that big—

*Stop! You're over him. You're done with him and his big... thing.*

"Morning," I say cheerfully, keeping my focus on Mackenzie as I manage to avoid looking at him at all—other than the ass shot, of course. I'd have to be dead not to notice that, and I'm done, not dead.

"Hey, Addie," Mackenzie says. "I put a few calls through to your voice mail this morning already, and you've got two deliveries in your office."

"Thank you."

"Addie," Hayden says, "could I have a minute?"

"Can't right now," I say, breezing by him. "Got a conference call in five minutes that I'm not ready for."

"Oh. Okay. Later, then."

"Sure," I say, though I'm thinking *when hell freezes over*. This might be a good time to mention that while Flynn is my boss and my number-one priority, in addition to what he pays me to be his beck-and-call girl, I also collect a salary from Quantum to assist the other principals as needed. So *technically* Hayden is also one of my bosses. Technically, however, he can kiss my ass. I've got nothing to say to him, even if my nipples tingled at the sound of his gruff voice saying he wanted to talk to me.

Fuck. Him.

I go into my office and shut the door, hoping he and everyone else stays out and leaves me alone until I get my shit together. I wish I had a conference call to lose myself in, but I have nothing on my calendar until the ten-o'clock foundation board meeting and I took care of everything for that on Friday. Damn my blasted efficiency.

It occurs to me then that he'll be able to tell I'm not on the phone when the red light for my extension isn't on. I pick up the phone and press the button for an outside line and then hit the mute button before placing the receiver on my desktop. Whatever it takes to avoid him.

I dive into my email, which includes a long one from our publicist Liza, outlining the four million interview requests Flynn has received since winning the Oscar. He did several of the big ones yesterday, but there are many more who want him. I print a copy of the email to give to him when I see him so he can choose what he wants to do—and what he doesn't. There will be far more in the latter category, as he's been burned by the media so many times that he's extremely choosy about who he talks to.

I can't say I blame him, especially after the recent feeding frenzy that erupted when Natalie's painful past was sold to the highest bidder. Natalie's father murdered the unscrupulous lawyer who sold her out to the media. I'm still trying to get my head around that part of the story and how her father killed the lawyer for besmirching the man who attacked Natalie. Speaking of fucked up…

How she can be the generous, thoughtful, beautiful person she is after what she endured as a teen is admirable, to say the least. They are so blissfully happy together, despite what they both went through before they met. She's absolutely perfect for him, and their story gives me hope that someday I might find the man who's perfect for me.

One thing I now know is that man will not be Hayden Roth. And I'm fine with that. A tingle of sensation between my legs takes me right back to the early hours of Monday when he was deep inside me as I writhed under him, seeking relief from the almost painful pleasure of his possession. And just that quickly, I forget all about my plans to forget all about him.

Dropping my head into my hands, I focus on breathing, on thinking about anything other than *him*. I hate him. I love him. I want him. I hate him. I love him. I'm a hot fucking mess over him, and I hate *that* most of all. I don't go crazy over men, and I never have. It isn't like me to obsess over *one* of them when there're so many to choose from. So what is it about Hayden that makes me nuts?

Before Monday morning or since then? Before Monday, when I thought of him—far too often—it was always his eyes that got to me. One minute so icy blue and the next minute hot and passionate, and then just as quickly, wounded and fragile. You have to know him, really *know* him, to ever catch a glimpse of his wounded or fragile side, but I've seen it. I know it's in there while the rest of the world mostly sees the ice.

Since Monday, I've got a whole new set of images to add to my mental library, none of which will be helpful to my forget-he-exists campaign. As much as I loved it as it was happening, I wish with every fiber of my being that I never slept with him. This crush or obsession or whatever you want to call it was bad enough before I knew what it was like to kiss him and touch him and…

A moan escapes from my tightly clenched jaw. I can almost feel the intense stretch and burn of him burrowing into me, ruthless and relentless and yet somehow tender at the same time. It had been earthy and erotic and dirty and sexy, and God help me, I want more of it. Maybe it would be enough to be his fuck buddy if it meant getting down and dirty with him once in a while. Wouldn't that be better than nothing?

No, it wouldn't be better.

Someone knocks on the door, forcing me out of my increasingly desperate thoughts to remember I'm at work. Hoping it's not Hayden, I say, "Come in."

Mackenzie sticks her head in, notices the receiver sitting on my desk and then looks at me. "Flynn is wondering if you're coming to the board meeting."

"Crap, is it already ten?"

"Ten after."

"Ugh, tell him I'll be right there."

I begin gathering up the agendas and other items I printed at Natalie's request on Friday and rush out of my office where I crash into someone in my haste. *Him.* Of course I crash into *him*, and my papers fly out of my hands, and it's all I can do not to break down right in front of him. At least I didn't drop my laptop, too.

Squatting, I gather the papers, thankful that I stapled everything on Friday, so it isn't a total disaster.

He squats next to me, helping.

I want to tell him not to bother, that I've got this, that I don't need his help or anything else. Remember the part about him being one of my bosses? Yeah, that's why I don't say any of those things. Rather, I take the papers he hands me without actually looking at him and mumble my thanks.

We both stand.

"Addie—"

"I'm late for a meeting."

I brush by him, hating the way my body reacts to even that slight contact. I hate him. I hate myself. I hate walking into the conference room now twelve minutes late when I'm never late for anything—ever. That's Hayden's fault, too. Everything is his fault. I hate that Natalie, Flynn, his parents, sisters and the other Hollywood heavy-hitters he recruited for the foundation board stop their conversation when I enter the room probably looking as frazzled as I feel.

I'm never going near him again.

And then he walks into the room, smiling as if he hasn't a care in the world. "What'd I miss?"

I hate him.

# CHAPTER 5

*Hayden*

She won't look at me. I know this because I haven't taken my eyes off her since I came into the conference room to officially join the board of Flynn and Natalie's foundation. I wasn't going to attend the meeting until I saw an opportunity to be in the same room with Addie for an hour to gauge what's up with her.

She's ignoring me. That's what's up with her.

And why does that bother me so much when it's exactly what I want her to do? It's what I *need* her to do. Except, the thought of losing my friend Addie is excruciating. Goddamn, I fucked this up so bad by having sex with her in the first place, then sneaking out and going silent on her afterward. I suck. I know I do. But better she find out now that I'm no good than to let her think I'm someone I'm not.

Now she knows exactly who and what I am—someone who would fuck his friend and then go silent on her when I know she has feelings for me that go beyond friendship. I've known that for a long time. Hell, I have those feelings, too. I feel more for her than I have for any other woman. She's amazing and smart and scary efficient and beautiful and so fucking sexy she makes me drool—and that was before I had the sublime pleasure of seeing her naked and losing myself in her.

And the pleasure was sublime. It's all I've thought about since the early hours of Monday when I took what I've wanted for so damned long. Though I keep thinking about what a heartless, selfish bastard I am for fucking her, I can't forget the way she took the lead, how she offered herself to me.

In addition to being a selfish bastard, I'm also no saint. When someone I'm painfully attracted to offers herself to me on a silver platter, I'm going to indulge like the glutton I am.

Staring at her now as she studiously avoids me, I remember every detail of what happened in her bedroom. I remember every sound and every touch. I remember how tight and wet she was, how she struggled to take all of me and what it felt like when she came so hard she tested my legendary control. More than a day later, I can still taste her sweet flavor.

I thought maybe if we indulged, if we did what we've both wanted to do for years now, that maybe I could put this ridiculous fascination with her in the past where it belongs. But that's not what happened. No, after having her, I only want *more* of her, and that *cannot* happen. It just can't. Look at how pissed off she is with me now. What would she think if she knew the full truth about me, about my true desires? She'd hate me even more than she already does.

You know that short list of people I love? Addie is right up there on the top of that list, and I can't bear to think I've caused a permanent rift with someone who's so important to me. *You probably should've thought about that before you fucked her and walked away.*

No shit, really?

I want to tell my conscience to fuck off and leave me alone, but the thing of it is, my conscience is exactly right. Flynn was exactly right when he got in my face the other night and told me to leave her alone if I wasn't interested in everything with her.

The cold shoulder is the least of what I deserve from Addie. I've got to fix this. I've got to repair our friendship, at the very least. I have no idea how I'm going to do that when she won't even talk to me, but I'll think of something.

I tune into the conversation the board is having about a kick-off event that will set the tone for what the foundation hopes to accomplish—raising money for hungry kids without spending hundreds of thousands on fancy Hollywood galas.

"What about a carnival?" The idea is out of my mouth before it's fully formed.

Everyone looks at me, except for Addie, who types on her laptop, presumably taking notes—or composing a manifesto on the many ways Hayden Roth sucks donkey balls, which is one of her favorite expressions.

"What do you mean?" Natalie asks.

"You don't want to do a gala, and on behalf of all of Hollywood, I thank you for one less formal event to attend. How about doing something fun for the population we hope to serve by hosting a carnival with rides and games and face painting and other stuff kids love? We could get someone to donate their estate for the day and turn it into a playground for kids. We'll invite celebrities to come and bring their kids and contact agencies that support needy kids and get them there, too. Lots of press and photos and TV coverage."

By the time I finish spewing, everyone is looking at me, including Addie, who stares at me with an intrigued, arrested expression that makes me want to grab her and drag her from the room so we can deal with the terrible awkwardness. But I can't do that, so I stare back at her until she looks away, busying herself with her laptop once again.

"That is an amazing idea," Natalie says. "What does everyone else think?"

"I like it," Flynn says. "It would be fun and keep the focus on the kids, which is what we want."

"How would we make money from it?" Flynn's sister Ellie asks.

"We'd charge the celebrities to attend," Flynn's mother, Stella, says. "They'd pay to be seen at something like this, and their kids would love it, too. It would be great publicity for them to be embracing such a worthy cause, and it would show them as down-to-earth parents who actually play with their kids."

I grunt out a laugh. Neither of my celebrity parents ever "played" with me, not that I can recall, anyway. One of the nannies, whose name I can't remember, took me to a park a few times, but my parents never did anything like that. They were too busy chasing careers that didn't pan out and romances that ended in one epic disaster after another. Their kid was an afterthought in the midst of all that drama. That's exactly why I'll never have kids of my own. I'm too selfish to give them the attention they deserve.

Flipping a pen between my fingers, I watch Addie take frantic notes as the carnival idea takes off within the group. How is it that even the way she types is sexy? So is the furrow that forms between her brows when she concentrates, and the pucker of her sweet lips.

I'm hit with a desperate feeling of dread as it occurs to me that I might not be able to fix the damage I've done. That can't happen. No matter what, I need her in my life as my friend.

With that in mind, I withdraw my phone from my pocket, and, keeping the phone under the table where no one can see what I'm doing, I arrange for the delivery of two hundred dollars' worth of multicolored roses. I'm taking a huge risk sending them to her at the office, which is why I don't sign the card. But I don't need to. She'll know who they're from because of the simple message I've included—*I'm sorry. Forgive me?*

I pay extra to have them delivered within the hour, so maybe she'll think I arranged for them before I knew she was so pissed at me. When I've filled in all the fields, I stare at the Place Your Order button for a long moment before I press it to submit the order. She'll get them soon, and then we'll see what happens. I hope it works, because I don't have a plan B.

*Addie*

He stares at me throughout the entire meeting. Even though I studiously avoid him, I can feel him watching me. He blew me off, so why is he staring? I want to scream at him to look at someone else, but of course I can't do that with Natalie and Flynn and his entire family in the room, not to mention the producers and actors Flynn has recruited to sit on the board. And speaking of that, this is the first time Hayden has attended one of the board meetings, despite repeated invitations from Flynn to participate.

What's that about? Why did he suddenly decide to come today? Ugh, he drives me *crazy*! That's probably why he came—to irritate me. Well, it's working. Yes, it is, even if I adore his idea about the carnival. See, that's the thing with Hayden—he can be so exasperating one minute, and in the next minute, he gets it just right.

We end the meeting with plans to keep in touch about the carnival. Flynn and Natalie personally thank everyone who came as they file out of the room. I gather my belongings and make the mistake of looking to see if Hayden is still there. Of course he is, and he's still staring. He smiles at me—a small, intimate smile that includes his eyes, which are now warm with affection that infuriates me.

He can stuff his affection straight up his ass. I'm all set with him and his *affection*. Whatever.

I take my papers and laptop and leave the room.

He's right behind me. "Addie."

Ignoring him, I go directly to the one place he can't follow me—the ladies' room. We share it with another company, so he won't come in here. Dropping my stuff on the counter, I close my eyes and breathe through the anger and agony that overwhelm me. I may tell myself that I hate him, but the truth is I still love him as much as I did before we had sex and ruined everything.

Then tears are rolling down my face, and I want to scream with frustration. I don't cry at work. I'm not that girl. I've never been that girl. I actually can't stand that girl who lets her emotions rule her life. That's never been me, until I had sex with Hayden Roth.

Using my sleeve, I wipe my face as the door opens to admit Natalie. Great. She immediately sees that I'm crying and comes over to me.

"Addie? What's the matter?"

I force a smile for her benefit. "I'm hiding."

"From?"

"*Him.*"

"Oh. So it didn't go so well the other night?"

"It went great."

"Then what's wrong?"

"He left without saying good-bye, ignored a text from me yesterday and today he wants to 'talk.' I wanted to talk yesterday. Today I have nothing to say to him."

She winces. "Ugh. So you guys actually…"

"Did it? Yeah, we did, and it was incredible, amazing, life changing, everything I thought it would be. It was like a dream come true, until I woke up alone." Fucking tears. They make me so damned mad!

Natalie closes the small space between us and hugs me. "I'm so sorry."

I appreciate the comfort and friendship she offers. "It's okay. I'll be fine. He's an ass. I suspected it before I screwed him. Now I know it for sure."

"What can I do?"

"This helped, thank you. I need to get myself together before Leah arrives after lunch."

"I can't wait to see her. I'm so excited to have her here."

"We'll take good care of her." I wet a paper towel and use it to mop up my tears and the mascara that has collected under my eyes. I look like hell. This day just keeps getting better. "He had a good idea in the meeting."

"He certainly did."

"At least he's good for something."

Natalie laughs and gives my arm a squeeze. "You know where I am if you need to talk."

"I do. Thank you, but I'm all done talking about him. It's time to cut my losses and move on."

We leave the restroom together, and I'm relieved to see no sign of Hayden in the hallway. Natalie smiles at me before she ducks into Flynn's office. I love her, but I can't stand that she feels sorry for me. I don't want her or anyone to pity me. I got exactly what I wanted the other night. If I haven't gotten what I wanted since then, well, so what? I'll survive. I always do.

In the next couple of hours, I throw myself into work. Flynn and Natalie are going to Italy in March for the wedding of Dylan Martin, an actor he's worked with several times. I plow through the scheduling of the plane, the reserving of a suite at a hotel under a fake name and confirming the wedding itinerary with Dylan's assistant.

I move on to reviewing the details of Flynn's schedule for the promotion of the film that defies naming. It'll be out in July, and Liza is already arranging interviews and appearances around the premiere. After five years of working for Flynn, the cycle of shooting, postproduction—which he has a hand in when he's also producing—promotion and premieres around the world has become somewhat predictable. It's always a little different from one film to the next, but the steps involved don't change much.

I've got a list of questions for Liza, things I anticipate that Flynn will want to know. I'm ten minutes into composing an email to Liza when Mackenzie appears at my door carrying a massive and colorful bouquet. They positively dwarf her petite frame, and when she peeks around them, her brown eyes dance with glee.

My heart staggers when I realize they're for me.

*Goddamn him.* Goddamn him and my staggering heart.

Mackenzie puts the vase on my desk. "Someone has been keeping secrets."

"Not me. I have no secrets."

"Who're they from?"

"I have no idea. Is there a card?"

Mackenzie points to the envelope buried between yellow and pink roses. The fragrance overpowers my senses as I reach for the envelope. I'm afraid to open it in front of her in case he's signed it. He wouldn't do that, would he? "Um…"

"Oh, okay. So it's like that, is it?" Winking, she smiles and turns to leave the room.

We're friends, and we talk about guys and hookups and other such things. But there's no way I can talk about *this* guy or hookup with her or anyone else tied to Quantum. It's bad enough that Natalie knows—and if she knows, Flynn probably does, too. Moaning at the mess I've made of things, I open the envelope to read the message: *I'm sorry. Please forgive me?*

I drop into my chair, undone by the simple sentiment and the grand gesture of four-dozen roses, delivered to the office, of all places. "Damn you, Hayden." He's got my attention, that's for sure. Now what?

I have no time to answer that question or to think about Hayden and the flowers or his note or anything else, because I'm needed at the luncheon to welcome Leah to the Quantum team. Leah, who's tall and lean and adorable with curly brown hair and big blue eyes, is so excited about her new job that she all but bounces with unrestrained glee.

Once she gets past being starstruck by her new employers, I think Leah will make a great assistant to Marlowe. She's bright and intelligent and eager to learn. Thankfully, Hayden is reportedly upstairs in the editing suite and doesn't attend the luncheon. Flynn, Natalie, Jasper and Kristian are all there representing

Marlowe, who's in London for a premiere. She'll be back at the end of the week, so I've got a few days to get Leah up to speed.

I keep today focused on the basics, setting her up with email, business cards, a company iPhone and a file containing passwords she'll need to work on Marlowe's behalf. I help her activate her new American Express black card and take her through the Quantum employee manual.

Emmett Burke, our chief counsel, arrives with the confidentiality agreement that Leah is required to sign as a condition of her employment. Emmett goes over each element of the agreement, emphasizing the requirement for complete discretion at all times.

"I need you to understand what that means," Emmett says. "Your friends are going to be fascinated by your new job. They're going to ask you about Marlowe and Flynn and Hayden and the others. They'll want you to tell them things no one knows about the stars you now work for. By signing this agreement, you indicate that you understand the implications of talking about the Quantum principals, their family members or their personal business to anyone. Ever. If you do—"

"I won't."

"I'm sorry, but I'm required to inform you of the consequences of violating the agreement." He outlines the legal steps the principals would take in the event of a breach of the confidentiality agreement.

I know them by heart. I've never forgotten my orientation or the fear of God that Emmett put into me with threats of legal action that would effectively ruin my life. I've never breathed a word of Flynn's business or the business of any of the Quantum partners to anyone, and I never will.

With the fear of God instilled in her, Leah signs the agreement, her hand trembling ever so slightly as she does.

"I'm sorry to start your first day with such dire warnings." Emmett tucks the documents into a leather portfolio. "But I hope you understand that it's not something we can postpone."

"I do, and I assure you, you'll never have a reason to enforce that agreement."

"I'm sure I won't." He shakes Leah's hand. "Welcome to Quantum. Look forward to working with you."

"Yes, me, too. Thank you."

As Emmett leaves the conference room, Leah watches him go. "Is being insanely hot a prerequisite to working here?"

I laugh, because I can see why it would seem that way to an outsider.

"What's his story?" she asks.

"Emmett? He's been friends with Flynn and Hayden forever, since high school, and he's worked for them since shortly after he graduated from law school. One thing I can tell you is he knows this business inside and out. He's my go-to person for information I can't get anywhere else."

"Good to know," she says with a coy smile that makes me laugh. "I have a feeling I'm going to have a *lot* of questions for him."

# CHAPTER 6

*Addie*

I spend the rest of the day orienting Leah to the routine of assisting one of Hollywood's biggest stars, sharing tricks and tips I've learned during five years of working for Flynn. Everyone is different, and what works for Flynn might not do for Marlowe. I emphasize that it'll take some time to master Marlowe's preferences, and Leah's job will get easier once she has a handle on the little things that mean so much in the chaotic life of a movie star.

"Here's a list of everything I know about her." My "list" is twelve single-spaced pages. Marlowe has been one of the most important people in my life since my mother died while Marlowe was filming a movie with my dad behind the camera. At that time, she was "no one" by Hollywood standards, but she quickly became everything to a motherless twelve-year-old girl. If it wasn't for Marlowe's unwavering friendship, I have no idea what would've become of me. She's the one who suggested Flynn hire me after I graduated from UCLA.

Leah scans the first page of my report on Marlowe and then glances at me. "I think I love you."

I smile at her and hope I've made another new friend. My dad always says you can never have too many friends.

By the time I leave the office, it's nearly eight o'clock and dark, too late to run on the beach or Rollerblade on the boardwalk. That leaves me with yoga videos in my living room. Finding my Zen will be a challenge tonight, but I'll give it a whirl.

The one good thing about working late is I've missed the worst of rush-hour traffic, and I'm home in twenty minutes. I unbuckle the roses that I've belted into the passenger seat and carry them to the elevator, emerging on the fifth floor to find Hayden sitting outside my door.

I'm so surprised to see him that I nearly drop the heavy vase.

"I guess the fact that you brought them home means you like them," he says as he stands.

"They're nice." I focus on not dropping them as I juggle my purse and keys and open the door. "What're you doing here?"

"I was hoping we could talk."

"I was hoping for that yesterday."

He gestures to the flowers. "I said I'm sorry."

"I know."

"You promised you wouldn't hate me."

"I don't hate you because we had sex."

"But you do hate me."

"I hate the way you treated me afterward, as if I don't matter at all, as if I'm just another of your random bimbos."

"You're neither of those things."

"And yet your silence told me I was both. You see my dilemma?"

"I don't want you to hate me."

"Okay, I won't."

"Why don't I believe you?"

The roses have begun to get heavy, so I take them inside and put them on the kitchen counter. I slide open the door to my deck, which overlooks the Pacific, letting in the fresh air and buying myself another minute to prepare to deal with him.

I turn to find him standing directly behind me. His hands land on my shoulders, and I want to shake him off, to tell him he doesn't have the right to touch me like that, but I'm frozen. When I see the stark, naked desire in his heated gaze, I can't seem to breathe, let alone speak.

"I'm an asshole, Addie. You knew that before."

Shaking my head, I say, "No," in the softest possible whisper.

"Yes, you did. You know me."

"Not like this. I didn't know you this way before."

His hands frame my face, his thumbs stroking my cheeks. "I never meant to hurt you. I promised Flynn I wouldn't, and then I did. Because I'm a selfish asshole who has no idea how to do something like this."

"Something like this?"

"Something real. Something that matters."

I can't hear this if he doesn't mean it or if he means to end it. As tears flood my eyes, I start to shake my head, but he tightens his hold on my face, keeping me from moving and anchoring me for a soft, sweet, devastating kiss. I want to tell him to stop, that he can't do this to me, but then my arms are around his neck and my mouth is open to his tongue, and I'm lost in him all over again, as if the last two torturous days never happened.

He kisses me as if I'm the most precious thing in his world, and for that moment, I allow myself to believe that maybe I am. That's the only way I can silence the frantic protests coming from my better judgment. I can either lose myself in the fantasy or go crazy wondering what it all means.

His hands fall from my face to grip my ass as he lifts me without breaking the kiss. Then we're moving through my dark condo, the same way we did the other morning, only everything is different now. *He* is different. We come down on the bed, still kissing deeply, but it's not like before. This time he's softer, sweeter, gentler. There's none of the frantic urgency that had us ripping clothes off each other's bodies the first time.

All he's done is kiss me, and I already know that if he disappears again after this, it'll ruin me. Still, I don't put a stop to it. Not then and not when he begins to undress me while continuing to kiss me with deep thrusts of his tongue. My breasts are freed from my bra, and his hands cover them, singeing my skin with his heat. I want to beg him to hurry, to kiss and suck and bite my nipples the way he did the last time, but he's not in that mood tonight.

He breaks the kiss and moves down, dragging the tip of his tongue over my throat and chest to the valley between breasts.

I arch and stretch, trying to get him to notice the way my nipples have tightened for him. He notices, but he doesn't immediately give me the relief I need so desperately.

"Addie," he whispers, "you're soft and sweet and beautiful. You need someone better than me."

"No." I'm left stunned by the shock of pain that ricochets through me at the thought of anyone but him touching me this way ever again. "I need *you*. I've always needed you."

Bending his head over my belly, he leaves a trail of fire on the way to the waistband of my skirt. "Not good enough for you."

The despair I hear in his voice has me blinking back new tears. I want to soothe and calm him. I want to fix whatever he thinks is so wrong with him. Seeing his vulnerability—hearing it in his words—I fall more deeply into the kind of love that lasts far longer than one lifetime.

He turns me over to unbutton and unzip the pencil skirt I wore to work, easing it down over my hips, leaving me wearing only a red thong. His hands cup and shape my ass, his tongue sliding over my back, straight down the center of me, leaving no part of me untouched. Again, I'm shocked by the erotic thrill of his tongue in a place no one but him has touched. And he doesn't just touch me, he worships me, until I'm crying and screaming and begging for sweet relief from the sharp, aching need.

He holds me wide open for his fingers and tongue, and when he sucks hard on my clit, he sends me into orbit. I come so hard that I lose all sense of place and time. I forget how much I hated him earlier. The love is all I feel, all I know, all I want. *He* is all I want.

I'm marginally aware of him moving behind me, the rustle of clothing, the pillow he shoves under me, the knees that push my legs wider apart, the hands that grasp my hips and the searing pain when he pushes his cock into me. I cry out, and he stops.

"Ah, fuck, you're hurting, aren't you?"

"Please, don't stop. *Please*."

"We'll go slow."

I'm so wet that I take the first part easily, but then the battle begins anew, a push-pull of want and need and ache and astonishing pleasure that only comes after the struggle to take him.

For a long time after he finally enters me fully, he stays still, pulsing and throbbing and expanding within me. His big body covers me, his hands grasping mine tightly as he waits for me to catch up. I'm so surrounded by him, so overwhelmed by his distinctive scent, the feel of his chest hair against my back, the tight grip of his hands on mine, and a wild, desperate need for more. I can't move or speak to tell him what I want or need, but he knows.

He flexes his hips, surging deeper into me, touching a spot that only he has ever found. I've barely moved, and I detonate, coming in a way I wouldn't have thought possible before he showed me what I'm capable of. I don't have the time or capacity to process that discovery, because he starts to move, riding the waves of my orgasm, keeping with the slow and tender theme that's ruined me from the first second he touched me tonight.

Unlike the first time, which went on forever, tonight he shows me some mercy. He gathers me up, his arms tight around me when he gives in and takes his own pleasure, flooding me with the heat of his release. Afterward, he holds me so tightly I can barely breathe, but it doesn't occur to me to tell him so. Nothing in my life has ever felt better than being surrounded and possessed by Hayden.

I grasp his arm, hoping to keep him there as long as I can, because I'm afraid of what happens next. Will he run away like he did before, or will he reluctantly try to give me what he thinks I need? Neither option works for me, but I don't know how to make him want me the same way I want him.

"Do you forgive me?" His voice is gruff, and the heat of his breath against my ear makes my skin tingle with goose bumps.

"I want to."

"You really, *really* should. I can't handle you hating me."

"How do you know I hated you?"

"I know you. I know your death stare. I've seen you use it often enough on people who try to go around you to get to Flynn."

"Why did you run?"

"I didn't know how to handle something like this. I still don't."

Not that I want him to move, but I need to see his face for this conversation, so I give him a little nudge.

He takes the hint and withdraws his still-hard cock—and how exactly is that possible?—and turns onto his back.

I push myself up onto my elbows and study the face that is at once so familiar and still so mysterious at the same time. "Something like this? What does that mean?"

He seems to force himself to look at me. "Something that matters. *You* matter, Addie. You matter way more than you should."

That, I realize, is the closest he'll probably come to telling me he cares about me, but it's enough to give me hope. "You say that as if it's a bad thing."

"It is. For you. And for me, too, if the last couple of days are any indication."

"What happened the last couple of days?"

"I couldn't stop thinking about you, about what we did and how soft your skin is and your taste…

I swallow hard, moved beyond measure by his heartfelt words. "What about it?"

"I couldn't get the taste of you off my tongue, and I didn't want to. I wanted to remember it and savor it because I knew I'd be lucky to ever get this close to you again."

Hearing him say such things, I need to touch him, so I snuggle up to him, making myself at home with my head on his chest and my hand on his upper abdomen, just above the head of his cock.

His arm comes around me, bringing me in even closer to him, and I exhale a long deep breath. At least he's not running. Not yet, anyway. "Why do you expect it to be such a bad thing?"

"I don't do this stuff, Addie. I don't do relationships or feelings or romance or any of that shit, and that's what you deserve. You need a guy who'll go all-out for you. That's not me."

"Maybe I need you more than I need that stuff. Has that occurred to you?"

He shakes his head. "No, it hasn't. You shouldn't need me. I'm not capable of what you want." His hand slides from my shoulder down to grip my ass. "This, right here, is what I'm capable of. Wanting more than this isn't wise."

"If you've never done it, how do you know you can't?"

"You'll have to take my word on that. There're things about me you don't know, and if you did… Well, you wouldn't want me the way you do."

"Haven't we always been friends? From the first time my dad brought me to work with him on one of your films, haven't we been friends?"

"Not always," he says with a low chuckle. "At first, you used to annoy the shit out of me with your ten million questions and endless curiosity about what I was doing and why. I wanted to muzzle you."

I laugh at that, as I always do whenever he reminds me of what a pain I was on that first set. I was seventeen, he was twenty-four, and I was desperately in love with him from the first time I laid eyes on him in all his exquisite male beauty, not that he knows that. In the ensuing years, we did become friends, even as I dated other guys and he "dated" every vagina in Hollywood—or that's how it seemed to me.

"I grew up, you grew up, and we did become friends. Admit it."

"Of course we're friends, Addie. We're close friends, which is what puts you off-limits to me. There's so much at stake, not just for us but for people we care about. People we love."

"You mean Flynn."

"Among others. He's not comfortable with me seeing you, because he knows you deserve better than me."

"He's your best friend. Why would he say such a thing about you?"

"Because it's true," he says with a sigh. "I never should've touched you the first time, and I certainly shouldn't have done it again."

"You say that as if it was totally up to you, as if I had no say in it."

"You definitely had a say, but as amazing as it is to be with you this way, it can't happen again."

My heart shatters into a million tiny pieces that can never be put back together. It takes every bit of the skill I've picked up from being around actors all my life not to show him how devastated I am to hear him say that. What's so wrong with me that he's unwilling to take a risk with me? So what if it's complicated because of Flynn and our other mutual friends? We're all adults. Or I thought we were.

Though he's drawn his line in the sand, he makes no move to leave. If he doesn't want me or this, part of me wishes he'd just go already and leave me alone. But the other part of me, the part that has loved him for so long, wants to hold on tight and never let him go now that I have him in my bed.

If this is all we're ever going to have, I want more, damn it. I curl my hand around his cock, loving the sharp gasp of his inhale.

"Addie—"

"Shut up, Hayden. If you're telling me this is all we're going to have, then let's do it up in style, shall we? Let's do everything."

*Hayden*

She has no idea what's she saying or who she's saying it to. The words "let's do everything" are to me what a red flag would be to a bull. During both encounters with her, I've kept in mind who she is to me and who she isn't. She's not my submissive, as much as I might wish otherwise. My dominant side has no place in her bed. But when she says those three little words, my inner Dom roars to life, and all bets are off.

"Put your hands over your head. Hold on to the headboard."

Her expressive eyes widen ever so slightly, her lips part and her nipples tighten. Holy fuck, does she *like* being told what to do in bed? No, no, *no*. Just no. It doesn't matter if she likes it. It doesn't matter if she's the world's most willing submissive. She can never be *my* submissive. I can't go there with her. Anyone but precious, beautiful Addie. The thought of marking her soft skin or torturing her with my kink is beyond my ability to comprehend.

I can do those things with other women because I don't love them. This woman... She has my heart and my soul and my love and, if I were capable, everything I have to give, except my dominance. But she asked for more. I can give her that without giving her everything.

Eyeing me with trepidation that makes me harder than I already was, she does what I've asked, slowly raising her hands up and over her head to grasp the wrought iron rails of her headboard. The movement puts her spectacular breasts on prominent display. I wish I had my clamps with me. I wish I had my floggers, ropes and plugs.

I'm out of my mind with lust at the thought of doing those things with her, even though I never will. But I can give her *more* without taking *everything* she has to give.

"Do you have lube?"

Her face flushes with the sweetest blush I've ever seen. "In the drawer."

Fuck, I hoped she'd say no, so I wouldn't be tempted. But she didn't say no, and I'm sorely tempted. She liked when I licked and fingered her there. I'm experienced enough to know when anal play turns off a partner, and Addie was incredibly turned *on* by it. Wait until she sees what "more" entails.

*You just told her you can't do this anymore, and you're going to do* that? I actively hate the inner voice inside my mind that calls me out on my mixed messages. This is the last time I'm ever going to touch her, and yes, I'm going to do *that* because she'll love it and so will I. It's one of my favorite things to do in bed, and why shouldn't I do it with her when she's already shown how much she likes to be touched there?

*Stop rationalizing and just do it, will you?* The devil in me always wins out over the angel. Always. Propped up on one hand, I reach for her bedside drawer and find the lube along with a box of condoms and a rabbit vibrator. I grab all three and drop them on the bed.

Her breathing becomes more rapid when she starts to figure out what I have in mind.

"You still want more?" I ask her as I roll on a condom and take the lid off the lube.

She eyes the lube and the vibe, and then she looks up at me with those big, bottomless eyes and nods.

"Words, Addie. Give me words."

"Yes, Hayden, I still want more."

"And you know this is it, right? No more after this."

"You've made that perfectly clear."

I can deal with my conscience tomorrow. Tonight, I'm going to give her an experience—and an orgasm—she'll never forget. And then I'll let her go because it's the right thing to do, not because it's what I want. No, if I could have anything in this world that I want, it would be her. However, I'm a realist, and I know how things work in the world I live in. I can't have her and still be me, too. I can't drag her into the dreck that is my life, my family or my kink. She's so clean and lovely and sweet. I can't be responsible for causing the inner light that shines so brightly within her to dim with disappointment and regret.

Her body is on high alert for immediate attack, so I surprise her with softness and sensuality. I start with her lovely pink nipples, which I lave with my tongue until she's squirming beneath me, her hips rising, seeking my cock. I add suction and the gentle pinch of my teeth, and she cries out. Moving down, I keep my fingers wrapped around her left nipple, keeping up the tension as I focus on her core. I tongue her clit in soft, persuasive strokes until the first orgasm rolls through her, making her gasp and pant, among other noises that I commit to memory for all the nights I'll have to spend without her.

I drive two fingers of my free hand into her pussy, which pulses with the aftershocks of her orgasm. Then I feel her hands in my hair, tugging and pulling. I withdraw from her to deliver a short, sharp spank to her right ass cheek that startles her.

"Hands over your head."

I notice her hands are now trembling when she returns them to the iron rods. Rubbing the spot where my hand marked her tender flesh, I turn the pain to pleasure.

"Hayden…"

"Shhh. No talking. Just feel. If you want to stop, say the word 'red,' and everything comes to a halt, okay?"

She nods rapidly.

"Words, Addie. Give me the words."

"Yes, okay."

"Unless I ask you a question, the only word you're allowed to say is red. Got it?"

"Yes."

"Now relax, and enjoy."

Her small laugh tells me she's a long way from relaxed, but I'm determined to make sure she enjoys this. In my perfect world, I would've prepared her with plugs and repeated sessions that work up to what I'm about to do. But my world with Addie is not perfect, and if this is all we're ever going to have, I want her ass. I've obsessed about her ass to the point of madness. And when she offers me everything, goddamn it, I'm going to take it. See what I mean about being a selfish bastard?

But because I love her so damned much, I'm going to make sure it's amazing for her. "Has anyone ever touched you here before?" I press two lubed fingers against her anus and push.

"N-no. Never."

"But you like when I do, right?"

"Y-yes. I like it."

"Mmm, you get so wet when I fuck your ass with my fingers." I lean in to run my tongue through her copious dampness. The more I stroke her with my fingers, the wetter she gets. I push the vibe into her pussy and turn it on, her low moan making me even harder than I already was. Fucking hell, I can't get any bigger or I'll cripple her. She holds on tight to the iron rods, but her body twitches and writhes on the bed. Her hips come off the mattress as she tries to find relief from the ache of her desire.

I slide my fingers back into her ass, suck hard on her clit and make her come again, her ass muscles clamping down tight against my fingers. I can't wait to feel that on my dick.

Pushing the vibe in and out of her, I say, "You still want more, Addison?"

"Yes," she says through gritted teeth. "Give me more."

Fucking hell, she's amazing. Maybe she could be everything I need and want—

*No. Don't go there. One more time, and then it's over forever.*

My hands tremble ever so slightly when I apply a generous amount of lube to my cock. She's tight, I'm big, and this is going to be a battle royal. I can't wait. "It'll hurt—a lot—at first, but the more you relax and push back against me, the easier it'll be. You got me?"

"Yeah," she says, panting, "I got you."

"It's going to be so good, so hot, so amazing, but not at first." With the vibe making the squeeze even tighter than it would be without it, I press the tip of my cock against her tiny opening and push into her.

She screams so loudly I worry her neighbors will call the cops.

I withdraw, grab my T-shirt off the bed and give it to her. "Bite down on this."

Her body is one big quiver as she puts the T-shirt in her mouth to bite down on it.

I start over, giving her the first two inches in one thrust.

The shirt muffles her scream, and her hips come up off the mattress again, seeking something more. She's not ready yet for more, so I remain still while her body stretches to accommodate me. I press my thumb to her clit, stroke the vibe into her and then back out, and another inch of my cock sinks into her ass. Watching her tiny hole stretch and open to allow me in is one of the hottest things I've ever seen—and I've seen a lot of hot things in my life. But because it's her, because I love her, this is off-the-charts hot.

Still teasing her clit with my thumb, I pulse into her in small increments that make her mewl into my shirt. Those noises, those incredibly sexy noises, send a new burst of blood and heat to my cock, making her moan when she feels me expand within her.

"Addison."

She opens her eyes to meet my gaze, and the fierce determination I see in her eyes does crazy things to my heart. I love her so fucking much. What would it be like to be with her this way every day? To have her in my bed and in my life, to make love to her my way, her way and every other way we can think of? It's just a fantasy, though. Real life doesn't work that way. Real life is a mess, and I can't make a mess of something so perfect.

"Are you okay?"

She removes the T-shirt from her mouth. "Mmm. Yeah." Her words are choppy and breathy.

"More or stop?"

"M-more."

I give a little push of my hips to remind her of where I am, in case she's forgotten. That thought nearly makes me laugh. "You're sure?"

"Y yes."

"You're so fucking sexy, Addison. You have no idea how hot you are taking my cock in your ass." I frame her face with my hands and use my thumbs to wipe away tears that flow freely down her cheeks. "Why're you crying?"

"Overwhelming."

"Not painful?"

"Some."

I keep one hand on her face and use the other to apply more lube. The last thing I want is to cause her real or lasting pain. All I want is her ultimate pleasure, and I'm determined to get it.

Bending over her, I take a nipple into my mouth, tugging and sucking until it's standing up tall and proud. Then I bite down on it, just hard enough to take her mind off the pressure down below. As she gasps, her back bows, and I push deeper into her while turning on the vibrator at the same time. I switch to the other side, repeating the process until she's taken all of me.

"You did it," I whisper, my lips brushing against her ear.

"I need…"

"What, honey? What do you need?"

"Touch you."

"Go ahead."

Her arms come around my neck, her muscles tightening into a noose as she holds me close, maybe so I can't move or do anything to disrupt the fragile accord we've reached. "You've got to let me move, baby."

She moans, and the sound goes straight to my dick, which expands inside the tight confines of her ass. She grunts and mutters something unintelligible, but it might've been about breaking her in half.

I love this so much. I love giving her a new experience. I love the noises she makes, the intensity, the earthiness, the dirtiness. I love the way her muscles milk me and her body trembles uncontrollably. I love the feverish heat coming off her skin and the flush that tints her complexion. And yes, I love the touch of fear in her eyes as she looks up at me, wondering what's next, wondering if this is it or if there's more.

*Oh, baby, there's so much more.*

"You've got to let me move," I say, kissing her face and then her lips as I work myself free of her tight hold. Propped up on my hands, I look down at her. "Spread your legs as far apart as they'll go."

Moving tenuously, she does what I ask her to, her legs trembling madly.

"Now keep them there. Hold on to my shoulders and bite down on the T-shirt if you need to scream. We don't want to freak out the neighbors."

Her lips move in silent inquiry. She's probably about to ask what I'm going to do. Why tell her when showing her is so much more effective? As I withdraw from her slowly, her fingernails bite into my shoulders. And then I slam back in while pressing my thumb against her clit. She explodes.

I fuck her harder, giving her deep thrusts while continuing to massage her clit and move the vibe, keeping her coming almost the entire time. She's screaming and crying and scratching me, but she never says the word that would stop everything. I fucking love her. I love the way her body takes me when she shouldn't be able to. I love that she seems to love this as much as I do. I love the way she comes and comes and then *comes* some more. I love the way she tests my control with the tight fist of her ass muscles squeezing my cock so hard that I cry out from the supreme pleasure of having her this way.

And then she breaks me with three little words.

# CHAPTER 7

*Addie*

How to describe the indescribable? I've had sex. I've had amazing sex—most recently with him. But I've never felt anything like this. At first, it hurt so much I didn't think I'd be able to do it, but he takes his time and masters my body the same way he's mastered my heart and soul. I take him. I take all of him. But that's the easy part. This part, the part where he hammers into me while I come constantly, is something else altogether. I need more air than I can get through my nose, so I tear the T-shirt from my mouth and toss it aside, grunting inelegantly with every deep stroke of his cock.

My body seizes and throbs, and I come *again.*

God help me.

I'm crying and moaning and clawing at him. Every emotion hovers at the surface, ready to break free. I can't handle his fierce possession and the swell of emotion, too. It's too much, and the words break free before I know I'm going to say them.

"Hayden, God, *Hayden,*" I say on a broken sob, "I love you. *I love you.*"

He drives into me one last time and comes with a low growl that reverberates through his chest into mine. I feel him everywhere, from the bottom of my feet to the top of my head and every pressure point in between. My ass and clit throb with the aftereffects of intense fucking and multiple orgasms. If I thought I was crippled after the first time with him, I'll never walk again after this.

He collapses on top of me, his body bathed in sweat, his breathing rough and choppy.

I hold him close, sensing he needs the contact as much as I do. I can't believe I blurted out those words, and he probably can't either. It's too much. It's not enough. It'll never be enough. He can't leave me now that he knows I love him. He can't walk away from what we could have together. I won't let him. He said this would be the end, but it's only the beginning of everything I've ever wanted. I can be what he needs. I can change his mind if I love him enough for both of us.

After what we just shared, I'm sure of that. I'm so sure that I'm willing to risk everything by saying it again, in case he missed it the first time. "I love you, Hayden."

He doesn't say anything, but he tightens his hold on me. It's all he's capable of. I get that, and it's enough. For now. I'll have all of him no matter what it takes. Anything less than everything will never be enough for me where he is concerned.

With a deep inhale, he rises up and begins to withdraw from me, slowly, carefully, making me moan from the agonizing drag of his big cock over my sensitive, tortured flesh. Then he removes the vibrator, too, leaving my body humming with aftershocks. He looks down at me for a long, charged moment before he leaves the bed and goes into the bathroom. I hear water running, and then he's back with a warm washcloth that he uses to clean me up. I'm so sensitive I want to beg him not to touch me, but I can see that it's important to him to tend to me. So I let him, wincing as he does.

When he's finished, he curls up to me, wrapping his arm and leg around me, bringing me in tight against him. I thought he would leave as soon as he could, so the intimate nature of this embrace brings a lump to my throat. He can run, but I'll find him. I'll go after him every time. I'll wear him down until there's nowhere left for him to hide from the fact that he loves me as much as I love him.

He's had me. Now I'll have him.

I'm emotionally and physically spent after what just happened, but I'm also buzzing with adrenaline that keeps me awake waiting to see what he'll do. He strokes my arm and back, his lips moving over my hair. The tenderness is what slays me. Even after he warned me that this was all we could ever have, he's still tender. He still cares. I can feel it in every breath he takes and every touch of his hands on my hypersensitive body.

We stay wrapped up in each other long enough that I lose track of how much time has passed. He never stops caressing me, and I float on a sea of contentment. This is how it could be, him and me, pushing the limits together, experiencing life's highs and lows and everything in between. I want that life with him so badly that there's nothing I won't do to get it. That sort of desperation is new to me.

His hand stills on my shoulder. "Are you asleep?" he whispers.

I start to reply, but something stops me.

After a long silence, he says, "I want to say it, too, and I'm sorry I can't. I don't know how to say it, because I never have before. I'm so sorry, baby."

While I hold my breath and blink back tears, he gets up from the bed. I hear him rustling around the room. I hear legs pushing into denim and the scrape of his zipper. His T-shirt is half under me, and he extricates it carefully. A few minutes later, I hear the front door click shut.

I want to beg him not to go. I want to beg him to give me—and us—a chance, but that battle can't be fought and won tonight. That battle is going to take some time and more patience than I've ever needed before.

But he's confirmed the one thing I need to know to make the struggle worthwhile—he loves me, too.

## Hayden

"*I love you, Hayden.*" It's all I hear as I drive through the dark night after leaving her. I'm too wound up to sleep or work, so I go to the one place where everything always makes sense to me—Club Quantum. Located in the basement of our Los Angeles office building, access is granted with a palm scanner that admits me to a special elevator that leads only to the basement.

The doors open into the club, which is busy for a weeknight. I wave to Kristian and Jasper, who are entertaining guests in the main room. At the bar, I pull up a stool and shake hands with Sebastian Lowe, who manages the LA club for us. He's tall, dark, muscular, scarred and ruthlessly intimidating. He also has a heart of gold and a loyalty streak a mile wide. Sebastian is one of my oldest and closest friends, and he's on that short list of people I love.

"Pappy?" he asks.

"You know it."

He puts a glass on the bar in front of me and pours. "Rough night?"

If you count having to tell the love of your life that you can't be with her a rough night, then yeah, it's been pretty bad. But I don't tell him that. I can't tell anyone that. "Not so much." In some ways, it had been a fantastic, magical night. I'll live off the memories of what we did for the rest of my life.

"Something's up," Sebastian says with the wisdom of someone who's known me a long time. His mother worked as my father's housekeeper for years. Sebastian and I grew up together, albeit on different sides of the Beverly Hills tracks. I credit him—and his mother—with bringing some normalcy to the chaos that was my life. They credit me with saving him from the lure of gangs by giving him a job at Quantum.

His mom has no idea what he really does for us, and she never will. Sebastian and Graciela Lowe are family to me, and as my brother from another mother, Sebastian knows when something's not right.

"Is it your mom?" he asks, painfully aware of the ongoing struggle of my mother's addiction to anything and everything addicting—booze, drugs, sex. You name it, she's hooked on it.

"All quiet on that front for the moment." I live on the razor's edge with her, constantly teetering between disasters. We've had three months of relative peace and quiet, mostly because she was in rehab for most of that time.

"You got eyes on her?"

"Yep." We both know having eyes on her hasn't prevented past disasters, and it probably won't prevent future ones either. But knowing someone is watching out for her allows me to sleep a couple of hours every night. The time I spent with Addie is the first peace I've gotten from the hell of that situation in ages. While I was lost in her, I wasn't thinking about my mother or worrying about when the next disaster will strike.

I think that's why I gave in so easily the other night. It's why I gave in again tonight after going there to smooth things over with her. I didn't go there to do what we ended up doing, which is further proof that I need to keep my distance or lose my resolve. Now that I know what it's like to touch her and kiss her and fuck her, I can't go near her again. My legendary control is nonexistent where she's concerned. She's my kryptonite.

"Is this seat taken?"

I glance over to see Cresley Dane, my close friend and frequent scene partner. "It is now." I lean in to accept her kiss to my cheek. I've touched every inch of her delectable body, but I don't feel anything more than friendly affection when I look at her world-famous face. "I didn't know you were in town."

She accepts a glass of the Belvedere we keep on ice for her, gifting Sebastian with the smile that's made her millions. He's not unaffected, but only I can tell that. The icy vodka is in sharp contrast to the warmth of her smile, the sweetness of her personality. Nothing about her screams fame or fortune or ego. I enjoy her tremendously, and I've loved the time we spent together in the dungeon. She's a complex woman who works at the top of her field by day, but willingly surrenders control in her personal life.

Under normal circumstances, I'd invite her to the dungeon to work out the frustration I feel about the situation with Addie. But I can't go from the bed of the woman I love to the arms of another woman and find the peace that eludes me. That's not going to fix what's wrong with me.

"You up for playing tonight?" she asks.

"Nah, I'm cooked. One drink and out for me."

Her lip rolls into an adorable pout. "What about my training?"

An odd pang that feels an awful lot like guilt takes root in my gut. The thought of touching Cresley—or any woman—after what I've shared with Addie makes me nauseated. I take a drink from my glass, and for once Pappy doesn't soothe me. "We might have to put that on hold for a little while." Just until I get my head together. I keep that part to myself.

She eyes me shrewdly. "How come?"

"I've got some stuff going on that's going to require a lot of time and focus. Can't afford any distractions." I'm making this up as I go, but it sounds convincing. To me, anyway.

"I thought that was the whole point, to reduce stress by cutting loose together."

"I… I need some time, Cres."

"How much time?"

"I don't know." I feel like shit for doing this to her when we're already well into the early stages of her submissive training. With her crazy life as an in-demand model and the single mom to a son, she doesn't take a lot of time for herself. This is important to her, and I hate that I'm disappointing her. But I can't imagine touching her now. As I stare into the eyes of one of the world's most beautiful women, my cock couldn't be less interested.

Fucking hell, is that what I'm doomed to now that I've had Addie? I can't get hard for anyone else? Suddenly, I'm angry with Addie for doing this to me. For wrapping her sweet, sexy self around my soul and working her way so deep inside me I may never get her out. And fuck, I don't want her out. I want more of her. I want her so badly, I burn with desire for her.

"I don't know what's going on with you, Hayden, but I hope you'll call me when you're ready to pick up where we left off."

I don't make promises I can't keep, so I stick to safer ground. "Say hey to Ty for me, okay?"

She smiles at the mention of her son, but I can see she gets that I'm ending our relationship—or whatever it was. "Yeah, you got it." She leans in to kiss my cheek. "Take care."

"You, too." I'm incredibly relieved when she gets up and walks away. Most Doms, myself included, don't like to share their subs with other Doms. But I hope that Cresley cuts her losses with me and finds someone else to play with. She's a smart, savvy woman, so I'm not worried about her safety. Right now, I'm more concerned about my own.

"Did you really pass up a chance to play with Cresley Dane?" Sebastian asks when he makes his way to my end of the bar.

"So what if I did?"

"So you're fucking crazy, that's what. What's up with you? You're like a pent-up tiger looking for a place to rage."

The thing about going way back with people is that they know you too well. At times like this, when I actually have something to hide, I wish I could be less obvious to my friends. "I'm fine. Under a lot of stress at work to name a film that defies naming, among other things."

"It'll come to you. Always does."

"Thanks for the vote of confidence. I'm going to head out." I clasp Sebastian's outstretched hand in a sideways bro shake. "Take it easy."

"You, too."

I feel his gaze on me as I wave to my partners and head for the elevator without stopping to chat with them. That, too, is unusual, but I'm all talked out tonight. I need to think, and I can't do that here with the music and the conversation and the temptation that surrounds me. I direct the Land Rover to my house in Malibu, in need of some time at the beach to clear my mind.

On the drive, I remind myself why it has to be this way with Addie. You see, I'm not all that different from my mother. I too have an addictive personality. I realized that when I was very young and tempted by all the same things that rule my mother. The only difference between her and me is that I've learned to manage my demons, whereas she never has. I learned what not to do by watching her self-destruct a little at a time until there's almost nothing left of her. As much as I love her—and I do in spite of everything she's put me through—I refuse to follow her path.

Control is the fine line that separates me from her. I rarely have more than a couple of drinks and haven't ever touched any kind of drugs out of fear that one taste would be all it took to ruin me. I'm so afraid of what might happen that I've never even smoked pot, which makes me a rarity in the indulgent world in which I live and work.

My mother can't control her demons. I'm not deluded enough to expect this latest honeymoon period after rehab is actually going to stick. The most I ever hope for anymore is that rehab will buy us some time.

I've lived in this state of petrified anticipation my entire life. Naturally, I try to control the situation by hiring people to watch her. Not that they can do a damned thing to curb her destructive tendencies, which is why peace of mind is a rare and fleeting thing in my life.

Control is my cornerstone, but I've lost control where Addie is concerned, and I can't let that happen. I've seen what happens when control is lost. I've lived the aftermath of disaster my entire life, and I refuse to be weak like my parents. I'm better than them, or at least I've always thought so. Recent events have me wondering if I'm not more their son than I ever wanted to be.

I direct so I can control every aspect of the films I create. I'm a dominant so I can control my own pleasure and that of my partner. I'm always in control of myself and my emotions. That's how I keep from becoming lost to addiction like my mother or a gluttonous failure like my father. Control keeps the demons at bay.

So you're probably thinking—he's a rich entitled prick who could have anyone or anything he wants. Why can't he just *have* Addie if she's what he wants? Those are good questions, and you're right about me being rich, entitled *and* a prick. I'd never deny I'm all that and many other unsavory things, too.

The answer to *why* I can't have her is simple. I can't *control* her. I can't control *myself* around her. I can't control the way she makes me feel—wild and *out* of control. I'm never out of control. And that's why I have to stay away. She scares the living hell out of me. I can't afford to lose control, so I can't afford her.

I say it's simple, though it's anything but. Staying away from her is going to be like telling my mother she shouldn't shoot smack and expecting her not to do it because it's not good for her.

Staying away from Addie will be the hardest thing I've ever done, but the alternative isn't an option for me as much as I might intensely wish otherwise. I want her in a way that I've never wanted anyone else, but I refuse to make an exception to the rules that have governed my life. Those rules are the difference between a life of success and a life of disarray.

After growing up the way I did, I'm afraid of very few things. I'm afraid of how and when I'll lose my mother. But I'm even more afraid of losing control of myself, of veering off the current path, of losing the life and career I've worked so hard to have. Too many people depend on me to let that happen. Sometimes, even rich, entitled pricks don't get everything they want.

I learned early on that life isn't fair. I'm not about to start fighting that battle now. I love her, but I can't have her. Somehow I'll find a way to live with that.

*Addie*

I almost call in sick this morning because I'm aching so badly from last night that I can barely move. Not that I regret it. I don't. It was the most amazing sexual experience of my life, and any aches or pains I have today are a small price to pay.

I don't call in sick, because I've got a lot to do at the office, and I need to start making plans for how I'm going to change Hayden's mind about us.

He needs me. I need him. I refuse to believe we can't find a way to be together. Resolved to my goals where he's concerned, I force myself out of bed and hobble into the bathroom to run the hottest bath I can stand. I fill it with eucalyptus oil, hoping it will take some of the sting out of my abused flesh. I lower myself carefully into the tub, sitting gingerly and sighing with pleasure as the hot water surrounds me.

I think it through from every angle. He's keeping things from me. That much I'm sure of. I have access to every kind of resource, including private investigators if it comes to that, which it won't. I can't take the chance of him—or Flynn—finding out if I were to have Hayden investigated. That would be a disaster for me professionally. I love my job—and the people I work for—too much to go there.

But damn, I want to. I want to know everything about him so I'll have the tools I need to see this through. I have to remove the obstacles he sees standing between us. How can I do that if I don't know what the obstacles are?

Part of it is most definitely rooted in his chaotic childhood. He was shaped, for better or worse, by the drama he grew up with. His mother has caused him endless heartache with her horrific addictions to drugs, booze and men. The scars he carries with him probably run deeper than anyone realizes.

"That's okay. I can work with scars. I don't need him to be perfect. I just need him to be perfect for me."

Before this day is out, I want to see my dad. He usually gives me good advice, and he will in this situation, too, as long as he doesn't know I'm talking about Hayden. For reasons he refuses to share with me, he can't stand Hayden. I try not to think about how difficult that'll be if I'm able to work things out with Hayden. I'm close to my dad, and it kills me that he hates the man I love. But even my father's certain disapproval is not enough to deter me from my goal.

When the water begins to cool, I rise up from the tub feeling marginally better than I did when I got in—until I step foot on the bathroom floor and pain radiates from my backside, making me wince and grit my teeth. *Ugh*. This is going to be a long-ass day. I giggle at my choice of words.

Standing in my walk-in closet, I start to reach for my most comfortable work clothes, the ones I wear at that time of the month, but then stop myself.

Pain aside, this is no time to fall down on the job. There's never been a more important time to look like two million bucks at the office. I grab a sexy black wrap dress and a pair of four-inch heels that do incredible things for my legs. Just in case this day turns out better than expected, I wear lacy black underwear that leaves very little to the imagination.

Each step in the heels hurts, but I soldier on, determined to make use of every tool in my arsenal, including my bruised and battered body, to get what I want. I decide to grab coffee at the office and head for the garage. As I make my way from the elevator to my car, I realize I'm actually limping. I'll need a story to explain that and settle on a Rollerblading accident. Everyone knows how much I love my blades, so it won't surprise anyone to hear I pulled a muscle while blading on the boardwalk. I can sell that.

Leah is moving into her new apartment today, so she won't be in the office, which is just as well. I have a ton of my own stuff to get done.

By the time I reach the Quantum parking lot, I'm in so much pain from sitting on my sore bum that I'm blinking back tears. I pull into my assigned space and am gathering my things when a big, black shadow falls over my car from Hayden's Range Rover pulling in next to me.

I'm surprised he's getting here so late. He's usually one of the first to arrive. I look over to find him staring intently at me and stare back at him, wishing I could read his mind so I'll know exactly what I'm up against. Since that's not an option, I get out of the car and make a huge—and painful—effort to move normally, to act like nothing hurts when everything does.

Grimacing all the way, I go inside ahead of him.

"Addie, wait up."

I turn and smile up at him. "Did you need something?"

"You… Are you… You're all right?"

"Of course I am. Why wouldn't I be?"

"I, um… Ah, no reason, I guess."

"How are you?"

He seems surprised by the question, and in the heartbeat of a second it takes for him to answer me, I see the anguish that grips him. I'm strangely satisfied to know he's agonizing over this situation as much as I am. "I'm fine." Dragging his gaze off my face, he lays his hand on the palm scanner and presses the up arrow to summon the elevator.

We wait in awkward and painful—in my case, anyway—silence until the elevator arrives with a cheerful ding.

Hayden holds the door open for me, and I proceed ahead of him.

And the Academy Award for Best Actress in a morning-after first-time anal sex scene goes to… Addison York. The crowd goes *wild*! I pinch my lips to keep from laughing out loud at the ludicrous direction my thoughts have taken.

"We need to talk," he says in a low growl that makes my nipples tingle. It's the same way he talked to me when we were in bed.

"About what?" I ask in my best nonchalant tone. I'm making this up as I go along, but it seems to rattle him that I'm not a hot mess after last night. Since my calm coolness is getting to him, I keep it up.

"You know what about."

"I don't need to talk, but if you have something on your mind, you know how to find me." It's physically and emotionally excruciating to have to pretend I'm unaffected by what happened last night. I want to throw my arms around him and love the wounded look right out of his gorgeous blue eyes, but if I do that, if I tip my hand too soon, I'll lose the edge I currently hold over him.

He's undone by my indifference. That much is apparent, so I lean back against the corner of the elevator to relieve the pressure on my aching body while we ride the elevator to the fifth floor. I watch the elevator's progress above the doors while he watches me. I can feel his heated gaze on me, and remaining indifferent takes everything I've got and then some.

"Tonight I'm coming over, and we're going to talk," he mutters before the doors open on our floor. "You hear me?"

"Uh-huh." My heart dances with glee and anticipation. For all his sophistication and experience with women, the poor bastard has no idea that I've already got him firmly ensnared in my web. Despite what he said last night, he's coming back for more. He thinks we'll talk. I've got other plans.

Note to self—take some painkillers later this afternoon so you can "perform" later.

We part company at the reception desk, where Mackenzie gives me an inquisitive look because I arrived with Hayden. If only she knew the real story.

"Hey," she calls after me. "Are you limping?"

"Rollerblading disaster," I say over my shoulder, continuing on to my office.

"Who had a Rollerblading disaster?" Flynn asks. Wearing faded denim and an old T-shirt, he's sitting in my visitor chair, feet on my desk, scrolling through his phone, looking nothing at all like the world-famous Academy Award-winning actor and producer he is. Today, and most days, for that matter, he's a regular guy who happens to have a blockbuster career. I love that he's so unaffected by his fame and success. I love the way he cares about his friends and family, and watching him fall madly in love with Natalie has been a beautiful thing.

"I did. One leg zigged while the other zagged, and well, ouch."

"Yikes. That sounds painful."

"You have no idea."

"Do you need a doctor?"

"Nah. Just some pulled muscles that'll be fine in a day or two." I drop my bag on the desk and remain standing so he won't see the full extent of my so-called injury. "What're you doing in my office anyway?"

"Other than the fact that I own the place?" he asks with a cocky grin.

"Other than that."

"Nat and I were talking last night about doing something to celebrate *Camo's* big win. We'd like to take everyone to Mexico for a getaway in the next couple of weeks. I was hoping you could help me with that."

"Is *help* a metaphor for plan and coordinate the entire thing?"

"Of course it is."

"Thought so," I say with a chuckle. It's a good thing I love him so much, or I'd want to have him killed half the time. "I can do that. No problem. And it's a great idea. You guys will have a blast."

"*Us* guys? You're coming, too, and so are Leah, Emmett, Ellie, Sebastian and everyone else who matters. I want the whole crew."

"I'll see what I can do." Coordinating a vacation for a dozen of the busiest people I know is going to take some doing, but it's a challenge I welcome on a day when I have too many other things vying for my attention. "And I'm delighted to be included. Thank you."

"Of course you're included. You're the best, Addie."

"I know. I tell you that every day."

Laughing, he gets up to leave. "You're sure you're okay?"

"I'm fine. Nothing to worry about."

"Okay, then. Keep me posted on the plans for Mexico."

"You know I will."

"You're coming to the meetings today, right?"

"Yep, I'll be there." He has a series of conference calls lined up to go over preproduction details for the new film he's due to begin shooting in Prague next month. This one isn't a Quantum production, so it requires a lot more external coordination ahead of shooting.

"Remind me to never again do a non-Quantum film."

"Funny, I was just thinking how much more 'work' it is when you take an outside project."

"It sucks," he says bluntly.

"Is Natalie going to Prague with you?"

"Yeah, she is. She can handle foundation business from there, and I won't lose my mind trying to work while wishing I was with her."

"You're pathetic."

"I'm well aware of that, and the happiest pathetic bastard you'll ever meet."

"Get your happy self out of my office so I can plan your vacation."

"I'm going, but before I do… I need to ask you something that's none of my business."

"Okay…"

"You and Hayden. Is that happening?"

I'm unprepared for him to ask me that so bluntly, and I have no idea what to say. Is it happening? Hell, yes, it's happening, but will it continue? That much I don't know, and I'm sure he can tell just by looking at me that I'm torn up about it. "Ah, well, we're in negotiations, I guess you could say."

"Stick to your guns and get what you want out of it."

"That's the goal."

"Love you, Addie," he says on the way out the door.

"Yeah, yeah," I mutter. "Love you, too." He's the best boss and friend anyone could ever have. We work hard, and we play harder. He includes me in all the fun stuff he and his friends do together, and I love being part of his inner circle. It's an honor I don't take lightly. After his disastrous marriage to Valerie blew up in his face, he became a lot more selective about the people he allows close to him, and we're all incredibly protective of him.

I sit, carefully and painfully, and boot up my computer. I immediately dive into the planning of the Mexican getaway by sending emails to everyone Flynn asked me to invite. Their replies begin rolling in immediately.

"Count me in," Jasper says.

"Yes, definitely YES," Marlowe replies.

"Love to," Kristian writes.

"God, yes," Flynn's sister Ellie responds.

"Um, let me think about it…" Emmett says. "YES!"

Leah's reply makes me laugh. "*Seriously*!?!? I *love* this job!"

"Well," I say to myself, "tell me how you really feel, people." I can't help but notice that Hayden hasn't replied to my email. I try to imagine the two of us in our current push-pull status together for a vacation in Mexico. How will we ever pull that off in front of our closest friends? He hasn't even said he wants to go, and I'm already anticipating disaster.

Just before eleven, I gather my stuff and head for Flynn's office to participate in the first of three calls he has planned for today. I'm about to knock on his partially open door when I hear Natalie's voice.

"Someone has to tell her," she says. "It's not fair that she's getting into this without knowing. Remember how the sin of omission nearly derailed us?"

"I remember, but it's not our place to share Hayden's business. It's up to him to tell her, not us."

"I hate that she doesn't know. It makes me feel like a bad friend to be keeping such a big thing from her when she's getting in deeper with him all the time."

*Holy fucking shit.* I have no idea what they're talking about, but I want to know—and I want to know right now. I knock loudly and enter Flynn's corner office with the spectacular view of the city. I couldn't care less about that spectacular view in light of what I just heard. "I'm going to put this right out there. I heard you talking about me, and I want to know what everyone is keeping from me."

The two of them stare at me, wide-eyed and slack-jawed. Eavesdropping on my boss and his wife is not the best way to get ahead in my career, but the door was open, and he knew I was coming for the meeting.

I look him dead in the eyes and say, "Tell me, Flynn."

"I-I can't." In all the years I've known him, I've never once heard him stammer. "I'm sorry. We shouldn't have been talking about you or Hayden. It's none of our business."

"No, it isn't, but the fact that he's keeping something big from me is very much my business in light of the fact that I'm sleeping with him."

That statement results in more staring and shocked silence.

"This is all my fault, Addie," Natalie says with tears in her big green eyes. "I never should've said anything. Not here, anyway. Please forgive me."

"Of course I forgive you. You're both concerned about me, and I appreciate that. But I don't appreciate my friends keeping things from me. So who's going to tell me the big secret?"

"Hayden has to," Flynn says. "It's not ours to tell."

Well, isn't this just fabulous? He said we're going to "talk" tonight, well, you bet your ass we're going to talk. He's going to tell me what he's been keeping from me if I have to beat it out of him.

"Fair enough. There's your call," I say when the extension on his desk rings.

Still looking rattled, Natalie kisses his cheek and squeezes my arm on her way out of the office. The friendly but sympathetic smile she gives me sends my nerves into the red zone. What the hell does everyone else know that I don't?

# CHAPTER 8

*Flynn*

*Fuck, fuck, fuck, FUCK.* I don't hear a word of the conference call as my mind races with the implications of what Addie overheard. Hayden is going to fucking kill me for this. I should've stopped Natalie the second she opened that line of conversation after I told her I was worried about Addie.

She said she hurt herself Rollerblading, but after hearing she's sleeping with Hayden, now I'm not sure I believe her. I said as much to Natalie, and our conversation took off from there.

So fucking stupid! I know better than to do that here, but I let my worries for Addie get ahead of my better judgment.

During the call, she glares at me accusingly. I don't blame her for being pissed. I'd be pissed, too, if she knew something about Nat that she refused to tell me. But telling her that Hayden is a sexual dominant is absolutely not my place. He—and only he—can tell her that—or not tell her. That's up to him. I want to text him to tip him off to what happened, but I'm afraid to do even that with Addie staring at me.

I bet she hasn't heard a word of the call either.

As it begins to wind down, I say, "Can you email a summary of everything we covered today?"

"Of course," the director's assistant says. "No problem."

"Thanks a lot. I look forward to seeing you in Prague next month."

"We're thrilled to have you on this project, Flynn," the director says.

"Happy to be part of it."

We end the call a few minutes later, and silence descends upon my office. Addie makes no move to leave. She continues to stare at me, seemingly without blinking. Wow, this is bad.

"Addie…"

"Unless you're going to tell me what you're keeping from me, don't talk to me."

Her unusually harsh words are like a knife in my heart. I hate that I've hurt her, even if it wasn't intentional. "I can't tell you. It's not that I don't want to, but it's not my place—"

"Right. So you said." She gets up to leave, gasping and reaching for the back of the chair to steady herself.

I move around my desk to grasp her elbow. "You need a doctor."

"No, I don't." Her face turns bright red, leaving me to wonder what the hell is really wrong with her. If Hayden did something to her, I'll kill him with my own hands.

"Let me call Dr. Breslow to see you."

She wrenches her arm free. "Mind your own business, Flynn, and stay out of mine—and Hayden's." Limping, she leaves my office, and I'm reaching for my phone before she clears the doorway. Though he hates to be disturbed while editing, I choose Hayden's number from my favorites, prepared for his fury when he hears about what happened.

The phone goes to voice mail, so I call again and again and again until he finally answers.

"*What?*" His roar actually hurts my ear.

"We've got a problem."

"What kind of problem?"

"Um, Addie…"

"What about her?"

"She might've overheard Natalie and me talking about the thing Addie doesn't know about you—"

"Are you fucking kidding me right now?"

"I wish I was. There were no specifics, but now she knows there's something."

"Fantastic, Flynn. That's just great."

"I'm sorry and so is Natalie. We weren't thinking."

"It's fine," he says with a sigh. "Don't beat yourselves up. It doesn't matter anyway. The thing with her is over. Mostly."

"Why is it over?"

"For all the reasons you never wanted it to happen in the first place."

"Does she know it's over?"

"Yes."

"Do you know why she's limping today?"

Complete silence.

"Hayden?"

"She's not limping. I saw her earlier. She was fine."

"She's definitely not fine, and when I suggested calling Breslow to look at her, her face turned bright red, she got royally pissed and told me to mind my own business."

"Fuck," he mutters.

"She said it was a Rollerblading accident, but it wasn't, was it?"

"I have to go. Don't worry about her. I'll take care of her."

"You'd better."

"I said I would, now butt out."

The line goes dead, and I'm left feeling unsettled about the entire situation.

*Addie*

Fuming and confused and in worse pain than I was in before I sat for an hour, I leave Flynn's office and go into mine. I'm in there for about two minutes before sheer frustration propels me out the door to the lobby.

I take the elevator to the sixth floor and invade Hayden's sacred territory by entering the editing suite. Everyone who works for Quantum is told on day one to stay away from the sixth floor when Hayden is doing postproduction or risk his wrath. I don't care if I'm bothering him. I don't care about the rules or anything other than whatever he's keeping from me that Natalie thinks I have a right to know.

When I walk into the suite, he's surrounded editors and sound people and others whose roles I can't recall off the top of my addled brain.

"Hayden."

When he looks up and sees me there, he doesn't seem surprised, which tells me Flynn has already gotten to him.

"Could I have the room, please?" he says softly, but everyone hears him.

People file out, each of them taking a look at me on the way by. The fact that I'm up here and that he asked for privacy will be all over the office within minutes. I couldn't care less. When the last person leaves, the door clicks shut, leaving us alone. Now that I have him to myself, I have no idea how to proceed with this conversation.

"Why did you lie to me?" he asks, breaking the charged silence.

"What?" I ask, genuinely baffled. "I didn't lie to you."

"You said you were fine, but Flynn says you're limping and that you told him you hurt yourself Rollerblading."

"I did."

He gets up, angrily tosses the headphones that were around his neck onto the control board and comes to stand in front of me. "That's a lie, Addison, and we both know it."

I force myself to meet his gaze without blinking. "Would you prefer I tell my boss and your best friend that I'm sore because we had anal sex last night?"

He makes a sound that's half groan, half laugh. "I'm sorry you're sore."

"I'm not sorry we did it."

His hands land on my shoulders. "*Addie…*" My name is a groan, an oath, a swear slipping from between his clenched lips.

"What does everyone else know about you that I don't?"

He's shaking his head before I finish asking the question. "It doesn't matter."

"It matters to me."

"We talked last night. We agreed that was the last time we're going to be together that way, so it doesn't matter."

"It's not the last time. It's the first of many times we're going to be together that way." Because I'm fighting for my life here, I brazenly cup his obvious arousal and run my fingernail down the full length of him, making him tremble in response. "You can lie to yourself, but you can't hide the truth. Not from me."

"You won't understand."

"I love you, Hayden. After last night, do you think there's anything you could ask of me that would be too much for me?"

His eyes flare with heat and desire, and his cock gets even harder under my palm. Before I have a second to anticipate what's going to happen next, he's kissing me with deep, desperate strokes of his tongue that send me reeling. I almost forget why I came up here. With that in mind, I turn my face away to break the kiss. "Tell me what you're hiding from me."

"No."

I squeeze his cock, and his fingers dig into my shoulders. "Tell me."

"Fucking hell, Addie. No, I won't tell you."

"I'm not leaving until you do." Before he can anticipate my intentions, I unbutton and unzip him and drop to my knees before him, taking most of his thick length into my mouth and then biting down gently but insistently.

He howls and claws at my hair, but I don't let up. "Fuck, Addie… *Motherfucker.*"

I raise my hand to his balls, squeezing the firm globes until he's leaking down my throat, on the verge of release. Massaging the spot behind his balls that turns every man to putty in the hands of a lover, I drag my teeth over his shaft, sending the not so subtle message that there's nothing I won't do to get to the truth. I want his truth—and I want it right now.

"All right! I'll tell you! *I'll fucking tell you!*"

Thrilled with myself and with him, I decide to let him come before he talks. I stroke him with my lips, tongue and hand while continuing to massage his pressure point with my other hand. He comes with a grunt and a sharp thrust of his hips, sending his cock so deep, my gag reflex is triggered. I battle through it to take every drop of his release into my throat, swallowing frantically.

When I release him, he stumbles backward, landing on the sofa where he's been known to sleep while editing.

He's sprawled on the sofa, his dick hanging out of his pants and still wet with my spit. I have a confession to make right here—I'm exceptionally pleased with myself as well as my powers of persuasion. To see such a big, strong man reduced to putty in *my* hands is rather satisfying, if I do say so myself.

"That was a dirty trick, Addison," he says in that low sexy growl I love so much.

Sitting back on my heels—a move I instantly regret—I shrug off the comment. "Desperate times call for desperate measures. Now start talking."

"It's really none of your business. You know that, right?"

"I'm making it my business." Moving slowly, I push to my feet and move to the sofa, wincing as I sit because I no longer need to hide how I'm feeling from him.

He takes hold of my hand. "I hate that you're hurting."

"You play, you pay."

With his gaze focused on our joined hands, he says, "That's what Flynn and Nat were talking about. Playing."

"How do you mean?"

"I'm a sexual dominant, Addie. Do you know what that means?"

As I'm still processing the words "sexual dominant," I don't immediately answer him.

"You're shocked, right? I know it's a lot to take in, but it's not really important that you fully understand it. It doesn't matter—"

"It does matter. This is why you keep telling me that what's already happening between us can't continue. You think I can't handle it."

"That's not it."

"*Right.*" I load that single word with every ounce of sarcasm I possess.

"It's so much more complicated than that."

"You know how I feel about you, Hayden. Don't I deserve more than platitudes? Tell me the *truth.*"

"Fine! The truth is we're incompatible. You're no one's submissive, let alone mine, and you can't be controlled. I'd be crazy to even try to dominate you. You'd fight me every step of the way, and we'd both end up hurt in the end. I can't go there with you, and I'm not willing to live without that side of myself. You wanted the truth—there it is."

It's a lot to wrap my head around. "So let me get this straight—you want and need dominance…" I swallow hard. "In bed."

"Among other places, including dungeons, playrooms, in public."

My brain nearly gets stuck on the word dungeon, but I force myself to listen and process everything he says. "But you don't want that with me."

"It's not that I don't want it with you, Addie. It's more that I've been in this lifestyle a long time, and I've learned how to judge compatibility. We're incompatible."

"That's funny, because we felt pretty damned compatible the last couple of nights in my bed."

"That's not what I mean. We have chemistry, attraction and desire to spare. I'd never deny that. But those things alone don't make for a successful dominant-submissive relationship."

"What does?"

He sighs deeply. "For one thing, a deeply held desire on the part of the submissive to turn over her well-being and control of her pleasure to her Dom. That's not you, Addie. You want to be an active participant. You want a partnership. I want utter dominance and complete submission."

The words, and the images that accompany them, make my nipples tighten. My clit tingles, and I shift in my seat, seeking some relief from the sudden hum of desire. "Th-that doesn't sound *terrible*. Could we try it?"

He shakes his head. "No."

"That's it? Just no?"

"Just no."

Now I'm pissed. "You say you don't want me to hate you, but if you refuse to even consider the possibility that we could make this work, I'm going to hate you."

"I'm sorry you feel that way," he says with weary resignation. That's when I realize this is hurting him almost as much as it's hurting me.

Why does it have to be this way? Before I can ask that, another thought occurs to me. "How do Flynn and Natalie know about this?"

"Before I say anything more, I need to be assured of your discretion. We're talking about people's lives and reputations here."

"I'm a little insulted that you think I'd repeat whatever you're about to tell me. I might remind you that I signed Emmett's rock-solid confidentiality agreement. Suffice to say I'm not looking to ruin my life or anyone else's by blabbing about what goes on here."

"I know I can trust you, but I have to say it anyway because of the sensitive nature of what I'm about to tell you."

"I won't tell anyone, Hayden. You have my word on that."

He hesitates before he says, "Flynn and Natalie know about this because they're in the lifestyle, too."

Even though I sensed he was going to tell me about Flynn, I'm shocked to hear that Natalie is part of it, too. Suddenly, a lot of things make sense. "This is why she left him, isn't it? She discovered he'd been keeping this from her."

"Yes. She found the room I keep at my Malibu place and asked him about it. He panicked and lied to her, and then Valerie called her and told her where to find the room in his house. When she confronted him about that, he lied again. As you know, they've since worked things out, and he's brought her into the lifestyle slowly but surely."

"So Natalie, the survivor of a violent sexual assault, can handle being a submissive to her dominant husband, but *I* can't handle being submissive to you?"

"It's not about whether or not you can handle it, Addison. It's about whether or not you're actually submissive. And you're not. That's not how you're wired."

"From what I know about your... lifestyle... people can be trained to be submissive, is that correct?"

"Yes," he says through gritted teeth.

"So you're saying I couldn't be trained?"

"I'm saying I'm not willing to train you."

"Fine," I say, getting up so quickly that I gasp from the pain. "Then I'll find someone who will."

He's right behind me, grabbing my arm and bringing his face right down to mine. "The hell you will."

"Why, Hayden, are you *dominating* me right now? Is that what this is?"

"No. This is me forbidding you to do stupid, dangerous things to get back at me for not being what you need me to be."

I raise a brow in stunned disbelief. "You're *forbidding* me? Isn't that rich? You don't want to be my Dom, but apparently you think you have some sort of right to order me around just because I fucked you a couple of times? What century are you living in?"

His face has gotten very red, and his eyes have never been bluer. "I'm living in the here and now, and I won't let you do this."

"Guess what? You don't get to tell me what to do. We're done, remember?"

"I take that back. We're not done."

I laugh at the sheer lunacy of this conversation. "You can't take it back. This isn't preschool, even if it's starting to feel a lot like it."

"Call it whatever you want, but you're *mine*, and no one else is touching you but *me*."

I think about what I'm going to say for a long moment, and then I force myself to look him dead in the eyes. "Last night, I would've loved to hear you say that. Now you're saying it for all the wrong reasons, and that's not okay. So I respectfully decline your offer to 'take back' what you said last night."

I'm almost to the door when he says, "This is not over, Addison. It's not even kinda over."

I resist the urge to reply to that comment and smile to myself as the door clicks shut behind me. All things considered, I'd say that went very well.

# CHAPTER 9

*Hayden*

I'm losing my fucking mind. The thought of Addie seeking out BDSM training from someone other than me makes me insane. As I zip up my jeans, I can't believe she blew the truth out of me, basically proving my point. Addison York is no one's submissive, and I have zero control over her.

Picturing her submitting to someone else, though… That kills me. I reach for my phone and call Gordon Yates, our director of security in LA.

"Hey, Hayden. Nothing new to report on your mom. She's had a quiet few days at home."

"Good to hear. I've got another situation I could use your help with. I need eyes on Addison York."

"Flynn's assistant?"

"Yeah." I grit my teeth to keep from correcting him. Yes, she's Flynn's assistant, but she's also *my* woman.

"What's the concern?"

"She's been making some questionable choices lately." I feel like an absolute shit for saying that, because the only questionable choice Addie has made is getting involved with me. "I want to make sure she's safe."

"Can you define questionable or give me something else to go on?"

"I want to be apprised of her whereabouts."

"Anything in particular?"

"All of it. Everything she does, I want to know."

"That's gonna cost you, my friend."

"Add it to my bill." I'm already spending a small fortune to keep eyes on my mother. What's another small fortune if it means keeping Addie safe and out of the hands of a Dom who doesn't love her like I do?

"You got it. I'll be in touch."

"Thanks, Gordon." Though I've got a million and one things to do and people waiting to get back to work on the film that defies naming, I take the elevator to the fifth floor. I pass Addie's closed door. Is she in there researching LA-area BDSM clubs? I want to break down the door to find out. Barely resisting the urge to storm in there to see what she's doing, I go down the hall to Flynn's office. The door is open, so I step inside and close it behind me.

I ought to be fucking furious with him for what happened earlier, but I've got too many other problems at the moment.

"Hey," he says, removing reading glasses. "Everything okay?"

"Everything is fucking fantastic." I flop into the chair in front of his desk. "She knows, and she wants me to train her."

"And you said…"

"No. I fucking said *no*, because as much as she cares about me—and she does, I know she does—she's not submissive. It'd be a disaster from the get-go, and I'm not going there."

Looking relieved, he sits back in his chair and puts his feet on the desk. "For what it's worth, I think you made the right call."

"I know I did, but guess what? She says if I won't train her, she'll find someone else who will."

He sits up so abruptly, his feet drop to the floor and his mouth hangs open in shock. "She said *what?*"

"You heard me. She's determined to find out more about the lifestyle, and if I won't teach her, then she's going to do her own research. What the fuck, Flynn? I'm fucking damned if I do, damned if I don't."

Leaning his elbows on the desk, he appears to mull it over. "Can I ask you something and will you tell me the truth?"

"Yeah, I guess."

"Do you love her?"

"Yeah, I do. I have for a long time. You know why I couldn't do anything about it, and now she does, too." I've never said those words to anyone before, and when I've heard them from other people, often it was because they wanted something from me. Except for the other night when Addie said them. That was real, and all she wants from me is *me*.

"Maybe, if you love her, you could train her—"

"No."

"Hear me out. She may not be classically submissive, but she might be able to get there because she knows how much it means to you."

I'm shaking my head before he finishes. "I'm not training her."

"You know Addie as well as I do. When she sets her mind to something, she doesn't back down. If she said she's going to find someone else to train her, she probably will. Are you going to be okay with that?"

"How okay would you feel about another Dom training Natalie?"

His brow furrows, and his expression is positively murderous.

"Exactly."

"So what're you going to do?"

"I've got Gordon watching her every move effective immediately, and if I hear that she's heading for danger, I'll intervene."

"Intervene how?"

"I'll go in there and get her."

"And when she has you charged with kidnapping and assault?"

"She won't do that."

"This is Addie we're talking about. I wouldn't put it past her."

"She knows what you and I deal with in regard to the press and the Hollywood gossip machine. She'd never do that to me—or to you through me. What happens to me affects you, and she cares too much about both of us to cause trouble for Quantum."

"Maybe so, but I'd still think carefully about this plan of yours. It's a recipe for disaster."

"What would be worse? Me going after her, or her getting hurt by a Dom who hasn't the first fucking clue how to properly care for a sub?"

"The latter. Definitely the latter."

"Remember how stupid and clueless we were at first?"

Cringing, he nods in agreement. His first marriage ended in disaster because he pushed his wife for way more than he should have—among other reasons.

"What if she encounters someone who doesn't treat her right?" I ask.

"We'll have him killed."

"Seriously, Flynn. The thought of that makes me crazy. She says I can't forbid her to do this, but you could. As her boss, you could tell her not to do it."

"*Whoa.*" He holds up his hands. "That's not happening."

"Not even to keep her safe?"

"Addie is a smart woman. She doesn't need me or you or any man running interference for her."

"She's a smart woman who has no idea what she's getting into by venturing into our lifestyle."

"I'm not going to tell her not to, Hayden. I'll tell her to be careful and do her homework, but I can't—and won't—intervene in her personal life."

I rub my fist over a sharp ache in my chest. "I feel like I'm having a heart attack."

"You did the right thing by putting Gordon on it. He'll let you know if she's venturing into trouble."

"What if I get there too late and she's hurt or worse?" I rub my chest more urgently. "I fucked this up so bad, Flynn. Last night, I told her we can't be together anymore, and then today she overhears you guys talking and forces me to tell her the truth. And then when I do, she won't let me take back what I said last night and... Oh my fucking God! Are you *laughing?*"

He's laughing so hard he can't speak.

It's all I can do not to reach across the desk and pound the shit out of him. "What the *fuck* is so funny?"

"You are," he says when he recovers the ability to speak. "You're always so cool and collected when it comes to women. Seeing you like this over someone we both love is refreshing, to say the least."

"I don't *want* to be like this. I don't want to be in a relationship with her or anyone else. That's not how I roll, and you know it."

"Then I guess you have no choice but to let her go and hope for the best for her and yourself."

"That's a shitty option."

"Let me see if I can sum things up for you. You fucked her, left her, refused to train her and now you're having a heart attack because she wants to find someone who *will* train her. Did I miss anything?"

"Yeah, you missed the part where I fucking pound you for gloating about it."

"I'm not gloating."

"What would you call it?"

"I'm summarizing a series of events for you. That's all."

"It's a series of very unfortunate events." But not all of it had been unfortunate. No, the hours I'd spent lost in her sweet body had been anything but unfortunate. Remembering how her tight pussy clamped down on my cock when she came has me hard as steel. I shift in my seat and cross my legs.

"I have to find a way to fix this before she does something that can't be undone."

"Have you tried groveling? Begging? Those things worked well for me when I fucked up with Nat."

"Hayden Roth doesn't grovel or beg."

"Then I guess Hayden Roth will have to be prepared to see the woman he loves tied to another man's St. Andrew's cross."

"Fuck you. Fuck you all the way to hell and back again."

Chuckling, he says, "It might be time to grovel and beg."

I hate that he's right, but I can't deny that the idea of groveling is far better than imagining her submitting to someone other than me. I push to my feet. "Fine. If that's what it'll take, I'll do it."

"Since you've never done it before, I can give you some pointers about how to really sell it."

"You're enjoying this way too much."

"I'm not enjoying the idea of Addie doing something dangerous. But seeing you out of your mind and in love with one of the best women I know? Yeah, I'm kinda digging that part."

"Fuck you," I mutter on my way out the door, slamming it for added emphasis. And here I thought he was my best friend. He's an asshole. I take the stairs to the sixth floor where everyone is waiting for me to get back to work, even though my concentration is blown to hell and back again. I'll get through the day, and then I'm going talk some sense into her.

*Addie*

From my office, I can hear Hayden shouting in Flynn's office. I hope they aren't at odds because of me. I couldn't help overhearing Flynn and Natalie, and when I realized they were talking about Hayden and me, well, what would you do? Flynn and Hayden get into it all the time, and they always bounce back. They will this time, too.

I'm thrilled that Hayden is so upset about my plan to seek training elsewhere. It's the least of what he deserves for being so obstinate. His behavior reminds me of being a little kid and fighting over toys on the playground. I don't want that toy, but I don't want you to have it either.

Part of me aches for him. His experience with functional relationships is limited to his Quantum partners and a few other friends. He's never had a long-term relationship with a woman that I know of, but he's never lacked for female companionship. He's in uncharted waters with me, and he has no idea how to cope with the emotional element. He's got the physical part down to a science, but since he's never done both at the same time, it's up to me to show him how.

In case you're wondering, I'm going to forgive him for being an idiot. Eventually. Why should I make it easy on him?

My gaze settles on a plaque one of my girlfriends gave me after a breakup years ago. It says, "I've tripped and fallen. My heart has been broken. But even when I was hurting, I always found a way to pick myself up and carry on. I am a woman. I am a strong woman. I will never give up."

On more than one occasion, I've needed the reminder that I can get through anything, and the current situation requires all my strength and fortitude. I'm determined to get what I want—and I want Hayden Roth. I want a life with him. I want to love him and have him return my love freely and without reservation. I want to be everything he wants and needs in a partner and a lover.

I pick up the phone to call my stylist friend Tenley, one of the best-connected women in all of Hollywood and one of the most sexually liberated women I've ever met. If anyone can help me find what I need, it's her.

"Oh my God," she says. "I was going to call you today. What's up with you kissing Hayden Roth on international TV?"

"Hello to you, too, and in case you didn't notice, *he* kissed *me*."

"I noticed, and so did the rest of the world. Are you two together? I had no idea!"

"Nah, we're just friends." I hate to lie to her, but Hayden and I are a long way from ready to go public with our relationship. "He got caught up in the moment."

"That looked like more than a moment, but if you're going to hold out on me…"

"No holdout. We're really just friends." Right at this moment, that's the truth. She doesn't need to know the rest, especially with what I'm about to ask of her. I don't need her putting two and two together to get that Hayden is a sexual dominant. "I've been asked to do some research in scouting locations for a scene at a BDSM club. I was wondering if you have any recommendations."

"What makes you think I'd know anything about BDSM?"

"Because you know something about everything in this town and because you've told me you're sexually adventurous."

"You're right on both counts," she says with a laugh. "You could check out Black Vice in the Hollywood Hills. It's one of the best clubs in town, and the owner, Master Devon Black, is a friend of mine. A *close* friend. I could introduce you and ask him to give you a tour."

The words "Master Devon Black" make my blood race as I wonder what he's like. "That'd be amazing. Would you mind seeing if you can set it up for tonight or tomorrow night?"

"You're in a big rush, huh?"

"Apparently, this scene was just added to the film at the last minute, so they need the info pretty quickly."

"I'll give him a call and see what I can do."

"If you could not mention who I am or who I work for, that'd be best. I'd hate to get the rags talking about the guys."

"Say no more. I understand completely. I'll get back to you shortly."

"Thanks, Tenley. I really appreciate it."

"Anything for a friend."

We say our good-byes, and I force myself to get back to work on the plans for the Mexico trip as well as Flynn and Natalie's trips to Rome and Prague. I have a long to-do list after yesterday's foundation meeting, too, including trying to find a place to hold the carnival. Flynn's parents offered up their Beverly Hills home, but he wants me to give the board several options to choose from before any final decisions are made. I think he's worried, and rightfully so, about inviting the public into his parents' home.

I hear back from Tenley after lunch that Devon Black will see me at ten o'clock tonight. My body tingles with anticipation of what I might learn from him.

"Do you want me to come with you?" Tenley asks.

I want that so badly I can barely speak. "Do you want to?"

"Sure. Sounds like fun. I'll pick you up at nine, and we'll get a drink before we go."

I'm more relieved than I let on that I won't have to go alone. "That'd be great. I'll be ready."

"See you then."

I'm not proud of how I spend the rest of my afternoon—surfing the Internet for as much information as I can find about BDSM, dominance and submission, the lifestyle itself, the people who enjoy it and the emotional as well as physical elements. As I read, my imagination runs wild as I picture myself at Hayden's mercy while trying not to picture Flynn and Natalie doing the stuff I'm reading about.

It's fascinating in every sense of the word. I drop so deep into the rabbit hole of intrigue that I'm completely startled when Mackenzie pops in to tell me she's leaving.

"You've been quiet today," she says.

I wonder if my face is flushed from my research. "A lot going on."

"Oh, well, see you in the morning."

"See you then." A glance at the clock on my computer tells me it's five thirty. I feel guilty about how I totally wasted this afternoon, but it was for a good cause. It's in the best interest of everyone at Quantum if Hayden is happy, and I intend to make him happy. I clear the history on my browser twice and then do a check for keywords to make sure it actually cleared. I shut down the computer rather than putting it to sleep, hoping that will provide even more assurance that no one will be able to see what I've been up to.

Not that I expect anyone will check on me, but one can never be too cautious when searching for information about BDSM while at work. I grab my keys and purse and head to the elevator, aching twice as much as I was earlier. I'm dreaming about the painkillers I left sitting on my counter at home when the elevator dings.

It opens, and there's Hayden, slouched against the back wall. He straightens when he sees me.

"You go ahead," I say. "I'll take the next one."

"Don't be ridiculous. We can share a freaking elevator."

"Fine." I step in and turn my back to him.

"So this is how it's going to be?" he asks on the way down.

"How what's going to be?"

"You and me, avoiding each other, not speaking, that kind of stupid shit."

"When did I avoid you or not speak to you?"

"Just now when you told me you'd take the next elevator." He moves closer to me. His lips brush against my ear and his hands squeeze my hips.

I want to sag into his embrace and let him hold me and comfort me and tell me it's all been a big mistake. Of course we're meant to be together. How can it be any other way? But I remain stubbornly still, hoping to send the message that I'm unaffected by his touch when I'm anything but. "I didn't want to bother you."

"I want you to bother me." He rubs his hard cock against my back, and just that quickly, my body says *yes* to him even as my brain says *hell no*.

The elevator arrives on the ground floor with a ding. Before the doors can open, he reaches around me to press a button that keeps them closed.

"Be with me tonight," he growls in my ear.

I want to. God, I want to, but we can't go forward until we accept each other for who and what we are. I want to accept who he is, and I want him to let me into that part of his life. Until he's willing to do that, freely and without reservation, I don't see a way forward for us. That thought depresses me profoundly, but it helps me to stick to my plans rather than giving in to his powerful allure.

"I've got plans."

"Cancel them."

"No."

"Addison, I'm coming over later—"

"Don't bother. I won't be home."

"I'll wait."

"It's your time to waste as you see fit."

I wrench free of his hold and press the button to open the door, walking out ahead of him. I'm acutely aware of his gaze on me as I walk to my car, trying not to limp as I go. When I reach my car, I glance over at him, prepared to tell him to have a good night. I catch him looking around the parking lot, his gaze landing on a nondescript sedan parked on the far side of the lot.

I immediately put two and two together to get that he's put me under surveillance. So that's how he's going to play it. Well, two can play at that game. I get into my car without another word to him. I drive away and watch the sedan pull out a short distance behind me, far enough that I won't get suspicious, but close enough that I can't get away.

I head to my dad's in Redondo Beach, fighting rush-hour traffic and paying no attention whatsoever to my tail. Gordon's team is top notch, but they're no match for me. I've already formulated my plan by the time I arrive at my dad's tiny house in the coastal town where I grew up. Though he's made plenty of money working as a cameraman and artist, he's never moved from the house where he lived with my mother before she died of a heart attack when I was twelve. He's never gotten over losing his young wife so suddenly, and to my knowledge, he hasn't been on a date in the fifteen years since she died. He doesn't talk about it, at least not to me, but I know he's still nursing his broken heart, and I hate that for him.

When he's not on location filming, you can find Simon York in his pottery studio, which is our fancy name for the shed behind the house where he creates his works of art. And they are art. He makes a tidy profit from selling his pots, planters, window boxes and other household items in Southern California galleries.

Ignoring the sedan that parks down the street from me, I walk through the house to the studio, where he's up to his elbows in muck as usual.

"This is a nice surprise," he says without looking up from his wheel.

I kiss his cheek and take a bottle of water from the small fridge. "Whatcha making?"

"A pot." He reaches a point where he can stop, and the whirl of the wheel goes quiet. That's when he smiles up at me. "How's my beautiful girl today?"

"Pretty good. How are you?"

Dark brows furrow over chocolate-brown eyes. Growing up, my friends used to tell me he was hot. I didn't want to encourage that line of conversation, so I didn't agree—or disagree. But I'm not blind. I can see that he's incredibly handsome. "Been wondering when you were going to show your face around here after kissing that jackass Hayden Roth on national TV."

*Ugh, here we go.* "I didn't kiss him. He kissed me."

"Either way, my beautiful daughter's lips were on his." This is said with a grimace.

"Oh please. You may be surprised to know that many people think Hayden is a catch."

He gets up to wash his hands. Over his shoulder, he says, "I hope you're not one of them."

"What if I am?"

"Oh, Addison, come on. You've got to be kidding me. You could have any guy in the world. Why do you want one who has a hair-trigger temper and a surly personality?"

"That's only one piece in a very complex puzzle, Dad."

"So you're saying I have something to worry about here?"

"It's nothing for you to worry about."

"Are you or are you not involved with him in a more-than-friends capacity?"

Flashbacks from last night pick that moment to appear in my mind, a glaring reminder of how involved I've already been with Hayden. "Define involved."

"Addison!"

"*Yes*, I'm involved with him. *Yes*, I have feelings for him, and I have for a long time. And he has feelings for me. We're figuring it out."

"He's going to hurt you."

"Give me a little credit, will you? I know how to handle him."

"If you say so."

"Let's talk about something else, such as when you're going to get a love life of your own so you won't be so concerned about mine."

He rolls his eyes. "I'm perfectly content on my own, as you well know."

"You could be happy rather than content."

"What's the difference?"

"There's a huge difference. Look at Flynn. He would've said he was perfectly content before he met Natalie, but now he'd tell you there're a million miles between content and happy."

"I hear what you're saying, but I'm not interested."

That's what he always says. Every single time this subject comes up, which isn't as often as it used to. I've begun to give up on my long-held hope that he might take another chance on love. We'll soon note the fifteenth anniversary of the day my mother died, and while I've moved forward, he remains firmly stuck in the past. It makes me sad when I think of him that way, but I can't deny that he leads a full life that satisfies him. He says it's enough. I try to believe him.

"You got anything to eat around here?"

"Always." I follow him inside, where we make dinner together and share a bottle of wine that goes a long way toward calming the nerves that attack every time I think about my plans for later.

"I need a favor," I say after we've washed and dried the dishes and tidied the kitchen.

"What's that?"

"Could I leave my car here tonight? I'm meeting Tenley downtown, and I don't want to drive."

"Sure. You need a ride?"

"Nah, I'll get an Uber." I withdraw my phone and use the Uber app to summon a ride. I intentionally give a pickup address on the next street over. "They'll be here in two minutes." I kiss my dad's cheek. "Thanks for dinner."

"It was definitely my pleasure. Be careful with Hayden, you hear me?"

"I hear you. Don't worry."

"That'll be the day."

"Love you."

"Love you, too, sweetheart."

I consult my phone and groan dramatically, which is all part of my master plan. "Damn it, they're on the wrong block. I'm going out the back to find them."

He sees me out the back door and watches as I go through the gate to the next block, where I find the black Toyota Camry idling at the address I gave. I jump in the car, and the driver takes off toward my address in Santa Monica. And just that easily, I dodge the tail Hayden has put on me.

# CHAPTER 10

*Addie*

I giggle to myself as I imagine his reaction at hearing they lost me. He'll be out of his mind, just the way I want him.

The car drops me outside my building, where there's no sign of Gordon's men. I shower and change into a sexy black dress and four-inch heels that seem fitting for the outing I've got planned. I head down to the street level to watch for Tenley.

She pulls up a short time later in the white Mercedes G-Class SUV she says is essential to her styling business. I jump into the passenger seat, suppressing a gasp as the hard seat connects with my tender ass. I take a careful look in the mirrors, trying to gauge whether we're being followed. I don't see any sign of the car that followed me earlier.

I breathe a little easier at knowing I've made a clean escape and shift in my seat, trying to find a comfortable position.

"You look hot," she says, casting a sideways glance at me as she darts through traffic.

"You always look hot." Her long dark hair is captured in a messy bun that's deceptively casual. I can't see her outfit in the dark, but I have no doubt she's perfectly turned out in something no one else has seen yet. Such is the advantage of being one of Hollywood's top stylists. As one of her close friends, I benefit from her designer castoffs.

"So this is all about research tonight, right?"

"Yep."

"That's all you can say?"

"Yep."

"You have the coolest job. You know that?"

"No, *you* have the coolest job."

"I've never had anyone ask me to do BDSM research in any of my jobs."

Neither have I, but that's not something she needs to know. The way I see it, this research is for a good cause. It's about convincing my future husband that I can be the woman he needs in every way that matters to him.

*My future husband...* Where in the hell had that thought come from? Well, isn't that what I want? Don't I want everything with him? Hell, yes, I do. I want everything. I want forever with him, and I'm determined to show him there's nothing he could ask of me that would be too much. Somehow I have to make him see that all I want from him is *him—all* of him.

I'm not blind to the faults my father has identified in Hayden. I've seen his foul temper and his surliness. But I've also seen the way he takes care of his mother, even after the many times she's disappointed him. He never gives up on her, and I like to think the care he shows her is a much more accurate picture of who he really is than his temper or surliness.

"You're quiet," Tenley says when we're stopped in traffic.

"Tell me more about Devon Black."

"He's hot as fuck, for one thing."

"Have you..."

"I'll never tell," she says with a saucy grin that tells me she definitely has.

"So you participate in the lifestyle?"

"You could say that."

"What's it like?"

"Well," she says with a sigh, "it's amazing and intense and a little crazy at first. Being submissive to a man in bed takes some getting used to when you're accustomed to calling the shots in the rest of your life."

"How did you decide to try it?"

"I met Devon at a party one of my clients had. I was immediately intrigued. He invited me to his club, and one thing led to another."

"Did he tell you about the club the night you met him?" I laugh at myself. "Sorry—I have so many questions."

"No problem. Ask away. I'm an open book. You know that. And yes, he did tell me from the beginning that he's a Dom and owns a club that caters to the BDSM lifestyle."

"That wasn't a turn-off to you?"

"Hell no. It was a turn-*on*. I'd never met a man who was so blatant about his sexuality. I mean, he owns a club that caters to his every desire. I liked that he was honest about it, you know? No games, no subterfuge. He was just out and proud. There's a lot to be said for that level of honesty."

"Yes, I can see the appeal." I also understand why Hayden and Flynn can't be out or proud. The Hollywood media would have a field day with that information. Still, Hayden could've trusted me with it. Who did he think I would tell? "So are you still seeing Devon?"

"I am. It's been almost a year now."

"I can't believe you've kept such a big secret from me for so long!"

"I'm still not sure where it's going, so I haven't said much about it to anyone. He hasn't met my family. I haven't met his. We've kept it between us."

"How come?"

"I'm not sure exactly. We don't really talk about it all that much. We're too busy having mind-altering sex."

We share a laugh at the blunt way she says that.

"Sex that lasts for hours doesn't leave much time for talking," she adds.

"Hours…" I think about the two times I've been with Hayden and his amazing stamina both times. "You like that?"

"I didn't think I would, but Devon has shown me the benefits of endurance."

"Do you do it in public at the club?"

"We have."

"Does the fear of being recognized scare you?"

She shrugs. "If someone recognizes me, it's not like they'll say anything. That's the fastest way to get thrown out of the club. Security, safety and privacy are Devon's top priorities at the club. It took me a while to believe I could really let go and submit in public without fear of it being all over town by morning.

But the more time I spent at the club, the more I encountered people with far more to lose than I'll ever have, and no one knew about them. Ugh, this fucking traffic. We don't have time to get a drink before we hit the club. That's okay. We can have one there."

"So you're an actual member now?"

"Yep. Got a card and everything."

"Would you do what you do with Devon with other guys, or is it just him?"

"We've decided to be exclusive for now, so no, no other guys for me, but he's offered to set up a threesome if I want to try it."

I'm more fascinated by the second with this whole new side to my friend. "Do you?"

She glances over at me before returning her attention to the stop-and-go traffic. "I'm thinking about it. He says it would be incredible, and I believe he'd make sure it was for me."

"What's stopping you?"

"I wonder how I'd feel the next day knowing I'd had sex with two guys at the same time."

"One of my college friends did it during Spring Break one year. Everyone knew, and she was mortified."

"Did she like it while it was happening?"

"I think she was too trashed to remember much of it."

"Ahh, so she went the liquid-courage route. That's not an option at Devon's club. They have a two-drink limit. Most of the better clubs do. They don't want people getting into alcohol-fueled situations they'll regret in the morning. Everyone has to be clearheaded and healthy to belong to his club."

"He requires proof of health?"

"You bet. They have doctors on staff who do exams right onsite, so there's no funny business with results. That's something Devon doesn't budge on. See our doctors, or no admittance."

I swallow hard at the thought of being poked and prodded in order to obtain training, but I'll do it if it gets me closer to understanding what makes Hayden tick.

We drive up into the hills, not far from where Flynn lives, and a few minutes later, Tenley takes a turn into a driveway that isn't immediately visible from the road. I'm not sure what I expected, but the vast estate that unfolds before me is a surprise. It looks like someone's house—a rich someone, but a private home nonetheless.

"We have to shut off our phones to go in there, so I always leave mine in the car."

"I'll do the same." I power mine down and then do hers for her. I put them in the glove box for safekeeping.

The house has a stone façade with pillars and a grand entryway that's staffed by handsome young men wearing black vests over white shirts with black bow ties.

One of them opens Tenley's door and greets her by name.

"Hi, there," she says. "This is my friend, Addison. Devon is expecting us."

"Yes, ma'am." He helps her out of the car while another hot young man helps me. "He let us know. You have a good night."

"Thank you." Tenley hooks her arm through mine as we make our way inside, where doors are opened for us by more beautiful employees—male and female.

"Is this where people who don't score acting jobs come to pass the time until they get their big breaks?"

She laughs. "I tease Dev all the time about hiring from central casting."

We reach a reception desk where Tenley presents her membership ID to be scanned by the attendant, another handsome young man. "I have a guest tonight."

I'm given a detailed confidentiality form that outlines the rules of the club, the importance of confidentiality and a warning that violators will be prosecuted to the fullest extent of the law. I sign and date it and return it to the attendant.

"Have a nice evening." He presses a button that opens frosted glass doors with half of the Black Vice logo on each side.

Tenley clearly knows her way around the club and leads me up the grand staircase to what was probably once a ballroom. Today, it's a fully functioning BDSM club. It's almost too much to take in at one time. There are multiple stages where various performances are taking place. One has a topless woman working a pole with amazing skill and athleticism that captivates me as well as the men and women who watch her.

On another stage, a naked woman is bent over a bench of some sort. A man in tight black leather pants and no shirt is spanking her with an implement that looks like a ping-pong paddle.

I tear my gaze off that scene to take in the action on a third stage. A woman dressed in a black leather corset with fishnet stockings and spike heels is standing over a man lying prone on the floor before her. She digs her heel into his back, making him scream from the pain. Then she flips her hand, and I see that she's holding a bullwhip. "She's not going to… Oh my God!" The whip comes down on his back, and he screams even louder than he did the first time. "*Holy hell.*"

"She's a dominatrix. Men pay top dollar to submit to her."

I'm so transfixed by what I'm seeing that Tenley has to take me by the shoulders to steer me toward the bar. The rest of the room consists of tables and seating areas where people in street clothes and bondage attire are conversing over drinks. If you were to remove the stages and the costumes, it might resemble a regular nightclub. But there's nothing "regular" about this place, at least not in my experience.

Between the low, sexy beat of the music, the décor that focuses on the color black and the fragrant flowers spread throughout the big room, every one of my senses is fully engaged. My skin tingles with the desire to know more, to see more, to experience it for myself.

I wonder if Hayden has figured out that I dodged his men. If so, is he worried about what kind of trouble I might get into? What would he say if he knew where I am right now? Imagining his reaction makes me smile.

"I take it you like what you see," Tenley says, misinterpreting my smile.

"I'm overwhelmed."

She hands me a gin and tonic with a twist of lime. "Most people are the first time they come here. It's a lot to take in if the scene is new to you."

I raise my glass to her. "Cheers."

"Cheers." She leans in closer to me. "Now how about you tell me what you're really doing here, Addie."

*Hayden*

"What the fuck do you mean you *lost* her?" I'm overcome with rage and fear at hearing that Gordon's men somehow managed to lose track of Addie.

"I'm so sorry, Hayden," Gordon says, his tone tight with displeasure. "My guys were on her. They followed her to her dad's place in Redondo Beach, but she gave them the slip by leaving through a back door. We checked with the cab companies and Uber, and Uber will only tell us they made a pickup on the next block over around eight o'clock, but they won't tell us who they picked up or where they took her. Calls to her cell phone are going right to voice mail, which means it's probably off."

"Son of a bitch." If she gave them the slip, not only did she make them, but she's probably up to something she doesn't want me to know about. My fear spikes into the red zone. "I want you guys checking every high-end BDSM club in LA until you find her."

"Umm, what makes you think that's where she'll be?"

"Her interest is the reason I wanted you on her in the first place."

"And you're sure that tracking her down at one of the clubs is the best idea?"

"*Yes, I'm fucking sure!* She could be in danger, Gordon. I want to know where she is."

"I'll get right on it and call you the minute I know anything."

"Thanks."

"I'm sorry again, Hayden. The men who were watching her have been reprimanded."

"Just find her. Please find her."

"I'm all over it."

I put my cell phone on the coffee table where I can get to it quickly if needed and go to the bar to pour a healthy shot of Pappy, noticing that my hand is trembling. Fucking hell… Taking the glass with me, I sit on the sofa and stare at the phone, willing it to ring.

But it stays stubbornly silent while my stomach churns and my brain works overtime, sending me images of Addie at the mercy of a Dom who doesn't love her, doesn't care about her the way I do, doesn't even know her. I shudder, and for a brief, terrifying moment, I fear I might vomit.

I put down the glass and drop my head into my hands, focusing on breathing my way through the nausea.

The phone rings, and I pounce.

"Whoa," Flynn says, chuckling. "What's with you?"

"Addie ditched Gordon's guys. She's out there somewhere on her own, and I have no idea what she's up to. I'm losing my freaking mind."

"Oh shit."

"Yeah, not so funny anymore, is it?"

"He's looking for her?"

"Yeah, they're all over it, but Flynn... I mean, Jesus... We both know what can happen if she ends up in the wrong hands."

"You have to have faith in her. She's a smart, capable woman. If she's venturing into our world, she'll do so carefully and cautiously."

"I'm ashamed to say I don't even know who her closest friends are outside our group."

He names a few people I've never heard of and then he gives me a name I recognize. Tenley Stewart, stylist to the stars and major Hollywood insider. "I had no idea she and Addie were close outside of work."

"Why would you know? You've gone out of your way not to encourage anything more than friendship with Addie, and when you're with her, you're usually with the rest of us, too."

"Still, I hate that I don't know these things about her. Do you know how to get in touch with Tenley?"

"Yeah, I've got her number. I'll give her a call."

"Let me know what you find out."

"I will. So... Listen, I was thinking after we talked earlier, and I know you're going to flip out when I say this, but I feel like I have to say it anyway..."

"*Okay.*"

"Which is worse? The thought of training her yourself, or the thought of someone else's hands all over her?"

Moaning loud enough for him to hear me, I say, "The second one."

"You know what you have to do, Hayden."

"I *can't.*"

"Yes, you can. If I could go there with Natalie, you can with Addie."

"What if…"

"What?"

"What if I do and I freak her out or scare her or turn her off me completely?"

"What if you don't and she finds someone else who will?"

"God, you're a fucking *asshole* today."

"According to you, I'm a fucking asshole most of the time."

"True."

His laughter echoes through the phone. "The main reason I called is I wanted to talk to you about my idea for doing a film about Nat's story. I've been thinking a lot about it, and I was hoping for a few minutes in the next few days if you can fit me into your schedule."

"Yeah, sure. We're going to be in even deeper shit if we can't name the other one very soon. The studio is threatening to name it for us."

"Let's put that on the agenda for tomorrow. We'll get this figured out."

"I can't really think about anything right now except for where Addie is."

"I'll call Tenley. Let me know what you hear."

"I will. See you in the morning."

"See you then."

I put down the phone and reach for my glass, taking a couple of easy sips until I'm sure my stomach isn't going to reject the bourbon. The heat of the liquor works its way through me, warming the pervasive chill that's overtaken me. I'm scared shitless, and I feel like I should be out looking for her, but I haven't the first idea where to start. It's been years since I've played in any club other than ours. I can't afford the potential exposure, so I'm extra careful and have become removed from the larger scene in the city.

When I was younger, I did it all without a care as to who might find out or who might see me. As my career grew along with interest from the paparazzi, I became much more circumspect about keeping my private life private.

I receive a text from Flynn. *Tenley's phone went straight to voice mail.*

Fuck!

*I texted a few of her other friends to casually ask if they've heard from her. I'll let you know if I hear anything.*

I text him back. *Thanks for trying.*

*Keep me posted.*

The phone rings, and when I see Gordon's name on the caller ID, my heart stops for a brief, paralyzing moment. I grab the phone and take the call.

"Hayden."

I can tell by the way he says my name that something is terribly wrong. "Did you find her?"

"No, but when we did the nine p.m. check on your mother, we found her unresponsive. EMTs are taking her to Cedars-Sinai. I'm sorry to have to tell you this—"

I don't hear the rest of what he says. Jamming the phone into my back pocket, I grab my keys and run for the door. The post-rehab calm has just given way to the storm.

# CHAPTER 11

*Addie*

"I don't know what you mean." Tenley's audacious question has thrown me for a loop. "I told you why I'm here. It's research."

"Flynn would never send you to a BDSM club by yourself to do research for him, so tell me what's really going on."

I'm cornered, and we both know it. "There's a guy. He's into this." I gesture to the goings-on around us. "I'm not sure how I feel about it, so I wanted to find out more."

"Is this 'guy' the same guy who kissed you on national TV the other night?"

"I'm not at liberty to discuss the business of the man who may or may not be that guy."

"Fair enough. As someone who keeps most of Hollywood's secrets, I can respect that."

"Thank you for not pushing me to say more."

"Your business is yours alone, Addie, and so is his. You know how I feel about the gossip in this town. The only reason I can freely explore this lifestyle is because Devon makes it easy for me. Without him, I doubt I'd take the risk."

Devon Black joins us shortly after ten, apologizing for being late for our appointment. He's everything Tenley said he would be and then some. Tall and fit with an arresting face, dark hair and even darker eyes that convey a sort of intensity I haven't often encountered. Wearing a gray suit with a black button-down shirt and no tie, he greets Tenley with a brief kiss to the lips that's somehow hotter than a deeper kiss would be from another man.

Tenley's face flushes when he kisses her, and her eyes brighten when she looks at him. Despite her nonchalance in describing her relationship, she seems to be a woman deeply in love.

"It's delightful to meet you, Addison." Devon kisses the back of my hand when Tenley introduces us. "Tenley talks about you all the time, so it's nice to finally put a gorgeous face with a name."

I fan my face. "Okay, I'm thoroughly charmed."

"Told you so," Tenley says, smiling.

Devon laughs at our commentary. A drink appears on the bar in front of him, and he checks to make sure we're set for drinks. "I hear you're interested in my club and what goes on here."

"You heard right."

"And you're new to the lifestyle?"

"I am."

"What do you think so far?" He gestures to the big room full of decadence.

"It's rather overwhelming at first." I take another look around, and this time I notice the waitresses have tails extending from between smoothly rounded ass cheeks. I point to one of them. "How is that possible?"

"The tail?"

I nod, feeling like a blushing virgin as he matter-of-factly explains the various types of butt plugs, including those that have tails. "I, um, oh. Well…"

"I take it the concept is new to you?"

"It's *all* new to me."

"This'll be fun," he says with a broad sexy smile for Tenley. "How about we take a walk so you can see the rest?"

"There's more?"

"Is there more, Tenley?"

"So much more," she says. "Wait until you see."

Devon offers each of us an arm. "Right this way, ladies."

On fire with curiosity, I take hold of his left arm while Tenley curls her hand into crook of the right one. I tell myself I'm not doing anything wrong by looking. I haven't betrayed Hayden or my feelings for him by further investigating a lifestyle that's important to him. I'm after information, and Devon Black is an excellent source.

He's patient as he explains everything we encounter. "That is what's called a spanking bench. Note the padding that ensures the comfort of the sub."

I hadn't noticed the padding because I was too focused on the bright red ass cheeks of the woman bent over the contraption. "Doesn't that hurt?"

"Tenley, do you want to answer that question?"

"It's sort of a pleasurable kind of pain. It's hard to describe until you've tried it."

"So you like it?"

"Mmm," she says with a low hum. "I like it."

Devon smiles and pats her ass proprietarily. "I like it, too, but it's not for everyone. That's one of the best aspects of our scene—everyone is allowed to pick and choose what works for them and what doesn't."

"So it's like a cafeteria plan," I say, resorting to humor to hide my nervousness. Devon laughs. "Something like that."

We take a flight of stairs to the next level, which is open-gallery style and looks down on the main room below. Here the corridor is lined with sets of doors. "At my club, the left side is always the playroom and the right side is the observation room. We allow intercourse in the rooms but not on the main floor." He opens the first right-side door. "After you."

My heart beats a crazy staccato as I follow Tenley into a dark room. My attention is immediately drawn to the scene unfolding on the other side of a huge window. It's a doctor's office, and a naked woman is on the table, her feet in stirrups, her nipples clamped with metal clips. A tray of tools and objects is positioned next to the table. The "doctor" is a man and the "nurse" is another woman wearing a sexy white outfit with a demure nurse's cap on her head. When she turns around, I see that the outfit is actually an apron with no back.

I'm not sure how to feel about what I'm seeing. Part of me is mortified to be witnessing this. But the other part is fascinated and aroused, if the sharp ache between my legs is any indication. The doctor and nurse torture the woman on the table with devices I never would've thought could be sexy, including a speculum that they use to open her vagina. She moans and thrashes and seems to be coming constantly as they "examine" every inch of her. I can't believe that watching this actually turns me on, but it does.

"Let's see what else is happening," Devon says after we've watched for about fifteen minutes. He leads us from that room into another one where we see a woman bound from head to toe in an elaborate maze of ropes. The only parts of her not covered by the ropes are her breasts and genitals. She's suspended from the ceiling, and her lover is whipping her breasts with something that makes her moan with pleasure.

"What's that he's using?" I ask, my voice huskier than usual.

"It's a flogger," Devon says.

"Does it hurt?"

Again he defers to Tenley. I can't believe she's done all this stuff. Girl's been keeping some big secrets. "It stings, but it doesn't actually hurt."

I have a hard time understanding how it wouldn't hurt to be repeatedly struck by something with a dozen or more leather tips, but I take her word for it.

"The most important thing to know is that everything you see happening has been negotiated in advance between the Dom and sub. We don't believe in surprises during a scene, and the sub can put a stop to it at any time with one word that's also negotiated in advance."

"What's yours?" I ask Tenley.

"Style," she says with a big smile.

"Why am I not surprised?" I ask with a laugh.

"Tenley told me I can speak freely with you," Devon says, "so I'll tell you that she was about where you are when we first met at a party. She'd never heard of most of what goes on here, let alone tried it. She didn't get to where she is now overnight. It's a process, often undertaken by two people who have a common interest in the lifestyle as well as each other."

"So Doms and subs are always in relationships?"

"Not in the traditional sense of the word," Devon says. "In some cases, the only time a Dom and sub see each other is here or at another club where they might share a scene. Others live in full-time Dom/sub or Master/slave relationships."

"Master/slave? Seriously?"

"Everyone is different, and this lifestyle caters to what makes us unique. What wouldn't work for you works beautifully for someone else."

As I wonder if Hayden is into the Master/slave thing, I return my attention to the couple in the next room and watch as he manipulates her suspended body so her legs are wrapped around his hips. Her mouth falls open when he enters her, and I watch, transfixed, as a blissful expression occupies her face.

"See that?" Devon says softly. "That's called subspace. She's been transported out of the here and now, and the pleasure is all there is. A lot of the subs I know are strong, competent people who love to be taken away from it all for a little while, knowing they'll be well cared for if they let themselves go."

As a woman who constantly keeps a thousand balls in the air, the thought of being able to let it all go for a while certainly has its appeal. "So that can work? A woman who isn't submissive in her real life can submit here?"

"I see it all the time," Devon says. "We have women—and men—from all walks of life who come here looking to experience something new and different. Our club's membership includes actors and actresses whose names you'd recognize, thus the confidentiality agreement you signed upon entering the club. We take privacy and security very seriously here. Any club that doesn't is one to be avoided."

Since I'm not planning to take a grand tour of LA-area sex clubs, I'm comforted by this club's high standards.

"I'm surprised to learn that men can be submissive, too."

"Absolutely," Devon says. "Nothing is unheard of here. You're as likely to see a female dominatrix here as you are to see a male Dom." After we watch the couple in the next room for a while longer, he says, "Let's move along, shall we?"

I take a last look over my shoulder to see the couple in the next room still fully engaged in coitus. The man has stamina to spare, like someone else I know. I try to picture Hayden in this setting and can't help but wonder what his preferences are. Is he into floggers or whips? Ropes or toys? Or maybe he likes it all. I shiver as I imagine experiencing such things with him. I want to experience everything with him, and after seeing what's possible, that includes exploring this world.

In the next room, we see a man shackled to a large X.

"You mentioned being interested in the concept of a man as a submissive." Devon says. "That's what is known as a St. Andrew's cross."

I remember seeing them online. "Why is he alone?"

"His Domme is keeping him waiting. She's building the anticipation, which is one of many tools in the dominant's war chest. I thought you might like to see an example of female domination."

Another five minutes go by, during which my anxiety spikes right along with the man strapped to the cross, before a door on the other side of the room opens. In walks a blond woman wearing platform heels and a leather outfit that accentuates her generous curves. The man on the cross begins to tremble at the sight of her, and I watch in stunned amazement as his cock hardens.

Devon presses a button on the wall that allows us to hear what they're saying.

"That's very unfortunate," she says, glancing at his cock with utter disdain. "It'll make getting this ring on very painful."

"No, Mistress, please. Please don't hurt me."

"You did this to yourself, so save the begging for someone who cares."

"She won't really hurt him, will she?" I ask, horrified for him.

"Just watch," Devon says as Tenley's arm encircles my waist.

I wonder why she feels the need to offer comfort, but soon I see why as the mistress works the tight rubber cock ring down the length of his cock. He screams and begins to cry. I don't know what to do. Surely Devon will put a stop to this before it goes any further.

But he doesn't make any move to leave the room. Rather, he remains still as the man in the other room sobs.

"There, now," the mistress says in a more soothing tone once the ring is secured at the base of his scrotum. "You did it. I'm so proud of you. That deserves a reward. How would you like to be rewarded?"

"I'll let my mistress decide."

She pets his face and wipes the snot from under his nose with a tissue, tending to him as if he were a baby. Dropping to her knees before him, she takes his grotesquely hard cock into her mouth and begins to suck him off. Judging by the tight expression on his face, he's experiencing more pain than pleasure. Tears begin to slide down his cheeks once again as she sucks him to orgasm. His shouts are so loud they almost hurt my ears.

She stands and reaches for something on a nearby table.

He sees what's in her hand and recoils as much as he's able to, tied as he is to the cross. "No, Mistress. Anything but that."

"What is it?" I ask in a whisper. My voice has abandoned me. My heart is beating so fast I'm afraid it'll explode, and beads of sweat roll down my back.

"It's a crop," Devon says.

"Like the ones used on horses?"

"Similar."

"What's she going to…" The words die on my lips as the crop connects with his balls. His screams are agonizing to listen to. "Oh. Oh *God*." The room closes in on me.

Accompanied by the shrieks from the man on the cross, Devon takes me by the arm. "Let's get her some air."

They hustle me out of there and help me into an upholstered chair in the hallway.

"Take some breaths," Devon says. "Deep breaths."

I'm embarrassed and horrified and unbelievably aroused. More than anything, I'm confused as to how I can feel all those emotions at the same time. "I'm so sorry."

"Don't be." Devon encourages Tenley to take the chair next to mine while he squats in front of us. "It's a very common reaction among newbies."

"You… you didn't put a stop to it."

"No, only he can, and he knows exactly how to stop it if and when it becomes too much for him. He and his scene partner have worked out the details in advance, including a safe word that would immediately put an end to all activity."

"He was screaming in pain."

"He gets off on the pain."

I shudder, recalling the man's apparent agony.

"Everyone is different, Addie," Tenley says. "The lifestyle celebrates those differences."

"That's right," Devon adds. "We encourage participants to be true to themselves and to fully articulate their needs and desires so their partner can give them what they want. Communication between partners is absolutely critical."

"So he *wants* her to take a riding crop to his balls?"

"Yes," Devon says bluntly.

"I don't get that, but I guess I don't have to."

Devon smiles. "No, you don't. The important thing to know is not everything will appeal to you. Correct me if I'm wrong, but I got the sense you might've been aroused by some of what you saw?"

"Definitely."

"Then you should focus on the aspects that interest you and forget about the parts that don't."

"It's really that simple?"

"It is. The last thing I or any good Dom wants is a sub who rolls over and plays dead. I want an active, willing submissive who participates fully before, during and after our scene. No one is looking for a doormat to abuse, at least not any Dom I know."

I'm incredibly comforted by Devon's insight.

"Do you have other questions?"

"Could I maybe run a scenario by you to get your take on it?"

"Of course. Let's go up to my place and have a drink." Devon extends a hand to help me up and then does the same for Tenley before leading us to an elevator tucked discreetly into a nook.

"This house is incredible," I say.

"It's got an amazing pedigree." As we enter the elevator, Devon names the Hollywood glitterati who've called it home over the last five decades. The elevator deposits us into a penthouse that overlooks the city below.

I gravitate immediately to the floor-to-ceiling windows that look down over his property. "Wow, this is beautiful." A pool is lit up from within, casting a warm glow over the tiled deck and lush landscaping that surround it.

"I like it," Devon says with the understatement that I've come to expect from him after a couple of hours in his presence. "What can I get you to drink?"

"Is a gin and tonic doable?"

"Absolutely. Coming right up. Tenley?"

"I'll have the same, please."

We settle with our drinks in a sitting area near the windows. Tenley sits right next to Devon, and he slips an arm around her. They make a gorgeous couple, and I wonder if he's as serious about her as she seems to be about him.

"I'm happy to answer any questions you have," he says. "One thing you'll quickly learn is people in the lifestyle love to talk about it."

"They really do," Tenley says with a laugh. "It took me a while to get used to the dinner party conversations in Devon's world."

The look that passes between them demonstrates a deep level of intimacy that makes me envious. I want that. I want it so badly, and I want it with Hayden. The thought that we could have what they have is so tantalizing and yet so out of reach at the same time.

"I have a friend," I begin haltingly, still hesitant to say too much out of fear of violating Hayden's privacy. "We have an emotional connection, I guess you could say, that's recently turned physical. Today I found out he's part of the lifestyle, and when I asked if he would share it with me, he refused. He said I'm no one's submissive. At the same time, he indicated how important the lifestyle is to him. So here I am, crazy about a guy who wants things he thinks I can't give him."

"That's a dilemma for sure," Devon says. "Did he say why he thinks you couldn't be what he needs?"

"I'm guessing it's because he's never practiced with someone he loves, and he's afraid of hurting me or scaring me off."

"It's a totally different experience when you're in love with your partner," Devon says. "I get where he's coming from."

"So how do I convince him to let me try? As soon as I told him I was going elsewhere to learn about the lifestyle, he flipped out and said he'd train me himself. I told him I don't want him agreeing to it only because he doesn't want anyone else to touch me."

"The poor guy," Devon says with a low chuckle. "I feel for him."

"You guys all stick together," Tenley says, amusement dancing in her dark eyes.

"It's a tough spot for him. He's in love for perhaps the first time in his life, and he's struggling with how to reconcile the emotion with the lifestyle." Devon takes hold of Tenley's hand and brings it to his lips. "I've been there. I get it."

"Oh," she says on a deep exhale. "You have?" Her voice squeaks uncharacteristically on the two small words.

"We'll talk about that later," he says to her.

"On that note, I should get out of your hair."

"Don't go yet," Devon says. "I'm having an idea… It's a somewhat dastardly idea and goes against everything I believe in when it comes to the bro code, but it might solve your problem."

"Can't wait to hear this," Tenley says.

"What if we made plans for you to receive training at my club, under the supervision of one of my staff members? You could do as much or as little as you want—everything from merely talking to actually participating in a scene. So the training would be legitimate, and it would be up to you to decide how you want to structure it."

"And she would tell her guy about the training?" Tenley asks.

"Eventually, when she's ready to. Then he would know she's truly interested in the lifestyle because she's gone so far as to arrange for training. Hearing that would spur me to action if it involved the woman I love. I'd be surprised if it didn't do the same for Addie's guy."

As I stew over Devon's idea, I chew on my thumbnail, a throwback habit to my angst-ridden teenage years. "I can't imagine letting any other guy touch me."

"You don't have to actually have sex to receive training."

"I don't?"

"Nope. So what do you think? Would you like to set up some training with a member of my staff?"

"Would I be able to meet him before I trained with him?"

"Of course. I have a few people in mind for you. Let me make a call."

"So like right now?"

"Are you doing anything?"

I swallow hard. "Um, no. No other plans for tonight." I think about Hayden telling me earlier he was coming over to talk. Is he waiting for me to get home? Is he worried about where I might be or what I might be doing? I feel terrible for causing him any concern, but he did push me into a corner earlier by refusing to share this part of himself with me.

Before I've had time to work myself into a full-on panic over Devon's idea, the elevator dings to admit three men, each more handsome than the next. They're shirtless and wearing tight jeans or black pants that leave very little to the imagination. It's a buffet of male beauty. I'm introduced to Tony, Justin and Andre. Tony has the blond, blue-eyed California surfer look down to a science, while Justin is the brawny body builder and Andre, who's also muscular with intricate sleeve tattoos on both arms, has the most gorgeous skin I've ever seen on a man. When I say so, he tells me his mother is Mexican and his father is black.

"I'm insanely jealous," I reply, as I realize I'm flirting with him. I immediately feel guilty, though I have no good reason to. Hayden has made no commitment to me. If anything, he's done the opposite, so I'm not doing anything wrong by enjoying a conversation with another man. But my heart belongs to Hayden, and that's why none of this feels "right" to me.

"I've asked you gentlemen to join us because my friend Addie is interested in training."

"Are you a sub?" Tony asks with genuine interest.

"I never have been before, but I'm interested in trying."

"There's a guy," Devon says. "He's a Dom, but he's not sure Addie can submit the way he'd need her to."

"If you were my sub," Justin says meaningfully, "I'd make sure you were fully satisfied."

"Phew," Tenley says, fanning her face. "It's getting warm in here."

Everyone laughs, which breaks the tension somewhat. The guys have a drink with us while we talk about innocuous topics such as the Dodgers and the latest Hollywood gossip before Devon politely requests that they leave us.

Each of them bends to kiss my cheek on the way out, telling me it was nice to meet me. The elevator arrives, and they depart.

"*Where* do you find these guys?" I ask Devon the second the doors close.

"They find me. More importantly, are you interested in getting to know any of them better?"

I think it over for only a moment because I already know which one I'd chose. "Andre." I felt an immediate sense of kinship with him, and I feel like we could be friends at the very least.

"Excellent. Come tomorrow night at ten, and I'll set things up for you."
I must look poleaxed or something, because he quickly adds, "If that's what
you want."

Is it what I want? Am I really prepared to go through with this? Am I doing
it for the right reasons? Will this do more harm than good for Hayden and me? Is
there even a Hayden and me? What choice has he given me?

"Addie?" Tenley says. "What're you thinking?"

"So many things. Most of all, I'm afraid I'll mess things up with him."

"From what you've told us, there is no relationship with him unless you can
overcome the obstacle the lifestyle has put between you," Tenley says. "Right?"

"Yes, I guess that's true."

"If I were in your position," Tenley says, "I'd feel I had nothing to lose by
continuing my research."

"Would that include allowing another man to touch me?"

"If it was for a good cause in the end and you both knew the restrictions going
into it, I can't see why not."

"You have to understand," Devon says, "that the rules of fidelity and
monogamy are looser within our lifestyle. I assume your friend has been in the
lifestyle for quite some time. Would you agree?"

"From what I can ascertain, I'd say that's a safe assumption."

"Then you could safely argue that you're playing catch-up so you can get on
the same page with him."

I smile at that. "That's kind of a stretch."

"Are you a practitioner of yoga?" he asks, surprising me with the sudden shift
in conversation.

"I have been in the past."

"Then you know how the skill set builds upon itself. The more you practice,
the more you can do. The more you can do, the greater the benefits. This isn't all
that different. Andre can help you master the basics so you can fully realize your
potential. Everything you do with him would be safe, sane and consensual. Even
if he never lays a hand on your body or you never touch him, he can walk you
through what to expect if and when you do venture into a Dom/sub relationship."

The yoga analogy resonates with me. "So you're saying it would be akin to working with a personal trainer. It's just that the training is sexual rather than physical."

"The training is sexual as well as physical and emotional. Everything comes into play."

"I'll admit to being sincerely intrigued."

"Would you like to get your medical exam out of the way now, so you're ready to play tomorrow?"

He says this the same way anyone else would offer another drink.

"*Now?*" It has to be close to midnight.

"I have a doctor here around the clock."

"Wow. You don't fool around."

"Well, he does, but not when it comes to safety," Tenley says. "The exam is quick and painless. Nothing you haven't had before."

I try to find my inner reserve of courage. Then I remember the condition of my um, areas, and I wonder if having the exam now is a good idea. But the thought of any more delays when I finally have a real chance with Hayden is more unbearable than the exam could ever be. "Okay. Now would be great."

Twenty minutes later, I'm seated on an exam table wearing a cotton gown and nothing else while I wait for the doctor. I've been weighed and donated pee and blood. Now comes the "fun" part. I feel like a nervous sixteen-year-old having my first pelvic exam when I'm more than a decade removed from that mortifying incident.

Thinking about Dad declaring it was time to get me a lady doctor makes me smile. The poor guy did the best he could with a broken heart and a teenage daughter he had no idea what to do with. Though I was twelve when she died, my memories of my mother are somewhat fuzzy. I've read a lot about grief and the way it screws with your mind. I think that's what happened to me. Her death was so traumatic that I blocked all the good stuff along with the bad.

Dad took me to a therapist after she died, and that helped somewhat, but it didn't bring back my memories. I have pictures that fill in some of the gaps. They're all I have of her, so they're my most priceless possessions. I keep them in a fireproof box so they'll be safe no matter what happens.

Why am I thinking about my mother right now? I'm still puzzling that over when a knock on the door makes me gasp. I'd almost forgotten where I was and why. The door opens, and another of Devon's DNA-blessed employees walks in. Naturally, the doctor on call is a man—a tall, gorgeous, blond man with a smile right out of a toothpaste commercial. My aching lady parts shrivel up in horror at the thought of exposing themselves to him.

"Addison, is it?"

"Yes. I go by Addie."

"Addie, I'm Doctor Byron." Fitting that he should have the face and name of a poet. He makes a note on a page on his clipboard. "Mr. Black said you need the new-member physical. I have a brief questionnaire, then we'll do the exam and get you out of here. Sound good?"

"Um, sure."

He asks the usual questions about my cycle, whether I've ever been pregnant—I haven't—and how many sexual partners I've had. Ahhh, I settle on twelve. A nice even dozen, and I note the slight lift of his brow that might indicate judgment. I'm immediately on edge.

"Last time you were sexually active?"

"Yesterday."

He makes another note. We go on to cover family history and other routine questions before he clicks his pen and stands to wash his hands. "You can lie back and scoot your butt toward the edge of the table. I'm sure you know the drill."

I know the drill, all right. Gritting my teeth, I move into the required position.

"Do you do regular breast self-exams?" he asks as he settles my feet into stirrups.

Define regular. "Yes."

"It's very important to stay on top of that."

"Got it."

"I have to ask… You appear bruised—"

"I had sex yesterday. Good sex. *Vigorous* sex."

"It appears you also had vigorous anal sex."

"I did. It was incredible." I prop myself up on my elbows, forcing him to look at my eyes rather than my bruises. "Have you had anal?"

His mouth opens, but nothing comes out.

"You can ask me. Why can't I ask you?"

"I suppose that's fair enough."

"Well?" I raise a brow in inquiry.

"I can't say that I have."

"You ought to give it a try sometime."

"Um, right, well, I'll keep that in mind. I'll, ah, use some lubricant on the speculum since you're bruised."

"That'd be very nice of you."

Despite the lubricant, the speculum hurts going in, and I lose some of my bravado. Every second it's in there feels like a week. He moves quickly to take the swabs he needs and removes the speculum. I release a long deep breath. My relief is short-lived, however.

"Two fingers to check your uterus and ovaries, and then we're done."

His fingers hurt almost as badly as the speculum did, but I grimace and bear it, telling myself it's for a good cause. He pokes around for a solid minute before finally withdrawing.

"Everything looks good. Your test results will be back by tomorrow afternoon." He hands me a slip of paper. "You can call the number there and give them the code to get your results."

"Got it, thank you."

He hands me a business card. "If I can be of assistance to you at any time, don't hesitate to get in touch."

Wondering what sort of assistance he thinks I might need, I take the card. "Thank you."

"A pleasure. Have a good night."

"You, too."

I can't get my clothes on fast enough. Suddenly, I'm out of steam with this day, and I want my bed. I step out of the exam room to find Tenley in the waiting area.

"How'd it go?"

"Oh, you know how it is when you have to spread your legs for a hot-as-fuck male doctor."

She laughs. "I've told Devon he needs to take mercy on us and hire female doctors. He swears he has them, but I got a guy, too." She glances around the corner to make sure we're alone. "Would you hate me forever if I don't leave with you?"

"I'd hate you forever if you did with that amazing man of yours waiting for you."

"He is pretty great."

"He really is." I hug her. "Thank you so much for this. I appreciate it."

"Happy to help a friend." She produces my cell phone. "I had a feeling you'd understand."

Smiling, I take it from her. "And how do you propose I get home?"

"Devon will get one of the staff drivers to take you."

She walks me out to the foyer, where Devon is waiting to see me off. I hug him. "Thank you."

"It was a pleasure. I'll look forward to seeing you tomorrow."

"I'll be here."

Devon tucks me into a silver Lexus SUV and tells the driver to take me anywhere I wish to go. I debate going to get my car and decide I'm too tired, too buzzed, too everything to drive. I give him my address at the pier and settle in for the ride.

I fire up my cell phone, and it goes crazy beeping with messages from Hayden repeatedly asking where the hell I am. I smile, listening to him get progressively more agitated and pissed off. God, I love him. I love every freaking thing about him, even the things I shouldn't love. Yesterday, when I hated him, seems like a long time ago now that I can hear his love for me coming through loud and clear in every message. The phone beeps with a final message.

"Addie, it's me." I sit up a little straighter at the sound of Flynn's voice. "I thought you'd want to know that Hayden's mother was taken to Cedars-Sinai earlier tonight. Gordon's guys found her unresponsive. I'm heading over there now."

My hands are shaking as I handle the phone. "Excuse me," I say to the driver, "could we please go to Cedars-Sinai instead?"

"Of course." At the next light, he makes a turn away from the coast to head into town.

I feel sick imagining what Hayden is going through. Getting to him as quickly as possible is the only thing that matters.

# CHAPTER 12

*Hayden*

Freaking food poisoning of all things. That's what put my mother in the hospital. I thought the worst on the way over here. I was so certain she'd fallen off the wagon—again—and that we were going to be plunged back into the rabbit hole of despair.

Apparently, she was sick all day but didn't want to "bother" me. Am I that much of an asshole that she wouldn't call her only child to let him know she was desperately ill? When I asked her that, she said of course not, but she knows how busy I am and that I have a film due soon.

I have to bite back a furious retort. I hate that after all we've been through together she would think my work is more important to me than she is.

As she rests in the hospital bed, her face is so pale she blends in with the linen except for the vibrant blue eyes that are the same shade as mine. She's hooked to IVs and monitors whose incessant beeping drives me fucking nuts. Her once-blond hair has begun to go gray, and she's letting it happen, preferring to age gracefully rather than fight it, or so she says. Despite her battles with addiction, she's still a beautiful woman, and I cling to the hope that maybe this time, her recovery will stick.

Flynn and Natalie were here earlier, but I sent them home when we found out she was okay. No sense in everyone losing a night of sleep. With the crisis passed, I glance at my phone to find nothing new from Gordon.

*God, Addie, where are you?* I'm half out of my mind with worry over where she might be and what she might be doing.

"You should go home, sweetheart," Mom says. "Get some sleep. I'll be fine."

They're giving her fluids and electrolytes to rehydrate her and keeping her overnight for observation.

"You can pick me up in the morning."

I take hold of her hand. "I'll stay for a while."

"Sorry to put you through this, Hayden. You have to be tired of getting emergency phone calls about me."

"I just want you to be okay. That's all that matters."

"I was doing great until I ate bad Chinese food."

I wince. "Yuck."

"You said it."

The door bursts open, and Addie comes into the room looking flushed and stressed and stunningly gorgeous. I'm so flooded with relief to see her that I can't move or speak. "I came as soon as I heard."

"Hi, Addie," Mom says. "It's so nice of you to check on me."

She rests her hand on my shoulder as she bends to kiss Mom's cheek. "You're okay, Jan?"

"I will be. Just a nasty bout of food poisoning."

"Oh," Addie says, exhaling in relief. "I'm so glad. Not about the food poisoning…"

"I know, honey," Mom says, her eyes full of understanding. She knows what everyone was thinking when we heard she was in the hospital again.

I want to lean into Addie's sweet body, to take comfort from her, but I have no idea where I stand with her. That she obviously came running when she heard about Mom is a good sign, but we still need to talk.

"You okay?" she asks, looking down at me with concern and love. The love is all I see.

"I am now." Two of the women I love best are safe. That's all I need to be okay. I can tell she gets what I'm saying, because her expression softens and her eyes do that sparkling thing that happens when she looks at me sometimes. I much prefer that to when she looks at me with disappointment, like she did earlier today.

"Will you please try to get my stubborn son to go home, Addie? He's refusing to leave when there's no need for him to stay. I'm absolutely fine."

Only because I need some time alone with Addie so badly do I allow my mother to talk me into leaving. I bend over the bed to kiss her forehead. "I'll pick you up when they spring you."

"I'll see you then. Try to get some sleep. Everything's fine."

She knows what I need to hear. "I will."

"Thanks for coming. Both of you."

"I'll check on you tomorrow, Jan," Addie says.

"I'll look forward to that."

I'm so lucky to have friends, including Addie, who've supported my mom and me through the worst of times. No matter how bad it gets—and it's gotten pretty fucking awful at times—they never judge or condemn, and for that I'm eternally grateful. My emotions are all over the place after the evening I've endured. Between worrying about Addie and then freaking out over my mom, I'm drained. Addie seems to sense that, wrapping her arm around my waist and leaning her head on my shoulder as we take the elevator to the lobby.

I'm too undone to resist the comfort she offers, and I'm so fucking relieved she's okay that I can't even find the wherewithal to be pissed at her for ditching the security detail. I'll have to take that up with her at some point, but not now. Not tonight.

"How'd you get here?" I ask her.

"I got dropped off." She doesn't say who dropped her off, and I don't ask, even though I desperately want to know.

I put my arm around her and lead her to the Range Rover, which is parked at an angle due to my earlier haste to get to my mother.

"You want me to drive?" she asks.

"Nah, I will." The ride to her place is quiet, but it's a comfortable silence. It's the kind of companionable silence I could get used to as long as I'm sharing it with her. The traffic is lighter at nearly two in the morning, and I pull up to her building a short time later.

"Come in," she says. "You shouldn't be alone tonight."

"I won't be very good company."

"You don't have to be."

And there in those five little words is another reason to love Addison York. She accepts me for who and what I am. The realization has me thinking that perhaps she could accept the rest of me, too. I'm too far gone tonight to give that thought the time or attention it will require to fully process.

She gives me the code to the garage, and I pull into one of the guest spots, still wondering if I shouldn't just go home before I do something to screw things up even worse between us. If that's possible...

Still in caretaker mode, she leads me upstairs and helps me out of my jacket and begins unbuttoning my shirt. Her mouth is set in an adorable expression as she concentrates on what she's doing. I can't resist raising my hand to tuck a strand of hair behind her ear. She looks up at me, seeming surprised by tenderness from me, and I vow to give her more of that. She deserves nothing but the best, and I want to be the one to give it to her.

After my shirt is off, she goes to work on my belt. I cover her hand to stop her. "I can take it from here."

With her hands on my face, she brings me down for a soft, sweet kiss that destroys the last of my defenses where she's concerned. I've got no fight left in me. I need her so badly. I need her to bring light to my darkness. I need her to bring sense to the madness that surrounds me. I need her to remind me to breathe when life is too much for me.

"Go get comfortable," she says, her lips still damp from our kiss. "I'll be right in."

I do what I'm told because there's nowhere I'd rather be than comfortable in Addie's bed. In her bedroom, I use the bathroom and then remove the rest of my clothes and get into bed, covering my eyes with my forearm as this endless fucking day comes to a close.

I'm lost in my own thoughts when I hear her enter the room. She goes into the bathroom and emerges a few minutes later. The mattress dips when she joins me. "Hayden."

I remove my arm from my eyes and look over to see her wearing a peach silk nightgown that's almost the same color as her skin. She hands me a glass filled with familiar-looking amber liquid.

"Pappy?"

"Of course." Smiling, she adds, "Having Pappy on hand wherever you're apt to be is part of my job."

"You're damned good at your job."

"Drink up. You seem to need it tonight."

"You have no idea." I sit up against the pillows and take a drink, sighing with pleasure as the heat of the bourbon travels through me.

"You thought the worst about your mom."

I note that she doesn't ask. "Yeah," I say after a long silence. "Her addictions are so insidious that I always think the worst."

"Insidious," she says, her lips pursing in thought.

"What about it?"

"That would make a good tile for the film."

I stare at her, half stunned because she's exactly right. "Fuck, Addie. That's brilliant."

Shrugging, she says, "I do what I can for the people."

"I can't wait to run that by the studio. I think they'll jump on it." I breathe yet another deep sigh of relief at having that monkey off my back. "Thank you."

"It's no big deal."

"Not just for suggesting a title that'll be perfect for the film, but for coming to the hospital tonight after the way we left things earlier. I didn't expect—"

Her hand on my chest stops me. "You can expect that I'll always show up for you no matter how we leave things between us. We're friends, and friends show up."

Overwhelmed by her sweetness, I cover her hand with mine and hold on tight to her while I finish the drink. I put my empty glass on the table and then reach for her, bringing her as close to me as I can get her. I'm not sure which feels better, the silk of the gown or the silk of her skin against mine. Definitely her. Nothing feels quite like she does. My cock is immediately hard for her, but for once, I'm not letting my cock rule me. My heart has far more on the line tonight.

"You gonna tell me where you were all night when I was looking for you?"

"We'll talk about it in the morning."

"Addison…"

"In the morning, Hayden, but I do have one thing I need to say to you right now."

"What?"

She swallows hard and takes a deep breath. "You've had me followed for the last time. Do you understand me?"

"I was out of my fucking mind worrying about you."

"I'm sorry about that."

"No, you're not," I say with a chuckle. "You knew I'd go mad looking for you, and you dropped off the radar anyway."

"That's not why I did it. I wasn't trying to make you crazy."

"Well, you did. I was losing it imagining you in an unsafe situation with nothing I could do to protect you."

"Give me a little credit, will you? I'm not an idiot. I'd never put myself in danger on purpose."

"Sometimes it's hard to tell what's dangerous in my world, sweetheart."

"You have nothing to worry about."

"That's where you're wrong. With you, I have everything to worry about."

"Aww, Hayden. You're such a romantic. Who knew?"

That makes me laugh when I would've said that nothing could make me laugh tonight.

"No more surveillance. I want to hear you say it."

"Fine," I say begrudgingly. "No more surveillance. Now can I kiss you?"

"I wish you would."

I prop myself up on one elbow and gaze down at her precious face for a long time before I lower my lips to meet hers. Addie's arms encircle my neck, and I end up on top of her for the sweetest, sexiest kiss of my life. All we do is kiss. Our hands remain stationary even as my cock throbs against her soft belly. I can feel her love in every stroke of her tongue, and her fingers in my hair soothe and calm the rage that lives within me.

The rage is exhausting, but I don't remember a time when I didn't carry it with me. I remember the red-hot heat of it from the first time my mother OD'd when I was five. It's intensified with every subsequent incident until it's as much a part of me as my blue eyes and dark hair. Sometimes I think the rage is partially responsible for my success as a filmmaker. I feel things more deeply than other people do, and that intensity comes through in my work. What I feel for Addie runs through me so deeply I'll never be free of it, and I don't want to be.

I ease back from the kiss, running my thumbs over her sweet face. "I care about you more than I've ever cared about anyone. No matter what else happens, I need you to know that."

Her eyes shine with unshed tears. "I do know, Hayden. I've known that for a long time. I love you so much. There's nothing I wouldn't do for you. I wish you'd believe me when I tell you that."

"I want to."

"You can."

"I'm trying."

"I know you are."

"Tell me where you were tonight."

She rubs shamelessly against my hard cock. "Aren't there other things you'd rather do right now than hear about my night?"

"Just tell me you didn't let any other man touch what's mine." I've never said such a thing to a woman before, and to me it's almost bigger to admit she's mine than it was to admit to myself that I love her.

"I didn't let anyone touch me."

The relief I feel at hearing that trumps every other emotion I've experienced during the last insane twenty-four hours.

Her legs curl around my hips in invitation. Her wet heat on my cock is irresistible, and I slide into her slowly and carefully, knowing she has to be sore. Whereas last night was about ravenous hunger, tonight is about sweet love. I almost have myself convinced that I could be satisfied if this is all it ever is for us, sweet vanilla sex with the woman I love.

If only I didn't know how much more is possible. But for tonight, for right now, this is more than enough. It's more than I ever hoped to dream possible. She moves with me in an effortless rhythm, her internal muscles snug around my cock, her heat searing and branding me as hers. It's true. As much as she's mine, I'm hers. I can no longer deny that, and I don't want to.

I find the hem of her gown and drag it up and over her head. Her lovely breasts bounce with every deep stroke of my dick. That plus the way the tips tighten into hard beads before my eyes mesmerizes me. Everything about her mesmerizes me. This, right here, is what it means to make love. I didn't think it would be different, but it is. It's night and day. It's my whole heart, soul and body engaged at the same time. It's what I would've said I didn't want until I had it, and now it's all I want. *She* is all I want.

She digs her nails into my back, which is sexy as fuck. Everything she does is a turn-on. Her scent turns me on. Don't even get me started on those little noises she makes when I'm deep inside her. God, I love them. I push my hands under her to grab her ass cheeks so I can go even deeper. I pull her open to take more of me, and she comes immediately.

I'm not nearly done with her, so I ride the waves of her orgasm and keep her coming by not letting up on the pace. She feels so good that I'm tempted to let go and give in to the need that has me right on the edge of losing my shit. But I want one more from her first. I slow down, press deep inside and stay wedged tight while her muscles work me over. If there's ever been anything that feels better than being inside Addie, I haven't experienced it.

Bending over her, I draw her left nipple into my mouth, licking, sucking and biting until it's standing up tall. Then I do the same to the right side.

"Hayden," she whispers.

"What, baby?"

"I want you to train me. Teach me. Show me what you want."

I shake my head. I can't. I just can't.

"Please," she says, her eyes filling. She grasps my face and forces me to look at her. "Please."

"No." I begin to move again, faster now, angry at myself and her. She's asking for more than I'm able to give. If she ever knew what I really want, she'd look at me with fear in those beautiful eyes. I couldn't bear that, so I take the coward's way out. I fuck her hard until she comes again, and this time I give in and take my own pleasure, losing myself in her

I come down on top of her.

She wraps her arms around me, her tears wetting my face. "Why?" she asks softly, so softly I almost don't hear her. "Is there something wrong with me?"

"God, no, baby." It kills me that she would think that. "Everything about you is right. You're perfect just the way you are. I'd be crazy to mess with perfection."

"I want to be perfect for *you*. I don't want to be put on a pedestal to worship and admire. I want to be your equal. Your partner."

"You're my equal in every possible way."

"But I can't be your submissive."

"No."

She pushes on my shoulder. "Let me up."

I withdraw from her, and she gets up. "Addie—"

"You need to go now, Hayden." She disappears into the bathroom, the door slamming behind her.

"Fuck."

# CHAPTER 13

*Addie*

I take a long hot shower as tears stream down my cheeks. I hate him and love him and want him and hate him. My emotions are a big disaster that circles around one exasperating man. I stay in the shower until the hot water begins to wane. My heart aches along with every other part of me as I towel off and put on a robe.

Certain he's long gone by now, I leave the bathroom and find him sitting on my bed, his head in his hands. He got as far as putting his jeans back on, but his chest is still bare. His defeated pose goes straight to my broken heart. Knowing he's hurting as much as I am makes it more bearable. But why is either of us hurting when we both know what we want? That's the part I can't seem to reconcile no matter how hard I try.

I sit on the bed next to him and put my arm around his shoulders.

"I couldn't leave it this way," he says after a long silence.

"That's an improvement from when you ran away."

"I don't want to hurt you, Addie, and I hate that I keep doing that."

"Then don't. Tell me what's stopping you from giving us a real, honest chance."

Releasing a deep breath, he sits up straight.

I keep my arm around him, needing the contact and hoping it helps to prop him up, too. He wants to tell me. I can see that. But he shakes his head. "You wouldn't understand."

"When you say that, I want to punch you, and I want to make it hurt."

A ghost of a smile occupies his lips. "I wouldn't blame you if you did."

"You're not being fair to either of us."

"I'm sure that's how it must seem, but I'm actually thinking of you when I tell you it'll never work. I'll disappoint you more than I already have. I don't have the settle-down-with-one-woman gene, Addie. Look at my dad—he's on his fourth wife, and because all they do is fight, I expect he'll be telling me any day now that they're splitting. And my mom—three husbands, three divorces. That's my gene pool. The Roths don't do monogamy or the kind of lifetime commitment you deserve."

"That's utter bullshit, Hayden. You're not your parents. If you were, you'd be in rehab with five kids to support. But you're not. You're their polar opposite, and you can't even see that. You're a successful, productive, healthy man who has many of the same friends he had in high school. You've never touched a drug, you drink only socially, and you take care of everyone and don't even realize it."

"What does that mean?" He looks genuinely baffled. "Who do I take care of?"

"*Everyone!* Your mom, Sebastian, Flynn, the Quantum team, me."

He shakes his head. "I do not."

"Hayden." I wait until he's looking at me. "You do, too. Everyone looks to you for direction at work—and not just when filming—and your mom would be dead without you. You're a caretaker. It's who you are. It's what you do. But who takes care of you?"

"I don't need anyone to take care of me."

"Everyone needs someone. Why won't you let your someone be me?"

"Because!" He gets up and stalks to the glass door to my deck. Hands on his hips, his every muscle rigid with tension, he says, "You think you know me, but you don't. You don't know how hard it is for me to…" He buries his hands in his hair, as if he wants to tear it from his skull, and then drops his hands to his sides, his shoulders sagging in defeat.

I get up and go to him, placing my hands on his shoulders and touching my lips to the indent between his shoulder blades. "What's hard for you to do?"

"This! Us. All of it. I don't know how to do this, Addie. I've never done it. I've never seen it done. I'll fuck it up so bad, and then you'll hate me for real, and I couldn't bear that. I just couldn't. If I lost you…"

I slide my arms around his waist. "You won't lose me, Hayden. I promise that no matter how badly you fuck it up, no matter how ugly it might get, you'll never lose me."

"You can't make that promise. You don't even know what you're saying."

"Tell me what I don't know. What big, dark secret are you keeping from me that'll prevent us from making a go of this?"

"There's no secret. You're asking me to be someone for you that I have no idea how to be."

"All I'm asking you to be is *you*. We'll figure out the details together, one step at a time."

"What if…"

"Say it. Whatever it is, put it out there." I feel like I'm fighting for my life by fighting for him.

He turns to face me, and the torment I see in his eyes sears me. "What if this isn't what I want?"

I force myself to remain calm, to not show him how much his question hurts me. "Only you can know that."

His hands land on my hips, keeping me with him when I would've turned away to get myself together. "I want you. I don't know if I want all the bells and whistles you're looking for, but God help me, I do want you."

"I want a chance to make it work. That's all I'm asking for, Hayden. A chance."

He stares down at me, and I hold my breath waiting to hear what he'll say. "Why me? Why in the world have you set your sights on me?"

"Why not you? Why do you believe that no one in their right mind would ever care about you or love you?"

"Because no one ever has."

"Your mother does."

He shrugs. "She has to. I'm all she has."

I stare at him, incredulous. "That's not why she loves you. She loves you because you never stopped believing in her, even when she gave you every good reason to turn your back on her. Flynn loves you. Jasper, Kristian and Marlowe love you. What about Sebastian? You saved his life, Hayden. Where would he be without you?"

All this talk of love makes him squirm. "You've built me up to be way more than I actually am."

"No, I haven't. I see you exactly for who and what you are, and *I* love you." When he would turn away from me, I stop him. "I love you, Hayden, and not because I have to, but because I don't know how not to. I've loved you, I think, since the first time I ever laid eyes on you, lording over one of your first sets, bossing everyone around. You blew me away with your passion and your intensity and your sexy blue eyes." I'm telling him far more than I ever intended to, but I sense he needs to hear it. "I don't remember a time when I didn't want you, and now that I've had you, I want you even more than I did before."

He stares at me, seeming stunned by my confession. "That long?" he asks, his voice hoarse.

"That long. So you see, you have to give me a chance or else—" I never get to tell him the "or else" because he's kissing me. His hands cradle my face as he devastates me with every stroke of his tongue. I cling to him, hoping this is his way of telling me I'm going to get that chance I want so badly.

His hands drop to my shoulders, and then his arms are around me. He breaks the kiss, his lips skimming over my face and neck. Only the tight hold he has on me keeps me standing when I'd otherwise slide into a puddle on the floor. His tender sweetness disarms me. I wonder if he's ever shown another woman this side of himself. Probably not. Look what it's taken to get him to be vulnerable with me.

"I want to give us the chance," he says haltingly.

The surge of joy that overtakes me has my heart on the verge of bursting. "But…"

With that one word, the joy is gone, replaced by anxiety. What now?

"I won't bring you into my BDSM lifestyle. That's off-limits."

He giveth, and he taketh away.

I let my arms fall from around his neck and take a step back. When he tries to come with me, I flatten my hands against his chest to stop him. "No deal."

"Will you listen to me?"

"No, I won't. I want all of you or none of you." As I say the words, a stab of panic hits my abdomen, leaving me reeling but firm in my resolve. "Your choice."

"Addie, please. Listen."

"You heard me. I don't see what else there is to say unless you're willing to give me everything."

"You're seriously going to tell me you've loved me for ten years and then walk away if I can't give you everything?"

I force myself to meet that intense blue gaze that shreds me. "Yes."

Shaking his head, a furious expression on his face, he stalks across the room to grab his T-shirt off the floor and puts it on—inside out. But he doesn't notice as he leaves the room.

I stand perfectly still until I hear the door slam behind him. My legs begin to tremble, and I stumble my way to the bed, where I sit and focus on breathing. One breath at a time, one second at a time. That's how I'll bear the pain that makes every part of me ache for what I just let walk away. Isn't some of him better than none?

"No," I say, moaning. "No, it's not enough." I don't know what to do with all the emotions running around inside me. I'm confused and despondent and furious. And sad. I'm incredibly sad for what could've been. My cell phone rings in the tone I've assigned to Flynn.

Another rule to being the successful assistant to the biggest movie star in the world is never ignoring a call from him, even when your heart has been shattered.

"Hey," I say. "What's up?"

"What's the matter?" he asks.

"Nothing, why?"

"You sound weird."

"I'm fine. I was working out."

"Are you lying to me?"

"What do you need, Flynn?"

After a long pause, he says, "I'm coming over. Don't go anywhere."

Before I can object, the phone goes dead. "Great." I put on a robe and head for the bathroom to do what I can to repair the damage before he gets here. I usually love the way he looks out for me, but tonight I want to be alone. I don't want to talk about it. What's there to say?

I love Hayden. He loves me. But we can't be together for some reason that only he seems to understand.

My face is swollen, my eyes are red, and I generally look like death warmed over. I suppose I should consider myself fortunate that it took twenty-seven years to have my heart broken. Sure, I've had boyfriends, a few I even liked a lot, but I've loved only one man. In the back of my mind, always, was the image of how my life would transpire.

Hayden and I would sow our so-called wild oats with other people, and then it would be our time. After a gorgeous, joyful wedding, we'd buy a fantastic house on the coast where we'd entertain lavishly and raise a family of blue-eyed babies. I'd hold down the fort at home with the kids while he was on location, and in the summer, when our kids were on vacation, we'd go with Hayden to exotic places where he'd create magic on film and our family would share in a grand adventure. There'd be delicious Thanksgiving turkeys and ten-foot Christmas trees and Easter egg hunts on our huge lawn. There would be friends and family and love and laughter and happily ever after.

I wipe away the new flood of tears that course down my cheeks as it becomes clear that none of that is going to happen. Not with him, anyway. The sad thing is, I can't imagine any other man but him playing the starring role in my fantasy life. I'm still in the bathroom and still weeping when I hear a pounding knock on my door.

I'm in no way prepared to see anyone right now, but I know Flynn won't leave until he's laid eyes on me. I tie my robe tighter around my waist and wipe my face—as if that will matter. I open the door to find Flynn, Natalie *and* Marlowe. Fantastic.

He gasps at the sight of me. "I'm going to fucking kill him."

"No, you're not." Leaving the door open for them, I turn away and head for the bar I keep in the corner of my living room. "Who needs a drink?" I pour glasses of prosecco for myself, Natalie and Marlowe.

"Yeah," Flynn says. "I'll have one."

I pour two fingers of Bowmore, his favorite single-malt Scotch, into a highball glass and hand it to him. He's pacing the length of my living room, clearly livid with Hayden. Part of me wants to set Flynn on Hayden and encourage him to beat some sense into his best friend, but what good would it do?

Marlowe hugs me. "What can I do?"

"Nothing. How was your trip?"

"Screw that. I don't want to talk about London. I want to talk about why you've been crying and what we're going to do about it."

"There's nothing we can do."

"What happened?" Natalie asks, her expression empathetic and kind.

I sit on a floral chaise and curl my feet under me. "He offered me eighty percent, and I said that wasn't good enough."

"What do you mean?" Flynn asks, his sharp gaze intently focused on me.

"It's sort of personal…"

"Come on, Addie," he says. "This is you and Hayden we're talking about here. We want to help."

Again I tell myself it doesn't matter if they know the truth, because there is no me and Hayden as anything other than "friends." I clear my throat and vow to get through this without tears, which also aren't helping anything. "He wants to be with me, but not in the way he is with other women."

Flynn stops moving, his entire body going still.

Marlowe's lips form a surprised O. "How do you know about that?"

"How do *you* know?"

The three of them exchange glances.

"*You, too?*" I ask, seeing my old friend in a whole new light.

"All of us, honey," Marlowe says softly.

"All… I, um, oh. Wow. I had no idea." And how is that possible that my closest friends and colleagues are involved in something I knew nothing about? Now in addition to being heartbroken, I feel stupid, too.

"Don't go there, Addison." It doesn't surprise me that Marlowe read my mind. She's been doing that for years now. "You didn't know because you didn't need to, not because people set out to intentionally keep something from you."

"What she said." Flynn uses his thumb to point at Marlowe. "It's not about keeping secrets. It's about respecting privacy."

"I respect your privacy. I respect everyone's privacy. If he thinks I'd ever tell anyone…"

"That's not why."

We all look to Flynn.

"You better explain what you mean," Natalie says to her husband, and I want to kiss her for articulating my thoughts.

"He's a very demanding Dom, Addie." To Natalie and Marlowe, he says, "You guys know what I mean. He's probably afraid to scare you off by showing you the true extent of who he really is."

"I already told him he won't scare me off."

"How can you say that when you don't know what you're signing on for?" Flynn asks.

"I do know. I've done some research. I've seen what goes on."

"When? Where? You just found out about this."

"I went with a friend to Black Vice and had a tour."

Flynn's face registers shock and disbelief.

"Don't act like it's so unbelievable that I would do that! I love him! I want to understand him! He's refused to train me, so I've found someone else who will."

Flynn drops his glass onto a table with a loud thunk. "No fucking way, Addison. This is not something you just go out and do."

"Give me a little credit, will you?" It's not often that I find myself truly furious with him, but this is one of those times. "I'm not an idiot, Flynn. I know exactly what I'm doing, and I'll be doing it in a safe, sane, consensual environment."

His jaw pulses with tension, and I can tell he's on the verge of losing it. So can Natalie, because she gets up and goes to him.

She puts an arm around him. "Settle down."

"I will not settle down when she hasn't the first clue about what she's getting into!"

"Yes, she does," Marlowe says. "We're talking about *Addie*. She's nothing if not thorough, and that's why you brag about her being the best assistant in

Hollywood. I have no doubt that whatever she's doing, she's researched it thoroughly and feels comfortable."

I smile at her. "Exactly that."

"I don't like it," Flynn says.

"You don't have to," Natalie says. "It's her life and her choice, and frankly, I don't blame her for doing her own research. That's what I would do in her shoes."

Flynn's low growl lets his wife know what he thinks of that statement.

"Tell me more about what you've got planned," Marlowe says.

"I have a date tomorrow night—or I guess it's tonight now—with one of Devon's staff members, who will oversee my training."

When Flynn starts to object, Natalie puts her hand over his mouth. His eyes flash with rage. I fear she'll be in for it when they get home, but judging by the dewy glow of happiness she constantly wears, she seems to enjoy his brand of punishment.

"And you feel confident that he's someone you can trust and who'll take good care of you?" Marlowe asks.

"I trust my friend, who trusts Devon Black, who trusts Andre, so yes. I feel confident." I don't, really, but I keep that to myself. The only man I want to surrender to won't have me.

"I agree that you're going to keep that date and find out more about what you'd be taking on with Hayden," Marlowe says with a calculating look in her eyes.

"What're you up to, Mo?" Flynn asks.

"What if you were to casually mention to Hayden that Addie has a date with a Dom at Black's place?"

"He'd fucking lose his mind!"

"Exactly," Marlowe says, smiling.

"So wait…" Flynn begins to pace again. "Are you suggesting we *set him up?*"

"That's exactly what I'm suggesting. He needs a nudge, and if this doesn't do it, I don't know what will."

Listening to Marlowe's plan, I feel a flutter of hope in the area of my breastbone. It's a delicate, fragile feeling that I want to hold tight to, even though I'm scared, too. Marlowe's idea goes much further than Devon's would have.

"Addie?" Marlowe asks. "What do you think?"

"Do I really want him if I have to trick him into wanting me?"

"That's not what you're doing," Natalie says. "Wanting you isn't the problem. If he actually sees you embracing his lifestyle, that might make a difference to him."

"I don't like the idea of her embracing the lifestyle outside of our clubs," Flynn says.

Once again, I'm stunned. "Wait a minute. There're *clubs? Where?*"

"Um, in the basements of the Quantum buildings here and in New York," Flynn says, seeming reluctant to share.

"*Are you freaking kidding me?*" This is truly shocking to me. "Right under my nose? When can I go there?"

Marlowe waves her hand. "Let's worry about that another day. Are you in on this plan or what?"

"You're sure it's a good idea?" The only person I trust more than Marlowe is my dad, with Flynn also at the top of the list. They've been the three most important people in my life for a lot of years.

"If I wasn't sure, I wouldn't have suggested it," Marlowe says. "You're just what he needs, Addie, and he's so afraid of screwing it up that he refuses to even try. We need to take that option off the table and give him no choice but to let you all the way into his life, which is where he wants you anyway. Don't you agree, Flynn?"

Other than when Natalie's painful past was being made public, I've never seen him so tense. "I'm not a big fan of game playing in situations like this, but I agree that Hayden's never going to come to this conclusion on his own, and a push in the right direction might be beneficial."

"Okay, so it's unanimous," Marlowe says.

Natalie holds up her hand. "Wait. Do I get a vote?"

"Of course you do, babe." Flynn is acting as if this is his deal rather than mine. But who am I to quibble over the details when I want to hear what she has to say?

"You know I want you to get everything you've ever wished for and then some, right?" Natalie asks me.

"I think so."

"I do." She crosses the room to sit at the foot of my chaise. "You've been such a good friend to me since Flynn and I got together, and I'd love to wave a magic wand and have this situation with Hayden magically resolved with both of you happy and in love and planning a future together."

Because that's what I want, too, I feel my throat tighten with emotion.

"I just don't know if this is the right way to go about it. I've seen his temper in action, and it's not something to trifle with. He's apt to kill someone if he thinks another guy is touching what he considers his."

"That's a good point," Flynn says.

"Then we bring Devon Black in on it," Marlowe says. "I know him. I'll give him a heads-up."

"It would be better if he knew," Natalie says.

"I'll make the call," Marlowe says. "So we're in agreement? We have a plan?"

All eyes turn to me. I realize this is probably the last chance I'm going to have to convince Hayden that I can be everything he wants and needs. I take a deep breath and release it slowly. "We have a plan."

# CHAPTER 14

*Hayden*

After I leave Addie's, I drive around aimlessly. I already regret leaving, and I hate that I hurt her. I suppose it was inevitable, which is exactly why I kept my distance for so long. Thinking about Oscar night, when she basically took the choice away from me, I realize I was powerless to resist her. I lost control, and I can't let that happen.

It was the right thing to leave, but even knowing that, I can't imagine living the rest of my life without touching her again. How will I go back to being just her friend after having experienced the exquisite pleasure I found in her arms? I feel like I'm going to be sick, and I pull off the road.

Throwing open the door, I breathe in the cool night air, wishing for comfort that I already know can only be found with her. Part of me wants to say fuck it, fuck it all, and go back.

God, if this is what it feels like to be in love, I want nothing to do with it. No wonder my parents couldn't manage to go the distance with any of their spouses. If this is what it was like for them, I don't blame them for bailing.

When it becomes apparent that the meager contents of my stomach are going to stay down, I close the car door and contemplate my choices. I need help, and I have no idea where to turn. My partners and friends at Quantum are too close to Addie to be objective. I have other friends, lots of them, but no one I would share something like this with. There is one person who has always been there for me in times of crisis, and knowing she's usually up half the night reading and watching TV, I put the car into gear to head for my home-away-from-home in Pasadena.

I don't want to scare her, so while I wait at a red light at the entrance to the 110, I text her to ask if I can stop by.

*You've got the code, honey. Come on in.*

*Be there in twenty.*

I pull up to the house seventeen minutes later and punch Sebastian's birthday into the keypad outside the gate, which swings open to admit me. I bought the Spanish hacienda-style home for Graciela with some of the first money I ever made on my films. I'll never forget the day I brought her here and handed her the keys. She cried so hard I worried I'd have to take her to the emergency room.

Smiling at the memory, I kill the engine outside the mudroom door that we use to come and go.

Thanks to my patronage, she doesn't work anymore. Rather, she donates her time to other youth in need, doing for them what she once did for me. Every time my parents forgot they had a son on a holiday or birthday, Graciela filled the void. She never forgot about me, and I've never forgotten her or what she did for me.

My family has no idea I'm still in touch with my father's former housekeeper, let alone that I happily support her. I enjoy imagining what my father would have to say about that since I've refused to give him one dime of my earnings—and he has asked plenty of times. Why should I? He barely acknowledged me until I had money, so I'm not inclined to share with him or his "real" family, as he once referred to his other kids while raging at me about something.

Wearing a robe and slippers, Graciela is waiting for me at the door and greets me with a warm hug. With her long dark hair framing her pretty, unlined face, she looks much younger than her sixty years.

"This is a nice surprise, hijo." I love when she calls me the Spanish word for son, which is what she also calls Sebastian. Funny how one small word can convey a world of meaning. Though she left Mexico with her family as a very young girl, her native tongue still makes an appearance from time to time.

She hooks her arm through mine and leads me to the cozy family room that's my favorite room in the house. The TV is paused on Jimmy Fallon's face. She records his show and watches after it's over so she can skip the commercials.

"What brings you out so late?"

"I need a shoulder."

"Mine are always available to you. You know that."

"Sorry to come at this hour."

She pours me a glass of Pappy and hands it to me. "You're well aware that I'm always up past my bedtime."

I gesture to the TV screen. "Still nursing that crush, huh?"

"You know it. I'd leave home for Jimmy."

"I told him that when Flynn and I were on the show last year. He said he's coming for you."

"My bags are packed."

I smile at the predictable reply as she curls up on the sofa next to me, hugging one of the plump pillows she has all over the house. Sebastian and I tease her about how many pillows one woman needs, and she says a body can never have too many. As far as we're concerned, she can have a million of them if that's what makes her happy.

"You didn't come here to talk about Jimmy Fallon."

"No." I focus on the movement of the amber liquid in my glass. "There's a woman."

"Ahhh," she says with a big smile. "I had a feeling. Is it Flynn's Addie?"

Startled, I look over at her. "How do you know?"

"The whole world saw you kiss her on TV, hijo. I was watching. One of my boys was up for the big awards. I saw the whole thing."

"That was the start of it. Well, it started a long time ago, if I'm being truthful, but that was the first time I acted on it."

"Why so long?"

"It's complicated."

"The best things usually are," she says with a knowing smile. She'd been wildly in love with Sebastian's father, who left her while she was pregnant and then came back ten years later to make amends to both of them. As far as I know, they're still together, but for whatever reason, they don't live together. She's private about her personal life, and I don't pry. "What's so complicated with your Addie?"

"What isn't complicated?" I take a deep breath and release it. "Other than what she means to my closest friends, she's Flynn's assistant and everyone loves her."

"Including you?"

"Yeah."

"Is that the problem?"

"Kind of."

"I've waited a long time to see one of my boys finally take the fall." Her smile is full of maternal delight. "It's high time, wouldn't you say?"

"It feels like total shit. Is it supposed to feel like that?"

She dissolves into laughter that infuriates me. How dare she laugh when I'm dead serious?

"Hayden, honey, it only feels like shit when you fight it. Why're you fighting it?"

"Because! It'll be a freaking disaster." I still don't dare say the actual F word around her after having my mouth washed out with soap as a nine-year-old trying out the word for the first time. "I'm not cut out for the things she wants from me. Look at my parents. Look at how I was raised. What do I know about relationships or making them work?"

"Seems to me you know quite a lot. How far back do we go?"

I eye her with disdain. "You know full well we go all the way back."

"And you still show up. You still care about Sebastian and me and your other friends, like Flynn, who you've known for twenty-five years. You've got more friends than anyone I know, and you're loyal to all of them, not to mention what you do for your mother."

"Addie says the same thing, but it's different with her. That's not the kind of relationship she wants to have with me."

"I should hope she wants a hell of a lot more from you."

"She wants everything."

"Would it be so hard to try, Hayden?"

"It would be hard if I tried and failed. Too many people who matter to me, including Addie, would hate me if I screw it up."

"The Hayden Roth I know and love doesn't care what people think of him."

"He cares what some people think."

"That's not enough to keep the man I know from being with the woman he loves. So what aren't you telling me?"

I take a drink from the glass and then put it on the table. For once, Pappy isn't doing a thing for me tonight. "I feel out of control when I'm with her, like everything is spinning away from me, and I can't seem to make sense of anything."

"Ahhh, I see," she says, nodding, an astute expression on her face. "That would mess with your equilibrium."

"Yes, exactly!" I'm relieved she gets it.

"Of course, you know that's total bullshit."

I'm not sure which shocks me more—that she doesn't actually get it or the words she uses to say so. "What does that mean?"

"No matter how hard you try, you can't control every aspect of your life. You can't control what other people do or feel. You can't control how you feel about some things. As much as you'd like to think you can, you can't actually stop the world from turning or bad things from happening. That's life, hijo. Shit happens. People fall in love, and they survive it."

"I don't know if I would. I have no idea how to do it. I don't know how to be what she wants and needs."

"Yes, you do. You know exactly how to love and be loved. You show up for me and for everyone you care about. You can do it for her, too. That's all you have to do, Hayden. Show up for her. That's what she wants from you."

"You make it sound so simple when we both know it's anything but."

"It's messy and complicated and painful and beautiful and joyful and agonizing all at the same time."

"Sounds like the flu," I mutter.

She laughs and shoves my shoulder. "Stop being such a grumpy old man. It's nothing like the flu, as you know, or you wouldn't be so torn up about it."

"I can't even bring myself to say the words she needs to hear, even though I feel them. I've never said them to a woman before."

"When the time is right, and the feeling is right, they'll be the easiest words you'll ever say."

In the scope of a minute, the time I've spent recently with Addie replays in my mind like the sweetest movie I'll ever shoot. In addition to the last few incredible days, I also see flashbacks from years of friendship, smiles and laughter and sunny days at the beach, nights on the town and so many memories that revolve around her.

"You need to give yourself a chance to be happy, Hayden. If anyone has earned that right, you have."

"That's not true. Lots of people have grown up worse off than I did."

"Not too many people I know."

I shake my head. I've never been able to handle people feeling sorry for the poor little rich kid whose parents ignored him.

"Let go of that rigid control of yours and let her in, if that's where she wants to be. Stop thinking about the worst that could happen and try thinking about the best."

"And what would that be?"

"A beautiful, sweet life with the woman you love."

Yearning so sharp and so intense takes my breath away. I can't recall ever wanting anything more than I want that sweet life with Addison. "I want that," I say in a gruff whisper. "I want her. I want her so much that it makes me feel powerless."

"You're not powerless, my love. You have the power to create a life that makes you happy and satisfied. There's no greater power than that." She holds out her arms to me, and I go to her, resting my forehead on her shoulder while she runs her fingers through my hair, mothering me the way she has my whole life, when my own mother has been unable to. "You'll never be sorry for taking a chance. But if you don't, I fear you'll regret it the rest of your life."

"I have the same fear."

"Then you know what you have to do."

It was, I suppose, inevitable. From the first time that bright-eyed teenager stepped foot on my set and drove me bonkers with her inquisitiveness, her questions and an overabundance of energy. She was inevitable. *We* were inevitable. "Thank you, Gracie."

"I didn't do anything but tell you what you already knew. You'll bring your Addie to me someday soon?"

"If she'll still have me."

"She'll have you."

"How can you be so sure?"

"After you kissed her on TV, you walked away to collect your award, but the camera remained on her for another second, and I saw everything I needed to see."

"What did you see?" I ask, stunned.

"The woman who's in love with my Hayden." She releases me to reach for her phone on the coffee table and hands it to me after finding what she was looking for. "See for yourself."

I press Play on the video she has cued up and watch as I kiss Addie. The camera stays trained on her for an additional second or two after I walk away. And in that second, I see what Graciela saw—surprise, yearning, love, affection, desire. I see everything I ever wanted and then some.

"Stop running from your destiny, Hayden. Run *to* her, not away from her."

"You really think I can do this and not make a total mess of it?"

"I have no doubt at all."

I lean into her one-armed hug. "Thanks, Gracie."

"Any time, amor mio."

*Addie*

I emerge from my building to find Hayden's Range Rover parked at the curb. He's asleep behind the wheel, and my heart turns over in my chest at the sight of him. I was awake half the night thinking about the way he looked when he left, Marlowe's plan and what I'll do if it doesn't work. The sleep I did get was checkered with dreams about Hayden interspersed with the things I saw at Devon's club.

I'm more exhausted than I've ever been. This exhaustion is pervasive—body and soul. I'm so tired of wanting someone who is perpetually just out of reach. Part of me wants to ignore the fact that he's outside my building and obviously waiting for me. But the part of me that loves him can't ignore him.

I rap on the passenger window, and he awakes with a start.

He turns the key, and the window opens.

"What're you doing here?"

"You need a ride to your dad's to get your car."

"How do you know where my car is?"

His cheek twitches as his jaw sets with tension. "Get in, Addie."

"I have an Uber coming."

"Cancel it."

"I thought you were done with me."

"I'm not."

"For how long are you not done with me?"

"What does that mean?"

"I'm just wondering—are you back for the day, the week or is the jury still out?"

"I'm back to stay."

"What changed?"

"Will you please get in the car, Addison?"

"Not until you tell me what brought you back when you said last night—"

"Forget what I said last night. Just forget it."

I want to. Dear God, I want to jump in that car and into his arms. I want to hold on and never let go, but more than that, I want assurances that he's not going to run again. "I wish I could."

"You can. Please, Addie. I want to talk to you."

"I wanted to talk to you last night, but you left."

"I know, and I'm sorry for that. Give me another chance."

"So you're ready to bring me into every aspect of your life?"

After a long hesitation—long enough to tell me he's not as ready as he thinks—he says, "Yes." His teeth are gritted, and that pulse in his cheek is working overtime.

"I need to think, Hayden, and I can't do that when I'm with you."

"What's there to think about? I said I was sorry for leaving, and I'm ready to be what you want. What else can I do to convince you—"

"Give me some space." This is killing me, but I need to go through with Marlowe's plan, or I'll never be entirely sure that he's come back for the right reasons. A black car pulls up to the curb behind Hayden's Range Rover. "My ride is here. I'll see you later at Flynn's?" He's planning a celebration for Natalie, who is due to get her driver's license today.

"Yeah." He throws the Range Rover into drive, his tires squealing as he pulls away.

"That went well." I feel sick and despondent as I get into the Uber car for the ride to Redondo Beach. On the way, I send a text to Marlowe.

*Hayden was outside my place this morning. He apologized and said he's ready to try.*

She responds immediately. *What did you say?*

*I asked for more time. I don't think he's ready for everything…*

*So you're going forward with the plan for tonight?*

*I think I have to or I'll never know for sure.*

*For what it's worth, I agree. He needs to see that you're serious about wanting to understand what drives him. Seeing you at Devon's club will get that point across better than anything else ever could.*

*I hope you're right.*

*When have you known me not to be right??*

*Ha!*

*Hang in there, kiddo. You'll have the answers you need tonight, one way or the other.*

*That's what I'm afraid of…*

*I think it's going to work out exactly the way it was always meant to.*

I want to ask her what she means by that, but before I can, she texts again.

*See you at Flynn's later?*

*I'll be there.*

*Great. We can finalize the plan.*

*You're enjoying this a little too much.*

*LOL! I love to see my friends happy.*

*That would be nice.*

*It's going to happen, Addie. I'm sure of it.*

*Thanks. Xoxo*

*Thank YOU for getting Leah off to such a great start. Already wondering how I lived so long without my own Addie.*

*Glad to hear it. She's fantastic. I like her.*

*Me too. Have a great day.*

*You too!*

Since my dad is usually up half the night working, I don't disturb him. After the Uber car drops me outside his house, I get in my car to make the trek back to the city in rush-hour traffic on the 5. The slow roll gives me far too much time to think about how this day might unfold. By the time I arrive at the office an hour after I left my dad's, I'm a nervous wreck. I pull into my spot next to Hayden's Range Rover and head into the building, paying attention to the other set of elevators for the first time. I've never once wondered where they lead, which is amusing in light of what I now know.

I'm filled with curiosity about the basement of the building where I've worked for five years and wonder if or when I'll ever see what goes on down there. Part of me doesn't want to know. I can't imagine seeing my friends in that context.

My day at the office is busy with final details for Flynn and Natalie's trips to Rome and Prague as well as plans for the getaway to Mexico. I order food and beverages for tonight's party at Flynn's Hollywood Hills home and coordinate with the event planner about setting up tables by the pool. It's supposed to be in the low eighties today, so it'll be a nice night to be outside.

After the word got out about the carnival the foundation wishes to have, I've been inundated with offers of properties. Everyone wants to be tied to the worthy cause of feeding hungry kids, and everyone in Hollywood wants to be in Flynn's good graces after the clean sweep of award season. The sucking up has gotten even more ridiculous than it was before, and that's saying something. In consultation with Flynn, I narrow down the choices to two estates—one in Calabasas and the other in Pacific Palisades. I make appointments to see both after we return from Mexico.

At about three o'clock, Flynn appears at my door, his smile stretching from ear to ear. "She passed."

"Of course she did." I'm thrilled for Natalie, who never had the chance to learn to drive the way regular teenagers do. When Flynn found out she'd never driven a car, he had me apply for a permit with the state of California so he could teach her himself.

"Perfect score." He's like a proud papa crowing about his wife.

"Congratulations. Is she here?"

"Nope. She's on her first solo ride home." He checks his watch. "And I'm waiting to hear she got there okay."

"You're too funny. She'll be fine, and everything is set for tonight."

"Thank you."

"Always a pleasure."

He comes in and shuts the door, leaning back against it. "Is the plan for later still a go?"

"It is."

"And you're sure it's a wise idea?"

"I'm not sure of anything except that I love him, he loves me, and this one thing is keeping us apart. I've got to do something drastic to get us over this hurdle."

"That one thing isn't a small thing, Addie. It's a big thing. It nearly ruined everything for me with Natalie."

"Because you kept it from her. Why do you guys think the women in your lives can't handle a little kink?"

He looks up at the ceiling. "I can't believe we're having this conversation." He brings his gaze back to me. "First of all, it's not 'a little kink.' It's a way of life, and it's not for everyone. Second of all, it's a totally different proposition when you're in love with your partner. It raises the stakes to a whole new level, and I'd never been there before Natalie, just like Hayden hasn't been there before you."

"I get it. I really do. But I wish he would trust me enough to know I can handle it."

"How do you know that? Have you done it?"

"No, but—"

"But nothing, Addie. Until you've actually *been* there and *done* that, you have no idea what you can handle, and neither does he. That's what's holding him back. He's afraid if he shows you the full extent of who he really is as a demanding, bold, sexual dominant, you won't love him anymore."

Flynn's description of Hayden has me tingling in places I never tingle when I'm talking to my boss, who also happens to be one of the sexiest men on the planet. I swallow hard as I try not to let my imagination run wild about the sexiest man on *my* planet.

"Hayden doesn't love easily," Flynn continues, seemingly unaware that he's set me on fire with his talk of Hayden as a demanding dominant. I wish I had a fan to cool my heated face. "He learned at an early age that love equals pain. I haven't talked to him about this, but I have no doubt that his biggest fear is losing your love."

"That's not going to happen," I say softly, tears filling my eyes. As if my heart will ever beat the same way for anyone but him.

"I know you want to believe that, but until you know everything, you can't say that for sure—and neither can he."

"A lot of things make more sense now. Thank you for spelling it out for me."

"After some initial hesitation, I'm really pulling for you guys. I think you'd be great together."

"I do, too." Or at least I hope so. Hearing Flynn's take on things, I'm filled with more doubts than I had before, but these doubts are about me rather than Hayden. What if Flynn's right? What if I can't take what Hayden is dishing out? What if I can't be what he wants or needs? What then?

The assistant who has plans for her backup plans has no idea what she would do then.

# CHAPTER 15

*Hayden*

The studio loves the name *Insidious* for the new film, resolving what had become a massive headache for me and the other Quantum principals. I send an email to my partners to let them know the good news, and I copy Addie on the message, giving her full credit for the idea.

I love seeing the flood of responses that congratulate her for doing what people far above her pay grade had failed to do—name the unnamable film.

*Insidious.* It's a good word. It certainly describes my lifelong interaction with addiction of all kinds. It also describes my experience thus far with being in love. I looked up the word on Webster's online dictionary, which defines it as "causing harm in a way that is gradual or not easily noticed."

She snuck under my skin when I wasn't looking, working her way in so deep I can never get her out, even if I wanted to, which I don't. I'm terrified that the harm, all the harm, will come from me to her, that she'll be my unsuspecting victim, that she'll regret giving her heart to a man as fucked up as I can be at times.

I can't recall a time in my adult life when fear crippled me quite the way it has lately. If anything, I'm known for being somewhat fear*less*. I don't dither over the hundreds of decisions I make in a given day. Most of the time, I don't give a rat's ass what people think of me or whether I piss off the establishment in pursuit of my agenda.

But, God, I care about her. I care about her more than I've cared about anyone ever, and that's what has me so paralyzed that I'm on the verge of losing her before I ever really have her.

Tonight, after the get-together at Flynn's, I'll convince her to come home with me. I'll take her to the place in Malibu where we're assured of complete privacy, and I'll begin to indoctrinate her into my lifestyle. I'll teach her what she needs to know to decide whether it's for her. At some point during the restless night I spent in my car outside her place, I realized there are degrees of involvement. I don't have to do everything with her to make her part of it.

I have to do just enough to make her believe I've given her everything. The rest can come later or not at all.

I remember when Flynn was falling for Natalie, and he told me he would live without the lifestyle before he'd live without her. I told him I couldn't do that. I need the control and the dominance too much to ever abandon the lifestyle that has defined me. But now that I've had a taste of sweet Addie, I'm no longer so certain. It has begun to settle in on me that I could more easily live without the dominance than I could without her. If you'd asked me that before Oscar night, I would've said that no one woman would ever be more important to me than the control.

But now nothing is as black-and-white as it was before that first night with her. I just don't know anymore what I would pick if faced with a choice—her or the dominance. The thought of living without either of them is unimaginable, which is why so much is riding on tonight. If I can give her a taste and test her reactions, I'll have a better idea of what might be possible for us.

During the early evening ride to Flynn's in the Hollywood Hills, I plan a scene that has me rock hard in anticipation. Picturing her wrapped up in my ropes, her nipples clamped, her ass plugged, her sweet pussy mine for the taking… *Fucking hell*. I'm out of my mind with lust and desire and overwhelming love. It's a love so big it takes up all the space inside me. It fills me in places I didn't know were empty until she loved me. All that matters at the end of this day is that she still loves me. I simply can't bear the alternative.

I put my desire on ice for the time being. Part one of this evening is about celebrating Natalie. Part two will be about worshiping Addison.

The whole gang is already there when I arrive, carrying the huge bouquet of flowers I picked up for Natalie on the way. Our guest of honor is positively glowing as she greets me with a kiss to the cheek. There was a time, not that long ago, when I wondered if she and I would ever be friends. That time already seems like ages ago. She's made Flynn so fucking happy, I can't help but adore her.

"For you." I hand over the flowers. "Congratulations."

"Thank you so much, Hayden! They're *gorgeous.*"

"You're welcome. So proud of you, Nat."

She hugs me tightly. "Thank you."

"Will you take me for a ride one of these days?"

"She will do no such thing." Flynn shoves at my shoulder to end the hug. "Get your filthy hands off my wife."

"Shut up, Flynn," Nat says, "and go put these in a vase."

I snort with laughter at how she handles him so perfectly. Watching them, I'm struck by the realization that Addie and I could be like them. We could find a happy medium where she's my sub in the bedroom, and I'm her slave in life. I could live with that. I seek her out in the group and find her talking to Marlowe and Leah and Flynn's sister Ellie, but she's looking at me, which brings an unreasonable amount of comfort.

Over the happy shouts of Flynn's nieces and nephews in the pool, our eyes meet, and I can't look away. I can't see anyone but her. The moment is broken when Flynn's parents arrive and his dad claps me on the back.

"I understand *Insidious* is the word of the day," Max Godfrey says in his big booming voice.

I force myself to look away from Addie to focus on Max. "You understand correctly."

"Perfection," Max says.

"Tell Addie. It was her idea."

"I shall do that."

"Hayden," Stella Flynn says when she joins her husband and me. "We heard your mother is in the hospital. Is she all right?"

"She's fine after a nasty bout of food poisoning, and as of four o'clock this afternoon, she's home. She kicked me out so she could get some sleep."

"Thank goodness she's all right," Stella says, gripping my arm.

I cover her hand with mine. "It's okay, Stel. You can say what you really mean. Thank goodness it was *only* food poisoning."

"That, too," she says with a warm smile. The Godfreys were close friends with my parents back in the day, before everything in my family went to shit, before my parents' epically ugly divorce and my mother's slide into addiction put a wedge between them and most of the people in their lives—including me.

We eat and drink—well, they do, I abstain because I want my wits about me for later—and we celebrate Natalie. Flynn makes a big production out of presenting her with the keys to his silver Mercedes sedan, which is now hers.

Watching them, I feel a kernel of hope take root deep inside of me. If they can make it work, why can't we?

My partners are thrilled with the title we've settled on for the new film, and when we're all sitting around the outdoor fireplace after a delicious steak dinner, Jasper makes a toast to Addie, who "saved our arses" with her great idea.

She blushes in embarrassment, but her eyes sparkle with pleasure at the well-deserved attention.

"Does anyone else love the way 'saved our arses' sounds so filthy when he says it?" Ellie Godfrey says.

"Me," Leah says, raising her hand.

The other women, including Addie, follow suit.

Jasper flashes a leering smile and waggles his brows. "I got a lot of filthy words where those came from, ladies."

Everyone else laughs, but I notice Ellie watching him the same way I imagine I look at Addie. I'd be much more interested in wondering what's going on there if I didn't have my own dragons to slay.

"So who else is counting the days until we leave for Mexico?" Kristian asks.

A chorus of "me" follows his question.

"I am so ready for a fucking break," Kristian says. "We can't keep up this pace."

"You wimping out on us, old man?" Flynn asks.

"Hardly," Kristian drawls, "but you've got to admit the last couple of years have been rather punishing."

"I can see how all that Oscar gold would be a major drag," Addie says, drawing laughs from everyone.

Kristian raises his glass to her. "Touché."

"I agree with Kris," Marlowe says. "I'm ready for a vacation. The Mexico trip couldn't come at a better time."

"Glad you agree," Flynn says. "Addie gets all the credit for throwing it together."

"That's *shocking*," Jasper says in a teasing tone. "And here I thought *you* were doing this for us."

"Har-har," Flynn says. "*As if.*"

We all have a good laugh at Flynn's expense, which is one of our favorite things to do. He says we keep him humble, and we say someone has to. The truth is, his fame has never gone to his head. In many ways, he's exactly the same guy he was before his career took off.

I give the party another hour before I'm ready to ask Addie to give me one more chance. I intend to make this chance count, except I can't find her. She's not in the house or out by the pool. "Where's Addie?" I ask Flynn when I've done a thorough search and come up empty.

"Oh, she left a while ago."

I can't believe she actually *left* without having said a single word directly to me while we were there. Has it really come to that? "Where'd she go?"

"She didn't say, just that she had an appointment."

"Who has appointments at ten at night? What've you got her doing?"

"It's not for me. I have no idea where she went."

Marlowe and Natalie come into the kitchen, bearing plates and glasses from the pool deck.

"Do you guys know where Addie went?" I ask them.

They exchange glances.

Marlowe is the first to look at me. "Um, well, I know, but she asked me not to tell you."

"She specifically said, 'Don't tell Hayden'?"

Marlowe looks at Natalie, who nods.

"That's what she said," Natalie confirms.

"Then you definitely ought to tell me." I can feel my blood pressure rising by the second.

Marlowe considers that. "Hmm, well, I suppose we could—"

"No, Marlowe," Natalie says. "She told us not to."

"I don't *care* what she said! *Fucking tell me! Right now!*"

"Watch how you're talking to my wife, man," Flynn says.

"Sorry," I mutter and force myself to chill the fuck out so I can get them to tell me what I need to know. "Please, I need to find her. I have to tell her... I... *Please.*" I can't believe I'm about to break down in front of them, but that's what's going to happen if someone doesn't tell me what I need to know. Right. Fucking. Now.

"You know Devon Black?" Marlowe asks.

All the oxygen leaves my body in a big whoosh that has my head spinning and my heart racing. I fucking know Devon Black. "What about him?"

"She's gone to Black Vice for—"

I have no idea how that sentence ends, because I'm out of there the second I hear the words Black Vice. I swear to God, if Devon Black lays one finger on her, I'm going to rip his fucking head off and shove it up his motherfucking ass.

Flynn comes after me, calling my name, but I ignore him and tear out of his driveway as if the hounds of hell are chasing me. The only thing I can process at the moment is the all-consuming need to get to Addie before it's too late. If she lets Black or anyone else touch her, I won't be responsible for what I do.

I know exactly where Black's place is because I've been a guest there. He's a friend, or at least I thought he was. If he's training Addie—

Christ, I'm going to be sick, but I don't have time for that, not when she's got at least a half-hour head start on me. When I think about what can happen in thirty minutes at a BDSM club, my entire body is gripped with agonizing pain. This is my fault. It's my own fucking fault that she's gone somewhere else for what I wouldn't give her.

I take the hairpin curves on the road that leads back to town going much faster than I should, but I can't bring myself to slow down. Not when Addie might be doing something foolish and risky.

Black's a good guy, I tell myself. He won't let anything happen to her. But he might touch her or let someone else touch her, and *that* would count as something happening to her—something that shouldn't happen with anyone but me. I push on the accelerator, endangering myself and anyone who has the misfortune of sharing the road with me. I'll take the time to feel badly about that later, after she's safely back in my arms where she belongs.

Thank God Black's place isn't far from Flynn's. I pull up the long driveway twelve minutes after I leave Flynn's, my tires screeching when I come to an abrupt stop. "Leave it right there," I say to the valet. "I'm not staying." I push past him through the main door.

A woman runs after me. "Sir, excuse me! You can't go in there!"

Devon Black comes through the doors that lead into the club.

"It's fine, Melanie. Mr. Roth is my guest."

"Where is she?"

"Who're you looking for, Hayden?"

"Addison York. I know she's here." I head toward the doors that lead into the club, but he stops me with a hand to my chest. "Don't fuck with me, Black. That's my woman in there, and anyone who touches her is a dead man."

"My club, my rules. Now unless you'd like to be physically removed from the premises, I suggest you calm the fuck down."

"I'm not calming down until I see her."

"Come with me." He takes me by the arm and jerks me toward a doorway to the right of the main doors. We enter a dark corridor, and I'm afraid of where it will lead. We stop at a large window that looks down upon a room where Addie is seated at a table across from a man. She's wearing a black silk robe, and her hair is tied back in a ponytail as she pores over paperwork.

"Take me to her."

"Not yet."

"I swear to God, I'm going to rip your fucking throat out."

"Try it. The entire place is monitored. You'll be dead before you can get a hand on me or anyone else in my club."

Rage throbs through my veins like an extra heartbeat. As always where Addie is concerned, I've lost control. Am I going to be forced to stand here and watch while another man indoctrinates her into the BDSM lifestyle? My chest is tight, and I'm having trouble getting air to my lungs. It's quite possible that I could be having a heart attack.

Sweat rolls down my back as I watch the woman I love talk and laugh with another man. He's shirtless, tattooed and has muscles on top of his muscles. Is that what she prefers? Is that who she really wants?

*No, she wants you, and you pushed her away. You let her think she wasn't good enough for you or strong enough to be what you need. You did this to yourself.*

I flatten my hands on the window as if that'll somehow bring me closer to her, allow me to touch her instead of the guy who's making her laugh. Then Black hits a button on the wall, and I can hear her. I can hear her going over the checklist of possibilities with another man. It should be me asking her how she feels about clamps and plugs and restraints and rope.

This is all wrong. It's so very, very *wrong*.

I start to scream and bang on the window, my palms flat against the glass, but she can't hear me. No, she can only hear *him* as he talks to her about safe words and the traffic-light system and the importance of articulating her needs to her partner.

*I'm* her partner. *Me*. No one else. I realize tears are running down my face, and I don't care that I'm crying for the first time in my adult life in front of someone I barely know. My heart breaks at the thought of her doing those things with anyone but me.

"Please, Devon," I say in a soft whisper because that's what's left of my ravaged voice. "Don't let this happen. Get her out of there."

He presses a button on the wall. "Andre, please bring Addison to my office. She has a visitor."

"Yes, sir, Mr. Black."

"Come with me." He leads me through another series of corridors until we reach his office, where he offers me a drink that I decline.

I use the hem of my shirt to wipe the tears from my face, lest she see the wreck of a man I've become because of her.

Black and I coexist in uncomfortable silence for five full minutes that feel like hours before a knock sounds at the door.

"Enter," he says.

Addie comes in first, and I go right to her, wrapping my arms around her sweet body and burying my face in her thick blond hair. As her familiar scent fills my senses, the tears begin to flow again.

I'm aware of Black leaving the room and taking the man named Andre with him. Good riddance.

Her arms come around me, holding me as if she still loves me. "Hayden? What're you doing here?"

I lift my head from her shoulder to look into her eyes. "What am *I* doing here? What're *you* doing here?"

"Devon is the friend of a friend. He offered to help me learn about the lifestyle."

"What friend of yours is a friend of Devon Black's?"

"Now, Hayden, you know I can't tell you that. I signed a confidentiality agreement."

"Whatever you signed here is null and void. You're coming home with me, and I'll train you. I'll teach you everything I know, everything you want to know. We'll leave no stone unturned, no kink unexplored."

"Is that what you want? Or are you saying that so I won't do those things with Andre?"

"You could really let another man touch you after what we've shared? I thought you loved me."

"I *do* love you. The only one I want is you. But you wouldn't teach me, so I found someone else who would."

Hearing she still loves me is the sweetest relief I've ever experienced. "I'll teach you, and I'll do it because it's what I want more than anything. It's what I've always wanted, but I was afraid…"

She brushes the dampness from my face. "Of what?"

"That I'd scare you so badly you wouldn't love me anymore."

"I'll always love you. That'll never change."

"Do you promise?"

"Yeah," she says, kissing my face and then my lips. "I promise."

"Will you come home with me, Addison?"

"Yes. Take me home, Hayden."

# CHAPTER 15

*Addie*

Our plan worked exactly as we hoped it would, but I'm unprepared for how undone Hayden is when I encounter him in Devon's office. I feel sick that something I did reduced my strong, confident man to tears. When I agree to go home with him, he picks me up and carries me out of Black Vice, cradling me to his chest as if I'm the most precious thing in his world.

I'm about to tell him that I need my things from the locker downstairs when a member of Devon's staff appears with a bag that is tucked into the backseat of Hayden's Range Rover. He puts me into the passenger seat and belts me in. I'm still wearing the Black Vice silk robe I changed into before my meeting with Andre and still holding the paperwork we were reviewing when Devon summoned us to his office.

I want to take a pause here to assure you that I never intended to allow Andre—or any other man—to touch me. I wanted information. I wanted to understand the process of entering into a Dom/sub relationship so if I got the chance to explore that with Hayden, I'd have a better appreciation for what it entailed.

The thought of any man but him touching me that way is unfathomable to me. In another life, one in which Hayden Roth doesn't exist, I might've found Andre attractive. I might've wanted to explore some of the things we talked about with him. But Hayden is the center of my world, and he's the only man I want touching me intimately.

It's funny to think that a week ago, before he kissed me and I decided to seduce him, he was always my fantasy man, the one I would choose if I could have anyone I wanted. But now that I've actually experienced the reality of him, I can't imagine allowing another man to ever touch me again. And I realize I need to tell him that before this goes any further.

"Hayden."

"Yeah?" He grips the wheel tightly, his gaze intently focused on the road as we drive to Malibu. I wondered if he would take me to his place in town or if we'd go to the beach. I'm glad he chose the beach.

"I need to tell you something."

"Okay."

"It's going to make you mad."

"Okay."

"I had no intention of doing anything with Andre."

He glances over at me, seeming to gauge whether I'm telling him the truth or not, and then he returns his attention to the road. "Then what was that about just now?"

"It was about showing you that I'm more than willing to be what you want and need."

"So it was a setup?"

"Sort of."

He's silent for a long time, leaving me to wonder what he's thinking. Is he pissed off? Will this change his mind about taking me home and teaching me about his lifestyle?

"So Marlowe and Natalie were in on it?"

"Possibly." I hate to throw my friends under the bus, but I'm determined to be truthful with him.

"And Black? He knew about this, too?"

"Possibly."

My stomach is twisted into knots as I wait to hear how he really feels about what we did.

"And Flynn," he says. "Of course he was part of it, too."

"Don't be mad at them. They were only trying to help us get over this hurdle so we have a chance of making a go of it."

"I'm not mad at them."

"Oh. So you're mad at me, then?"

He shakes his head. "I'm mad at myself. I should've had more faith in you from the beginning. What happened tonight… That was my own fault. I drove you to it."

I can't go another second without touching him. I release my seat belt and reach for him. "Hayden, I'm sorry. I hate that you were so upset by what you saw at the club."

"It nearly killed me to see you having that conversation with another guy when it should've been me."

"You're the only one I want. You're the only one I've ever felt this way about, and I'll never feel this way about anyone but you."

His arm comes around me, holding me tight against him. I feel his lips brush over my hair. "Same goes, baby."

For the first time since we hatched our crazy plan last night, I'm able to draw air into my lungs without a sharp pain of dread in my chest. This could've gone so wrong in so many ways, but it had gone exactly right.

"You need to let Flynn know that you won't be available tomorrow and possibly the next day, too."

Never has one sentence ever packed a greater wallop. "Oh, um… Okay. What about your deadline?"

"I'll make the deadline. Don't worry about that. You have far bigger things to worry about right now."

"Such as?"

"How I'm going to punish you for what you put me through tonight."

Every nerve ending in my body, especially the ones between my legs, tingle with awareness and anticipation. "Punish me?"

"Uh-huh. We've got a lot of options to choose from, but that sweet ass of yours is going to be mine one way or the other."

What does it say about me that I practically begin to pant with lust at the thought of him "punishing" me? Not to mention what the gruff, confident tone of his voice does to my system, which is already going haywire. My nipples are so tight they ache, and my clit is throbbing. His hand slides over the silk that covers me to cup my ass. He squeezes my cheeks, and lets his middle finger dip into the valley between them, and just that is nearly enough to make me come.

Dear God, what have I agreed to?

We arrive at his stunning home in Malibu, which is one of my favorites of all the incredible homes I've gotten to visit during my tenure as Flynn's assistant and friend. I love the sharp angles, the huge windows, the breathtaking daytime view of the Pacific, and the contemporary design. Though I've been here many times, I've never been upstairs, which is where he takes me upon entering the house.

Did I mention he insists on carrying me even after I tell him there's nothing wrong with my legs? *Swoon.*

I love him like this—dominant and insistent and in charge. He recovered quickly from the breakdown at Black Vice. Gone is the broken man I found in Devon's office. In his place is a man determined to finally get what he wants—and that's me. Holy shit is it exciting to experience this side of him.

I got a small taste of his controlling side in our previous encounters, but I already know that's nothing compared to what's going to happen now that he's fully committed to giving me all of him.

He puts me down on the biggest bed I've ever seen and sticks out his hand.

"What?"

"Give me those papers."

I hand over the contract Andre and I had begun to negotiate.

Hayden takes the paperwork and sits at the foot of the bed to review it. His brows knit in concentration and his lips pucker as he reads, occasionally glancing at me as he goes.

It's all I can do not to squirm under the intense heat of his gaze every time he directs it my way. This is what I wanted—his full and undivided attention. I wanted to *know* him on the deepest possible level, and now that I'm about to get that, I'm scared.

What if Flynn is right and I can't hang with dominant Hayden? What if I can't stand the pain? What if I break and disappoint him? My hands and legs begin to tremble as the possibilities run through my mind.

"You left your list of hard limits blank," he says, breaking a long silence.

"I know."

"So that means you don't have any?"

"I trust you to know what they are."

He shakes his head. "I have no way to know that, Addie. You have to tell me."

"I don't even know the full extent of what's possible. How do I know what my limits are?"

"So if I wanted to pee on you, you'd be fine with that?"

I can't help but wrinkle my nose at that.

He laughs. "Thought so."

My tongue suddenly feels too big for my mouth, and I swallow hard. "Do *you* like that?"

"Hell no."

"Oh, thank you, Jesus."

"This is what I mean when I say everyone has hard limits. What're yours?"

"It might be easier for you to tell me about yours."

"All right—I have zero interest in excrement of any kind, blood, animals, breath play, whips, gags, anything to do with rape or rape fantasy or humiliation."

"That's a good list."

"Now let me tell you what I *am* interested in—Kinbaku, which is a form of bondage and erotic tying that I've studied and practiced for years. It's one of my favorite ways to express myself as a dominant."

I'm transfixed as I listen to him and accept the beautiful gift he is giving me by sharing these facets of himself with me.

"Nothing turns me on more than having my partner completely at my mercy, submitting to whatever I might dream up for us." As he speaks, he seems to be somewhere other than here in this room with me. "I love toys of every kind. I love public scenes. I love to be watched, to know that what I'm doing is arousing not only my partner, but anyone who might be watching us. I used to love threesomes, but I won't share you with anyone." He turns that potent gaze on me. "You understand?"

I nod in agreement. I don't want him to share me with anyone.

"Did anything I just said give you pause?"

"I'm not sure how I feel about being watched, especially at a club where the people I work for are members."

"I understand, and we can work around that."

"How?"

He gives this some thought. "We could ask your buddy Devon Black if we could do a scene at his club."

"You would do that in a club you don't control?"

"I'd disguise my identity and yours, so no one would know who we are."

"Oh. Okay."

"If that's a hard limit for you, all you have to do is say so, and we take it off the table. That's how this works. We negotiate everything ahead of time so no one gets something they didn't expect. The idea is a safe, sane, consensual exchange of power."

"It's not a hard limit for me, but thank you for offering to make it one."

"You must have questions."

I have thousands of them, but when the time comes to ask them, my mind is completely blank except for one pressing thing. "What happens the rest of the time, when we're not having sex?"

"What do you mean?"

"Will you want to dominate me all the time or only in bed?"

"Our agreement only covers our relationship in the context of sex. It doesn't cover the rest of our lives." He finally leaves his post at the foot of the bed and comes to me, running his finger over my cheek. "I have no desire to see you become anyone other than who you are now—except for when we're naked together. Then you're all mine. I say what, I say how, I say how often, I say when we're done, I say when we're just getting started. So if you're not in the mood for all that, don't get naked with me."

His lips find a sensitive spot behind my ear, and I'm reduced to a quivering blob of need and want.

"Do we understand each other?"

"Yes."

"Yes who?"

"Yes, Sir."

"Mmmm." His voice is a low rumble next to my ear. "It makes me so hot to hear that one little word from you."

"What happens now?"

"Now we need to talk about a safe word—one word that puts a stop to whatever we might be doing. No matter what, if you say that word, it's done, so you need to be sure before you say it."

"What if I'm not sure I want it to end completely? What if I need a break or a breather or whatever?"

"That's what the traffic-light system is about. You say yellow if you want to slow down and red if you want to stop."

"That would work for me."

"Would you feel more comfortable if we signed a formal contract outlining what we've agreed to?"

"Would you?"

"In every other situation, I'd insist on it, but this is different."

"How so?" Of course I *know*, but I want to hear him say it.

"Because this, you and me, is forever. I hope you know you sealed your fate with your little stunt tonight." He runs his fingertip over my face. "Now that I have you, I'm never letting you go."

Thrilled to hear him finally say what I've always wanted to hear, I lock my gaze with his. "I'm counting on that, and I don't feel the need to sign anything."

"Okay." His fingertip moves from my face to my throat to my chest, sliding between my breasts and coming to a stop at the knot to my robe. "Now about that punishment you owe me."

"What about it?"

"It's time, Addison. And because I care so much about you, I'll let you choose this time."

I understand that's as close as he's able to come to telling me he loves me, and somehow it's enough. "What're my choices?"

"I can spank you with my hand, a paddle or a flogger."

"Which do you prefer?"

"I love them all, so you can decide."

"Which one hurts the least?"

Laughing, he shakes his head. "I'll never tell."

"That's mean!"

"Are you questioning your Dom, Addison? Because that would only add to your punishment."

"I would never question you, Sir." I lower my eyes in supplication and love the gasp my action draws from him.

"Send the text to Flynn."

I reach for my phone and type out a quick message to Flynn, letting him know I'll be unavailable tomorrow and possibly the next day.

He responds immediately. *Are you okay?*

*I'm fine.*

*Things went as planned, I take it?*

*Better than planned.*

*Glad to hear it.*

"Tell him to leave you alone now—and use those exact words."

*Hayden says you have to leave me alone now. His words, not mine.*

*Tell Hayden he'd better treat you like a queen.*

Hayden reads the text I share with him. "Tell him I said to fuck off."

"I'm not saying that to him."

He takes the phone from me. "Then I will." *This is Hayden. Fuck off.*

Flynn replies with laughing emojis.

"Now text your dad and tell him you had to go out of town unexpectedly and you'll be back in a couple of days."

"Why am I doing that?"

"So I can shut off your phone and not have you worry about anyone important trying to reach you."

I tell myself this is what I wanted—Hayden's full attention and his dominance. Now that I have both, I'm more than a little overwhelmed. I send the text to my dad.

*Travel safely, sweetheart. Call me when you're back in town.*

*Will do. Love you.*

*Love you, too.*

Hayden takes the phone from me, powers it down and places it on the bedside table. "Come with me, my sweet." He holds out his hand to me, and I'm left to wonder where we're going. But since I've agreed to go anywhere he wishes to take me, I grasp his hand and let him lead me into a large walk-in closet full of gorgeous clothes organized by color. I'm about to ask what goes on in his closet when I notice a door at the far end.

He pushes the door open and turns on the light, revealing a room full of BDSM equipment that I recognize from the hours of online research I've done since I first learned of his affection for the lifestyle. I see bondage equipment, a St. Andrew's cross, a spanking bench and a few other things I'm not familiar with. I have a feeling that'll be changing before too long.

"What're you thinking?" he asks after a long silence.

"How many other women have you had here?"

"You're the first. I built this room a year ago, and I haven't brought anyone here until now."

Though I know he's had many other partners, I'm comforted to know I'm the first he's brought here.

"There've been others in my playroom at my place in town, but it's been years since I brought anyone there. Okay?"

Nodding, I force myself to meet his intense gaze. He seems to be scrutinizing my every expression and reaction. His fingers tug at the knot on my robe until it falls open, and he pushes it off my shoulders.

I let it drop onto the floor and stand before him nude.

His eyes take a slow perusal from my face to my breasts to my groin and back up again. Every inch of me responds to the heated way in which he looks at me, as if he can't wait to devour me. I can't wait for that either.

"Are you scared?"

"Yes." This is no time to be anything less than totally honest.

"Don't be. I'll never truly hurt you, Addie. You have to believe me when I tell you the only thing I want is your ultimate pleasure."

"And my complete surrender."

His face lifts into a sexy grin. "That, too."

"What about your ultimate pleasure?"

He trails his finger around my left nipple, making circles that never seem to touch the part of me that burns for him. "Your ultimate pleasure will lead to mine." Leaning in, he kisses my neck on his way to my lips. "First things first." His thumbs caress my nipples, and I gasp from the heat that blasts through me. Then he takes me by the hand and leads me across the room to a set of drawers, opening the top one to reveal metal objects that I recognize as nipple clamps.

Now that the moment of truth is upon me, my legs are trembling so hard I can barely remain standing. I remind myself that this is exactly what I said I wanted.

"What're you afraid of?" he asks.

"That I went to all this trouble to get here, and I won't be able to do it."

"You'll be fine. Anything you can do will make me happy because it's you."

"What if…"

He cradles my face in his hands, making me feel treasured and safe. "What if what?"

"I don't know if I can handle the pain."

"I'll make sure it's not too bad. I promise."

He kisses me softly and tenderly, and I cling to him and his assurances. Then he breaks the kiss and takes something from the drawer before bending his head to lave my nipple. When it's standing up tight and proud, he affixes the clamp.

The pain is immediate and intense, but it quickly subsides into a dull ache that I can easily handle. He moves to the other side, and this time, knowing what's coming makes me tense up.

"Relax, sweetheart. I'll make it so good for you."

"I want it to be good for you, too."

"Having you here in this room with me is the best thing to ever happen to me as a Dom. I promise it'll be incredible for me."

The second clamp hurts as badly as the first—more so, really, because I know what to expect this time. But again the pain fades after a minute or two, leaving a pleasurable ache that has my full attention. He leads me next to a row of implements hanging from hooks on the wall. There are paddles in an array of shapes and sizes.

"See anything that interests you?" he asks.

"Um, if I say no, will that lead to more punishment?"

"You're a fast learner," he says with a low chuckle.

Anxious to get this over with, I point to one with the round face. It resembles a ping-pong paddle, like the one I saw used at Black Vice. "That one."

"Good choice."

"For who? Me or you?"

"Both of us."

He steers me toward the spanking bench. "Get comfortable."

I almost laugh out loud at that. Here I'm about to fold myself over a spanking bench for the first time in my life, and he tells me to get *comfortable*? Nothing about this is what I'd consider comfortable. I settle my knees on the supports, and Hayden adjusts the higher part of the apparatus so it falls in the center of my abdomen, forcing me to bend over it to settle my elbows on the pads below. My clamped nipples react immediately to the pressure of my breasts hanging low, sending a pleasurable thrum of desire to my clit.

The position leaves my ass completely at his mercy. I've never felt more vulnerable or aroused. "Is this good?" I ask, needing his approval.

His hands coast over my ass cheeks, squeezing and shaping them. "This is perfection." Then I feel his lips on my back, tracing the length of my spine and making me shiver with awareness. While I got settled on the bench, he must've shed his clothes, because I feel the heat of his erection against my bottom. My skin feels like it's been plugged into an electrical socket, with each caress seeming to register with every nerve ending I own.

"Do you feel the difference?" he asks softly.

I immediately understand what he's asking. We're still us, the same two people we were outside this room, but everything is more intense, more charged in here. "Yes, I feel it."

"I don't know if I can bring myself to punish you, Addison."

His hesitation is endlessly endearing. "Didn't I earn it by what I did to you at Black Vice?"

"You sure as hell did."

"Then you know what you have to do." I'm not sure where this bravado is coming from. I've never been spanked in my life. I have no idea whether I'll love it or hate it. All I know is that he has to do it, or this'll be just another exercise in frustration and futility. "Hayden?"

# CHAPTER 17

*Hayden*

Now that I have her exactly where I've always wanted her, I'm paralyzed with unfamiliar indecision. I've never once wimped out of a scene as a Dom, and I'm painfully aware that I can't do that now. This is no time to be a pussy who lets his heart rule his cock—or so I tell myself.

In truth, it's impossible to separate what I feel for this woman from what I want to do to her sexually. If there's any hope of a future for us, I have to do this. The sight of her perfect ass, waiting to be reddened by my paddle, sets me on fire with the kind of desire I've only ever experienced with her.

I need to hear her say she feels the same way. "Tell me you want this."

"I want it, Hayden. I want *you*. I want *all* of you."

Though her voice is strong and confident, I can see her legs are trembling violently. Despite her words of assurance, she's scared senseless. I want to make this amazing for her, and that determination fuels me. I take the paddle in hand and give her right cheek a short, swift spank, the kind that sends a message without causing great pain.

She gasps but otherwise remains silent.

I do the same thing on the other side, slipping into my zone after that second one. I let go of all the worries I had coming in here and do what I do best—bring pleasure to my sub with every tool in my arsenal. I keep up the paddling until her ass is a ripe rosy red and her pussy is so wet that I can see and smell her arousal.

Fucking hell, she's amazing, and she's all mine.

I drop the paddle to the floor, cup her heated cheeks and drop to my knees to lap up the moisture between her legs. The instant my tongue connects with her clit, she comes, screaming out her pleasure.

"Did I say you could come?" I ask, getting into it now. This is so fucking fun, especially because it's her first time.

"N-no, Sir, you didn't."

"You know what that means, don't you?"

"No, Sir. Why don't you tell me?"

"More punishment." I return to my drawers, where I keep toys of all sorts, and find one of my favorite plugs and take it and a tube of lubricant back to where she waits for me, her legs still trembling uncontrollably.

"What kind of punishment?"

"Subs don't ask questions. They take what their Dom is dishing out without comment or question. Do you understand?"

"Yes, Sir."

"That's my girl. You're very good at this."

"Am I?"

I rub my palm over her right cheek, offering comfort and affection. "You're the best."

"Somehow I doubt that."

"You're the best for me, Addison. Don't ever doubt that, or you'll be looking at even more punishments." After I thoroughly lube the toy, I squirt a healthy amount of lube on two fingers. Then I part her cheeks and press my fingers against her back door, pushing insistently until she yields and allows me in.

"Holy shit," she mutters. "A little warning next time would be nice."

"You aren't speaking out of turn, are you?"

"Would I do that?"

Smiling at her predictably saucy reply, I push harder, making sure she feels the full impact of my invasion. Then I pull back some before driving my fingers into her again. She raises her ass toward my fingers, which I take as permission to proceed—that and I haven't yet heard the word that would put a stop to this.

"What's your safe word, Addison?"

"It's 'red,' Sir."

"Do you need it?"

"No, Sir."

Pleased by her reply, I remove my fingers, cross the room to the sink to wash up and then return to her to replace my fingers with the wide, rounded edge of the plug. Her entire body goes tense as I take it nice and easy, giving her body time to adjust and stretch. A keening moan escapes from her that goes straight to my already incredibly hard cock. I draw out the insertion of the plug for a good ten minutes, wanting her completely focused on what we're doing.

By the time it's fully seated, she's panting and her inner thighs are wet from her arousal.

I love that she's so turned on. "Up you go, sweetheart." I help her up because I want to be able to look into her eyes for what comes next. Her face is flushed and her eyes are big as she adjusts to the dual sensations coming from her nipples and ass. She was upside down for more than thirty minutes, so I give her a minute to get her bearings.

"You feel okay?"

"Mmm-hmm." She blinks several times in rapid succession, and I see the beginnings of subspace.

Wanting to keep her there, I put my hands on her ass cheeks and lift her into my arms, forcing her to curl her legs around my hips and her arms around my neck. I walk us to an upholstered chair with no arms and sit, keeping her on my lap facing me. My cock is leaking profusely, wanting in on this right now. Unable to wait another second to be inside her, I lift her and bring her down on my cock.

She cries out from the tight fit made even tighter by the plug. "I *can't*!"

"Yes, you can. You already have. Relax and let me in." I give her a light smack on the ass to redirect her attention away from the stretch of her tender flesh. The spank startles her, and she yields another two inches to me. I'm hearing a whole new set of sexy noises from her, and they're wildly arousing. She grunts and moans and screams as I work my way in, one torturous inch at a time until I'm fully seated and she's having one orgasm after another.

"Mmm, someone's in the biggest trouble ever," I whisper harshly against her ear as I shamelessly ride her orgasms while trying to fend off my own. I'm nowhere near finished with her. Reaching around to her back, I play with the plug, drawing it out before pressing it back in again.

She's out of her mind, screaming and coming and clawing at my shoulders. God, I love her this way. I love that I've taken her somewhere she's never been before. I release the clip on her left nipple and watch her eyes fly open in shock a second later. Without giving her a chance to prepare or anticipate, I remove the other one, and she detonates, coming with a scream that seems to come from her very soul.

Holy fuck… I knew she'd be amazing, but this is something else altogether. It's like she was made for this, for me. I have to remind myself that this is still new to her. I can't go everywhere I want to take her tonight or even tomorrow. It'll be a lifetime journey of pleasure and discovery, but there's still a lot we can do tonight.

I keep up the slow but steady strokes into her as she comes down from the epic orgasm, her blissed-out expression making my heart ache with love for her. Her eyes flutter open, and I can see the exact moment when she realizes that only one of us has had epic orgasms.

She groans when I tug on the plug to remind her that we're not done yet. Far, far from it.

*Addie*

I have no idea if we've been at it for hours or days, but he doesn't let up. He owns me body and soul in that room, taking me places I never knew I could go. I'm outside myself, watching us, wondering what he has planned next as he takes me on the wildest ride of my life. My body is a big trembling nerve ending as one orgasm after another rips through me. He tells me I'm not allowed to come without his permission, but damned if I know how to stop it.

And I don't want to stop it. I want everything he has to offer and then some. With the plug still deep inside me, he positions me in a sitting position on a table, ensures my comfort and then begins binding me with soft ropes, starting with my wrists and working his way up to my shoulders and then down my torso.

Though I'm half out of my mind from what we've already done, I watch him closely, intrigued by his fierce concentration and attention to detail. His blue eyes are darker than ever, and a strand of silky hair falls over his forehead. If I were allowed to move, I'd want to brush it back with my fingertips.

With anyone else, the thought of being bound in any way would be terrifying. But with him, I'm not afraid. I'm thrilled to be sharing in his greatest desires, and I'm fascinated by the way the ropes come together in an elaborate pattern. I want to ask how he learned to do this, but I'm not allowed to speak unless I want to stop it, and that's the last thing I want to do. I'll have time to ask later, because now we have all the time in the world.

"Tell me what you're thinking," he says gruffly.

"I'm amazed."

"By?"

"You."

"How so?"

"I want to know everything about how you learned about this and who taught you and…"

"We'll talk later."

His tone is commanding and confident, both of which are a huge turn-on for me. I love him this way—completely focused on me and my pleasure. I love his tense control and the way he watches me carefully for signs of trouble. I'm in very good hands with him, and that gives me the ability to let go of my worries and enjoy every minute. Well, just about every minute. The plug that's still wedged in my ass is not quite "enjoyable," and it made sex with Hayden and his huge cock extremely challenging.

He may as well still be inside me from the way my body continues to contract with aftershocks.

Judging by the way his eyes glittered with passion, I could tell that he loved the challenge of getting me to take him while wearing the plug. I feel like I passed a test that led to what we're doing now with the ropes. He finishes with one knot to hold the entire scheme together, positioned directly over my clit. I'm immediately and uncomfortably aroused from the pressure on my most sensitive place.

"You look beautiful in my ropes." He takes a step back to admire his work before moving around the table to secure my bound hands to a hook above us.

The table that'd been holding me up is rolled away, leaving me suspended. I expected that would hurt, but it doesn't. As promised, he's made sure that nothing hurts more than I can stand. All the pressure is on my clit, which I now realize was intentional.

After taking a good long look at what he's created, he approaches me, still fully erect. "Does anything hurt?"

I shake my head.

"Use your words, Addison."

I love how he calls me by my full name, giving even more weight to what we're doing. "No, nothing hurts."

He raises a brow.

"Sir."

Smiling, he reaches out to tweak my nipple, which has been left exposed by the intricate web of rope. "I want to take a picture of you the way you look right now."

"How do I look?"

"Sensational. Sexiest thing I've ever seen. So a picture, yes?"

"For your eyes only."

"Absolutely."

"Okay."

While he goes to get his phone, I close my eyes and feel the presence of the ropes that bind my arms, hands, breasts, legs and the intense pressure on my clit. I take deep breaths in through my nose and out through my mouth and lose myself in the sensations that come from the bindings.

The next thing I know, his hands are on me, cupping my ass, which is still sensitive from the paddling. His fingertips caress the skin between the ropes, arousing me from the meditative state.

"Are you ready to take the picture?"

"I already did."

"Oh. Can I see it?"

"Later." He arranges me so my legs are on either side of his hips and presses his hard cock against my opening. Like before, the fit is tight and the pressure borders on pain. The knot is tight against my clit, making me feel everything even more intensely than I did before, if that's possible.

Hayden knows exactly how to position me for ultimate effect, and he enters me slowly but insistently, using the swing of the suspension to bring me in and then send me back. It's a thrilling push-pull that leaves me breathless with a kind of edgy, exciting desire that transports me out of myself and into a place where there's only him and us and how he makes me feel.

I'm not sure exactly what happens then. One minute we're making crazy love while I'm suspended, the next he's carrying me to bed, the ropes are gone, the plug has been removed and my body feels deliciously, gloriously used.

"Mmm, Hayden…"

"I'm here, honey. I've got you."

I glance at the bedside clock and see that it's after three a.m. when he tucks me into bed. Were we really in there for three hours? He holds a bottle of water to my lips and encourages me to drink. My throat is raw, as if I've been screaming. "Did I scream?"

"Yeah, baby." His brows are knitted as if he's concerned or anxious.

I trace my finger over the groove between his brows. "What's wrong?"

"You sort of punched out on me there for a while. Kinda scared me."

"Is that unusual?"

"No. They call it subspace, but you were really out of it." His fingertip caresses my cheek. "How do you feel?"

"I feel good. How do you feel?"

"I feel amazing."

"Will you come to bed with me?" I lift the covers to invite him in.

"I need a minute, and then I will." He kisses my lips. "Finish the water."

I watch him walk across the room and disappear into the bathroom, closing the door behind him.

*Hayden*

*Holy motherfucking hell…* That was… I don't have the words to describe my amazement and disbelief over the way Addie completely surrendered to me. I have to be honest—I didn't think she would. I figured it would be an endless struggle of me trying to control her and her trying to top me from the bottom.

But that's not what happened. She gave herself over to me, accepting my kink and my ropes and me. God, she was so accepting and peaceful, and when I felt her slip into deep subspace, I discovered that not only is she capable of being submissive, she's my perfect match.

I'm elated and exhausted and overwhelmed by the most satisfying sexual experience of my life. By the time I finally took my pleasure and let go of the control, I was like a tightly wound wire attached to a pile of dynamite.

I wash my face and hands and take a leak, thinking about how far we've come since the night of the Oscars, when I jacked off in the men's room rather than face up to what I feel for her. Now I don't have to hide it anymore, and the relief is pervasive.

I need to get back to her. Aftercare is a critical part of my responsibilities as a Dom. I spent forty minutes calming and soothing her in the playroom before I untied her bindings and carried her to bed. It's funny how I need her almost more than she needed me after our scene. I need to touch her and hold her and make doubly sure that she's all right.

Leaving the bathroom, I take a look outside on my way to bed and notice the stars sparkling brightly in the night sky. Will everything seem bigger and brighter now that I finally have what I've wanted for so damned long? Wouldn't that be something?

I get into bed and slide over to where she's curled up in a ball, kissing her cheek and the top of her head. My hand settles just below her breast, and the feel of her silky skin is all it takes to make me hard again.

"No," she says gruffly. "Just *no*."

I laugh and push my dick against her ass. "Remember the rule—if you don't want me, don't get naked with me."

"You didn't give me a choice about putting on clothes."

"Oh well, I guess you're stuck with me and my hard-on, then."

She moans. "You've got to be kidding me."

"Do I sound like I'm kidding?" I had absolutely no intention of making love to her again when I got into bed, but this is too much fun not to play it out. "You won't have to do a thing." Before she can object, I've lifted her onto my lap with her back reclined against my chest.

"You're insane."

"Maybe so, but you've made me that way." Taking myself in hand, I press into her, and she moans. "Does it hurt?"

"Yes, it hurts!"

I freeze and begin to withdraw.

"If you stop, I'll kill you."

Well, alrighty then. I press on until she takes all of me, which is a struggle as always, but I love that struggle. I love every single thing about being with her this way. Her internal muscles go crazy, and it's like being massaged from the inside. I cup her breasts and run my thumbs over her nipples, drawing yet another sharp gasp from her.

"Do they hurt, too?"

"Mmm, a little."

I slide my hand down the front of her to tease her clit. "How about here?"

"Everywhere."

"I'm sorry about that."

"I don't think you're one bit sorry."

Laughing at her testy tone, I fall deeper into the kind of love I've never experienced firsthand before. I now understand why people do all sorts of foolish things to get and keep this powerful feeling of unity and oneness and undeniable rightness.

She sits up a little straighter and leans forward, taking me deeper inside her.

I grasp her hips and hold on tight while she rides me, her plump ass cheeks tight against my groin giving me all sorts of ideas. After running my fingers through the dampness between her legs, I press them against her ass, and she bucks wildly on top of me, damn near finishing me off long before I'm ready to let go.

"My baby likes when I play with her ass."

"So what if I do?"

Smiling, I press my finger into her while using my other hand to caress her clit. The combination has her coming in under a minute. I could keep this up for hours still, but I know she's achy and tired, so I join her, letting go of everything to focus on the almost unbearable pleasure.

God almighty, I've never felt anything like it, and after tonight, I'm officially ruined for all other women.

*Addie*

I wake to the sound of Hayden's deep voice. He's on the phone outside the bedroom, barking out orders to some poor bastard at the office. "I want to see what you've got by five o'clock today. No more delays." After a pause, he adds, "I'm working from home today, so let me know when it's ready for viewing."

A glance at the clock has me sitting up straight in bed. It's *noon* already? What the hell? When was the last time I slept until *noon*? College? I went to work for Flynn shortly after I graduated, and he's kept me hopping ever since. I start to get out of bed but am forced to stop when every muscle in my body screams in protest. Erotic images from the night with Hayden resurface to remind me of how I got this way.

I thought I was in good shape until I went a few rounds with him.

Wearing only boxer briefs, he comes into the room carrying his phone and wearing a frown. "Did I wake you? Sorry."

"It's okay. I can't believe I slept until noon."

"We were up late."

I try to find a more comfortable position and wince from the burn between my legs.

"You're hurting."

"A little."

"A lot. Don't lie to me, Addison."

"I don't want you to think…"

His fingers find my chin, compelling me to look up at him. "What don't you want me to think?"

"That I can't take what you're dishing out."

The way he looks at me… I can truly die happy if he'd just look at me that way every day for the rest of my life. "As I recall, you took what I had to offer extremely well. So well, in fact, I can't wait to do it all again."

"Really?"

"Addison," he says with the tender smile that makes me melt. "Yes. A million times yes. In fact, I owe you a huge apology."

I'm genuinely baffled by what he thinks he needs to apologize for. "How come?"

He cups my face in that proprietary way that I've come to crave and runs his thumbs over my cheeks. "I never should've doubted that you're exactly what I want and need. I should've trusted my heart, because it kept leading me to you, even as I told myself I needed to stay away from you."

This deeply wounded man who is incapable of saying the three little words that would seal our deal manages to convey everything I need to know with one perfect sentence. I blink furiously, determined not to break down in front of him. When his thumbs sweep away tears from under my eyes, I discover that I've failed to hide my emotional reaction.

I reach for him to draw him back into bed with me. "This, right here, is all I've ever wanted from you. Everything else is a bonus. I just want you, Hayden. I don't care about all the reasons why I shouldn't."

"You're way more than I deserve. You know that, don't you?"

"No." With every muscle I own screaming in protest, I turn over so I can see his face. "I'm exactly what you deserve."

"No one has ever cared about me the way you do."

"And no one else ever will."

He stares into my eyes. "I keep thinking I'm going to wake up and it'll be the day before the Oscars and none of this will have happened."

"It happened. It's real. I'm real. *We're* real." I caress his chest and belly, noting that his cock is hard—again. Before I can tend to that, I have questions, lots of them. "Will you tell me how you discovered the lifestyle and the Kinbaku and everything?"

He gazes over my shoulder at the view of the ocean through the uncovered window, seeming to collect his thoughts. "It started when I was twenty-one and spent the summer on location with my father in Amsterdam. I became friends with the lead actor on the film, someone whose name you'd recognize, and he introduced me to the scene. I was instantly fascinated and captivated. Here, finally, was something I could control. I was obsessed after that."

"So you've had a lot of practice?"

"I've never claimed to be a saint, Addie. You knew that about me before any of this happened."

"I know." My mind is racing with more questions I'm not sure I have a right to ask.

"Say it. I can feel you spinning."

"You can't feel me spinning."

"I know you, and I know you have questions. There's nothing you can't ask me."

"Will it be enough for you? Just me?"

His big hand cups my cheek, compelling me to look at him. "If I have you, I have everything I want and need. You never need to worry about me wanting someone else. I've had plenty of others, and nothing compares to you."

"Okay, that's a good answer."

Smiling, he kisses me. "What else do you want to know?"

"The Kinbaku. How did you learn about that?"

"Early in my career, I was the assistant director on a film shot in Japan. While I was there, I sought out the scene and met a Kinbaku master who taught me almost everything I know about erotic tying. I've studied intensively with some of the top practitioners in the world and spent years perfecting my craft." Before I can ask, he continues. "It's the ultimate exchange of power when a sub surrenders to be bound by her Dom."

I slide my hand lower to wrap it around his incredibly hard cock. "It turns you on to talk about it."

Gasping as I stroke him, he says, "It's the ultimate turn-on." He shudders and stops my hand from moving. "What did you think of it? Tell me the truth."

"I was scared at first, but I loved it. I would've been terrified with anyone but you."

"You'll never do anything like that with anyone but me," he says in a low, menacing tone that makes me smile.

"I don't want to."

"I love to hear you say you loved it. That means so much to me."

"When can we do it again?"

"When you've had time to rest and recover from the first time." He runs his fingers through my hair as he looks at me intently. "What do you see happening now?"

Because I know he's asking about much more than our sex life, I bite my lip to keep from pouring out my heart to him, still afraid that maybe he doesn't want the same things I do.

"Give me the truth, Addison. I want to know."

I summon all the courage I can find to share my ultimate dream with him. "I see a big house on the coast, a bunch of kids with insanely blue eyes like their father. I see parties on the lawn, family holidays, the biggest Christmas trees we can find. I see you on location and us with you in the summer when our kids are on vacation. I see one grand adventure after another. I see the family we'll make together and the family we already have with our Quantum friends."

"A bunch of kids, huh?"

Smiling, I say, "Did you hear anything after that?"

His hand slides down my arm to link his fingers with mine. "I heard every word you said."

"And?"

"I think it's time I had a talk with your dad."

"Oh." All I can think of is how intensely my dad dislikes Hayden, for reasons he's never shared with me. "You don't have to do that."

"Trust me, when a man wants to marry another man's only daughter, he asks permission first."

Hearing him say the word "marry" in a sentence that refers to me is almost too much for my fragile heart to handle.

"That is what you want, right?"

"Yes, Hayden," I say on a deep sigh. "It's what I want."

He brings our joined hands to his lips, running them back and forth over my knuckles. Just that slight contact is enough to make my nipples and clit tingle. "So if I were to ask you the big question, I'd get the answer I want?"

"Is it what *you* want? Because I wouldn't want you to feel pressured into something you're not ready for."

"Oh, you wouldn't? Is this the same woman who basically tricked me into making her my submissive last night?"

"That's different. That's sex. This is your whole life we're talking about here, and you should spend it exactly the way you want to."

"Would you like know how I want to spend it?"

I'm afraid to breathe, let alone speak, so I nod.

"I want that big house at the coast, only it has to have a pool, too, so I can teach all those kids of ours how to swim. I see you lording over the entire thing, large and in charge, running roughshod over me and our family and friends. And then I see us in bed where I'll run roughshod over *you* every chance I get."

"Your vision looks an awful lot like mine."

"You noticed that, huh?"

"Please don't ask my dad," I say, filled with dread as I picture the reception he'll receive from Dad. "It's nice of you to think of the courtesy and everything, but—"

"He hates my guts."

I push myself up onto one elbow. "*Why* does he hate your guts?"

"That's a long story, and it's one that would be better to stay between him and me. You don't need to worry about anything. I'll work it out with him."

I don't like that answer, but I'm too close to having everything I've ever wanted to poke at it. Now that I know we have a chance at forever together, there'll be time enough to figure out why there's bad blood between the two men I love best.

# CHAPTER 18

*Hayden*

I'm a nervous wreck as I drive to Redondo Beach two days after that monumental conversation with Addie. I finally had no choice but to return to real life today with the final cut of *Insidious* due to the studio early next week and final edits still needed to get it just right. Not to mention Flynn was losing his mind trying to live without Addie managing every aspect of his life for him.

My phone rings, and I take the call from Flynn's brother-in-law on the Bluetooth, welcoming any distraction that takes my mind off the task that lies before me with Simon York.

"Hey, Hugh, how're you making out?"

"I've got a few things for you to look at whenever you're ready."

"Already?"

"We don't mess around when Hollywood's top director comes a'calling, and he's planning to propose to the woman who keeps my brother-in-law sane."

"That's good to know," I say, smiling. "At times like these, it's nice to have one of Hollywood's top jewelers in the family."

"I love a happy ending. Let me know when you want to come in to take a look."

"How's tomorrow afternoon around four?"

"I'll make a point to be here."

"Thanks again, Hugh."

"My pleasure."

I press the button on the wheel to end the call, excited to see the ring, to ask her, to make it official. But first I have to get past her dad. I'm well aware that it's the new millennium and I'm being somewhat old-fashioned by asking for his permission, especially knowing there's not a snowball's chance in hell he's going to grant it.

I've known Simon most of my life. He was a friend of my dad's at one time, before my dad's life went off the rails and many of his old friends moved on without him. When I was putting together the team to make my first film, I called on Simon to be my lead cameraman. I'll admit that first shoot was rocky. I was in way over my head and let my arrogance get the better of me.

Things went from bad to worse when Simon caught me fucking one of the craft services girls in the men's room. What can I say other than I was young and dumb and full of cum? In the few times my path has crossed Simon's since that shoot ended, he hasn't had much to say to me. Not that I blame him. If I were him, I'd think I was a douche, too. But I'm hoping I can appeal to his sense of fairness. All that happened a long time ago, and I'm not that guy anymore.

I know where Simon's place is, because I gave Addie a ride down here once to pick up her old car after her dad did some work to it. That was before Flynn bought her the Audi, and she was still trying to keep her 1998 Toyota on the road. The working-class neighborhood hasn't changed much in the years since I was last here. She tells great stories about growing up at the beach and the innocent "trouble" she and her friends got into.

She doesn't know trouble, not like the kind I grew up with. Sometimes I wonder which one of us had it worse—her because her mother died suddenly when she was twelve, or me watching my mother die a slow death from addiction all these years.

At least she had Simon to fill the void, while I had Gracie and Sebastian to make me feel part of a family when my own rejected me time and again. I'm struck by a paralyzing bolt of fear at the thought of the family Addie wants to have with me. What do I know about how to be a family man?

*Stop*, a voice inside my head says loudly. *You know how. You saw how Gracie was with Sebastian, and you've had a front-row seat with the Godfreys, too. You know what you need to do, and you'll do whatever it takes to make her happy. That's all you have to say to Simon.* I get out of the car determined to do the right thing here, but to leave with my intentions toward her still intact no matter what he might have to say.

My phone rings with a text from Addie.

*Are you there yet?*

*Just now. Wish me luck.*

*You know I do, even if we're still in the biggest fight ever.*

Laughing, I type out my reply. *I'll make it up to you tonight.* After that crazy first night in my playroom, I refused to make love to her during the day we spent together yesterday. I knew how sore she was, even if she said otherwise. So we did a lot of talking, a lot of kissing, a lot of touching and not much else, which left her furious with me in the best possible way. I love that she begs me for it, and I plan to use that to my advantage the next time we're alone together. Tonight can't get here soon enough for me.

*You'd better bring the big guns to make this right.*

*Don't I always? Isn't that why we're having this fight? My big gun made you sore.*

*Arrogant bastard.*

*You love me.*

*Yes, for some strange reason I really do.*

*Thank God for that. I'll see you soon.*

*Call me after…*

*Ok.*

Fortified by the exchange, I stash the phone in the back pocket of my jeans and make my way around the house where Addie told me I'd find Simon, tucked away in the studio he uses to produce his pottery when he's not on location. I hear classic rock coming from the small building that takes up most of the sparse backyard and knock on the door.

"Come in!"

I open the door and stick my head in.

He's sitting at a worktable with a beer and the sports page spread out in front of him. "What the fuck are you doing here?" he asks in a low growl.

"I was hoping we could talk."

"I got nothing to say to you."

"I know you don't, but I have a few things I need to say to you if you can spare a few minutes."

"Now's not a good time."

I have to remember to keep my temper in check, because that's got no place in this conversation. "Cuz you're busy?"

"Yeah. I'm busy."

"When will you not be busy?"

"For you? Never."

"Simon, you know why I'm here."

"Yep, and I don't want to hear about how you're in love with my daughter and want my blessing and yada yada yada. Ain't gonna happen—not in this or any other lifetime."

"Even if it's what she wants?"

"She's infatuated. She'll get over it."

His certainty that she'll get over me is like a knife to my gut. "I don't think that's going to happen."

"So now you know my daughter better than I do?"

"In some ways, yeah, I do."

His brows narrow, and his eyes flash with fury. "You'd better get the fuck out of here before I decide to kick your ass for daring to lay your filthy hands on my daughter."

"Are you the same person you were at twenty?"

"What the fuck is that supposed to mean?"

"You're judging me for things you saw me do thirteen years ago when I was barely an adult, trying to find my way. I'm not that guy anymore."

"No?" He raises a brow and seems amused. "So what they say about you isn't true?"

I swallow hard while trying not to reveal my panic. "What do they say?"

"That you're a kinky motherfucker who likes to tie women up. You gonna tell me that's not true?"

I've got two very distinct choices here—concede to the truth or lie my ass off. Neither is all that appealing. I guess I hesitate long enough for him to draw his own conclusions.

"Get out of here, Hayden. My daughter can do a thousand times better than you. I don't care how many golden statues you got sitting on your desk, a scumbag is still a scumbag no matter how much time goes by."

I'm cut to the quick by his sharply spoken words. He's not saying anything I haven't told myself. But then I remember Addie's vision for our future, and I want that sweet life with her so badly I can taste it.

"Thanks for your time, Simon. Sorry to intrude."

I go back the way I came, ducking around the tiny bungalow where Addie grew up, returning to the Range Rover, where I sit for a long time trying to get myself together before I make the drive back to the city, where she's waiting for me to tell her how it went with her dad.

And what am I to say to that? *It went great, babe. He's thrilled for us.* I can't lie to her, and I certainly can't tell her the truth. This is a fine predicament. What if she feels she has to choose between her dad and me? How can I compete against the guy who raised her, who is her only family?

Thinking about the things he said makes me feel sick. I can't believe he knows about my sexual preferences. I've been careful—really careful—about how and when I let people into that part of my life, but I suppose it was inevitable that someone would talk.

I slam my hand on the steering wheel. "Fuck. *Fuck, fuck, fuck.*"

*Addie*

Hayden is back in the office, but I haven't heard from him, which tells me things with Dad didn't go well. I wish he'd listened to me and skipped that part of the program, but he didn't, and now I have to deal with whatever fallout my dear old dad has left me with.

I pick up my cell phone and call the top number on my list of favorites.

He answers on the first ring.

"What did you say to him?"

"Who?"

"Don't do this, Dad. Don't play dumb with me. You know exactly who I'm talking about."

"I told him the truth."

"And that is?"

"You can do a million times better than him, and there's no way I'm giving my blessing now or ever."

*Oh God, oh God, oh God...* What he must be thinking!

"I can't believe you'd do this to me. You know how I feel about him."

"And you know how I feel about *you!*"

He's never in all my life yelled at me, not even when I was a rebellious teenager who gave him reason to every day.

"He loves me, Dad."

"And he's told you that?"

"Not in so many words, but—"

"Are you *listening to yourself*, Addison? You're planning to marry a man who *can't even tell you he loves you?*"

"You don't understand him. He's had it rough—"

"Are you serious right now? Are you honestly telling me that Hayden Roth, who was born with a silver fucking spoon in his mouth, has had it *rough? Rough* is losing your mother at twelve. *Rough* is having your wife drop dead in front of you when there's not a fucking thing you can do to help her. *Rough* is trying to raise a daughter on your own when you don't know the first goddamned thing about what makes a teenage girl tick. *He has not had it rough!*"

"His parents ignored him. They forgot about his birthday, left him alone with the housekeeper on holidays. His mother has OD'd four times, and he's had to clean up the mess every time." I know most of these things because Flynn told me, not because Hayden ever has. "You don't know everything there is to know about him."

"Do you? Do you know how he needs to tie women up to get off? Has he told you about that?"

I'm shocked speechless. "How... How do you know that?"

"People talk in this town, and that's what they say about him. You think you know him so well, but you didn't know that."

"Yes, I did. I know." I can't believe I'm actually having this conversation with my father of all people. I want to die of embarrassment, and I'm sick with fear over what Hayden must be thinking and feeling if Dad confronted him with this information.

"And that's okay with you?"

"It's… I… It's complicated." I can't very well tell my dad that I've done it and I love it, can I? No, I absolutely cannot.

He snorts with disbelief. "Can you even *hear* how you're justifying him, or are you so far gone that actually makes sense to you?"

Actually, all I can hear is the roaring in my own ears. The need to get to Hayden immediately, to fix the damage, trumps everything else. "I have to go, Dad."

"Addison, listen to me—"

"I heard you. I heard everything you said, and now I have to go. I'll call you soon." I hit the end button before he can reply, before he can say something else that can't be unsaid or unheard. I run for the stairwell and take the stairs to the sixth floor two at a time, the residual aches and pains from the other night forgotten in the midst of panic.

I burst into the editing suite, expecting to find Hayden surrounded by people the way he usually is at this stage in postproduction, but he's alone, staring at one of the big screens as the same cut of *Insidious* we watched the other night plays. Like all his work—and Flynn's—it's breathtaking, mesmerizing and sure to be another monster hit. But I can tell by the vacant look in his eyes that work doesn't have his usual razor focus today.

"Hayden."

He blinks several times, as if to clear his thoughts, before he looks up at me.

I stifle a gasp at the despair I see in his eyes, in his expression, in the rigid set of his jaw. *No, no, no!* Please, no. Not after how far we've come. Though I have no idea if I'll be welcome or not, I crawl into his lap and wrap my arms around his neck, kissing his face and then his lips. "No matter what he said, it doesn't change anything. I love you. I *know* you love me. That's *all* that matters, Hayden."

"No, it isn't. He matters to you. Please don't pretend his opinion has no bearing on us. It does."

"Only if we let it." I force him to look at me. I've never felt more desperate in my life than I am right now as I try to find the words to salvage us, if there's still an us to salvage. "I choose you. I'll *always* choose you."

He shakes his head. "I can't ask that of you. Someday you'd hate me for it."

"Never. I could never hate you, not when I love you so much it hurts to breathe when I think of losing you."

"And how do you feel about losing him?"

"I'll never lose him. I'm all he has."

"If he hates your husband, Addie, it'll never be the same between the two of you."

"So that's it? You're willing to abandon all our plans, our hopes, our dreams, because he doesn't approve?"

"That's not why."

The confirmation that he's abandoning me and us breaks my heart into thousands of pieces that'll never again be put back together. I'll never be the same after him. That much I know for certain.

"Why, then? If you're going to give up on us, at least have the decency to tell me why."

"He's right that you can do so much better than a guy who can't even bring himself to tell you how he feels about you."

"You *have* told me. You've told me you care about me more than you've ever cared about anyone. What else do you think I need to hear?"

He remains stubbornly silent.

I slide off his lap and drop to my knees before him. "Do I get any say in how my life unfolds, Hayden? Do I get a vote about what *I* want, or do you get to decide that for me?"

"I'm not deciding for you."

"If you tell me we're through because my father went off on you, then you *are* deciding. You're deciding for both of us, and I'm right here, looking you dead in your gorgeous blue eyes and swearing on my life that *you* are what I want. You are what I've *always* wanted. *We* are what I want. After having what we've had, I can't imagine seeing you with someone else or letting any other man touch me—"

A low growl erupts from his chest as he hauls me up and into his arms, his lips crashing into mine in a savage kiss that's all about possession and dominance and love. There's so much love here. He cups my ass and pulls me in tight against his erection as my heart soars with hope and more love than I knew was possible to feel.

His hands are under my skirt while his lips continue to devour me in deep, bruising kisses that I'll feel for days.

A quick knock sounds on the door before it opens. "Hey, Hayden—"

He rips his lips free of mine. "Get the fuck out and stay out. The next person who comes in here is a dead man."

"Gotcha." The door clicks shut again.

"That wasn't very nice," I mutter against his lips.

"Fuck being nice. I'd much rather fuck you than be fucking nice."

"So what's stopping you?"

Again, that low growl thing he does sets me on fire for him, and our hands collide as we pull at clothes to free the important parts. He lifts me up and onto his hard cock, and I bite my lip to keep from screaming from the burning ache of his entry.

"So tight, so hot, so wet and all mine."

I cling to him, one arm around his neck, the other hand fisting his hair. "Yes, Hayden, I'm yours. I'm all yours. Always."

He squeezes my ass cheeks as he lifts me up and drops me back down, forcing me to take all of him.

My head falls back and my mouth opens on a silent scream as I come instantly. I'm still in the throes of it when my dress clears my head and my bra is released, freeing my breasts to his ravenous mouth. That anyone could walk in here and catch us going at it doesn't faze me in the least. That's nothing when stacked up to how close I came to losing him today. I don't care about anything other than the tight squeeze of his cock inside me, the rough tug of his mouth on my nipple or the second orgasm that's about to boil over.

I ride him shamelessly. I want him to feel this every bit as intensely as I do. Judging by his groans and fierce, desperate kisses, he's feeling it. How could he not? And then I'm coming again, harder than before, and I can't stop the cry that's torn from my soul. He covers my mouth with his, and I'm glad that one of us is concerned about the scandal that's probably ripping through the Quantum building.

I don't care. I have him, and that's all I've ever wanted. Nothing, not even my beloved dad, is going to come between us. Not if I have anything to say about it.

## *Hayden*

I follow Addie up the stairs to the private plane Flynn chartered to take the Quantum crew to Mexico. We're all in need of a break after the last few insane months. As of midnight, when I turned in the final cut of *Insidious*, I'm on vacation. The gang is in high spirits as we buckle into our seats for takeoff and order drinks from the poor steward who drew the short straw for this trip. I hope Flynn is taking good care of him. He's going to more than earn anything he makes.

In addition to Flynn, Natalie, and myself and Addie, Jasper, Kristian, Sebastian, Marlowe, Leah, Ellie and Emmett have joined the party. It's like a freaking miracle that all of us could break free at the same time, but for once, the gods of schedules smiled down upon us, and we've got a whole week to spend together at Flynn's awesome house in Cabo San Lucas, one of my favorite places to unwind.

I've been tightly wound since the day Simon York handed me my ass and Addie refused to let me go like she probably should have. Though I'm deeply thankful that she's made up her mind that her father's disapproval isn't going to derail us, I wish I could be so certain.

Tucked into a secret compartment in my suitcase is the stunning ring Hugh and his team created for Addie. The three-carat emerald-cut diamond is flawless, and the platinum setting is one of a kind, just like the woman I love. I debated about the size of the stone, but I wanted her to be able to wear it every day, not just on special occasions. My Addie is endlessly efficient and productive, and she'd hate a big clunky ring that gets in her way. So I settled for a smaller but still gorgeous stone that I think she'll love if I can work up the courage to actually ask her.

I hope that'll happen in Mexico. I've had the ring for six days now, and there's been plenty of opportunity in that time, but something always stops me when I think the moment has come. All my insecurities where she's concerned come roaring to the surface any time I try to say what needs to be said to make her mine forever.

As the others laugh and talk and guzzle their drinks, I relive those painful moments in Simon's studio. His words have cut me deep, and the wounds are still open and festering despite Addie's best efforts to put her special kind of balm on them. I can't stop thinking about the things he said and the abject hatred that came through in every word. I keep telling myself all that matters is that *she* loves me. The whole rest of the world can hate my fucking guts for all I care as long as *she* loves me.

If only it were that simple.

The plane taxis to the runway, and the ground rushes by as we hurtle lift off into the heavens. Addie's hand covers mine, and I turn my palm faceup to rub against hers, looking over in time to see her smile at me. Everyone who works in the Quantum building knows we had wild sex in the editing room last week, but my partners have wisely refrained from comment. Perhaps they can sense how fragile our relationship really is. And it is fragile, despite the $200,000 ring I had made for her, despite the nights we've spent together, the love we've made. Underneath it all is a fragile foundation that could crumble at any second.

If I thought the ring could shore up that foundation, I would've put it on her finger the night I picked it up from Hugh. But it's going to take far more than a piece of jewelry or a lifetime commitment to fix this. I heard everything she said that day in the editing room. I heard her say she chooses me over her father, over anyone, and that's not going to change. I heard what she said, but I know her. I know how important her father is to her, how essential they've been to each other since they lost her mom. I remember their tight bond from the first time I met her, when she came on location with us and tended to Simon like a mother duck while he worked long, grueling hours.

A rift between them will lead to a rift between us. I'm as sure of that as I am that the sun will set tonight in spectacular fashion in Cabo. And therein lies the crux of my dilemma. How do I give her what she says she wants most without costing her a relationship she cherishes?

I can't get my head around it, no matter how hard I try to see it from all angles.

"I thought Aileen was coming with us," Kristian says when we reach cruising altitude and the steward returns with more drinks.

"She couldn't swing it with the kids in school," Natalie says of her friend in New York who has been battling breast cancer.

"Oh," Kristian replies. "That's too bad. Would've been nice to see her again."

I see Natalie and Addie exchange intrigued glances at Kristian's apparent interest in seeing Natalie's friend again. I'm sure they'll be matchmaking in no time with that little tidbit now out in the open. Poor Kristian.

Addie settles herself against me, her arm wrapped around mine. "You're quiet."

"Decompressing. Second-guessing."

"What're you second-guessing?"

"The film," I say, quickly realizing she thinks I meant us.

"What about it?"

"Oh, the usual… coulda, shoulda, woulda. After that last time through last night, I'll never watch it again."

She raises her head off my shoulder. "*Why?*"

"I'll see something that'll piss me off because I didn't fix it when I had the chance."

"When you look for the flaws, you run the risk of overlooking the magic."

Her wise statement applies to much more than my moviemaking-induced anxiety.

"How'd you get so wise?" I ask, cuffing her chin.

Smiling, she says, "I'm not all that wise."

Raising the armrest between us, I put my arm around her and bring her in as close as I can get her in the restrictive confines of the seats. "I think you are, possibly, the wisest person I know."

"And you are, without a doubt, the most brilliant filmmaker of your generation. *Insidious* is brilliant. *Camouflage* is brilliant. All your films are amazing, and so is the person whose vision makes them possible in the first place."

"I hate to point out that you may be a tad bit biased," I say, embarrassed by her effusiveness.

She sighs and puts her head back on my shoulder, making it impossible for me to read that ridiculously expressive face of hers.

"Why the deep sigh?"

"Sometimes I wish you could see yourself the way other people do."

I'm almost afraid to ask. "What do you mean?"

"When people say you're the most gifted director of your generation, they aren't saying that to blow smoke up your ass. They say it because it's true. I say it because it's true, not because I'm in love with you. I know your childhood was less than ideal, Hayden, but you grew up to be a very fine man who everyone on this plane is honored to call friend, partner, collaborator. You take care of the people you love even if you have trouble telling them how you feel. You're nothing at all like the people who raised you, and regardless of what you believe, I often feel like *I'm* not good enough for *you.*"

They are, quite simply, the most magnificent compliments I've ever received from anyone, and I'm rendered speechless. I tighten the grip I have on her shoulder.

She lifts her head off my shoulder to look into my eyes, which have to be shinier than they were a minute ago. "So shut up about the film being anything less than perfect, will you please?"

"Sure, baby." I smile at her, my heart full to overflowing. "Whatever you say."

# CHAPTER 19

*Addie*

The time in Mexico is pure bliss—sunshine, lots of laughter with most of my favorite people, amazing food, all the booze we can drink and some of the sexiest nights of my life with Hayden. He's lightened up somewhat since our talk on the plane, but he's still burdened by something—and I suspect that something is my father's disapproval.

Since that night at his place before he saw my dad, there's been no more talk of our house on the coast, the blue-eyed children or the life we might one day have, but that's okay. I'm giving him all the time and space he needs, hoping he'll relax during this much-needed getaway. I'm also trying not to think about how he'll soon be leaving town for a few months to shoot his next film in the Middle East.

The thought of all that time away from him makes me sick at heart. But we'll get through it. Even though we've had our ups and downs, I'm more convinced than ever that we belong together, and I'll fight to the bitter end to make that happen.

I've had a few tense conversations with my dad since the day Hayden saw him. I understand that he has a right to his opinion, but I've urged him to spend more time with Hayden and with the two of us together before he passes judgment. He's agreed to think about it, leaving us truly at odds for the first time in my life.

I'm not sure what I'll do if he never comes around to seeing what I do in Hayden, but I've made up my mind that if our relationship has to permanently change because of the choice I've made, then so be it. I'll miss the closeness I've always shared with Dad, but I won't sacrifice my happiness—or Hayden's.

A thunderstorm blows in after dinner on our fourth night in Mexico, and everyone is hunkered down in various corners of the big house. Jasper, Sebastian, Kristian and Emmett are playing an intense game of high-stakes poker while Leah, Ellie and Marlowe look on, taking sides, teasing and generally rabble-rousing. Natalie is in the kitchen cleaning up after dinner. She chased us all out when we offered to help, and we let her. I've noticed how much she enjoys mothering us all, and I wonder how long it'll be before she's mothering a baby.

"Where did Hayden and Flynn get off to?" I ask.

"I heard something about cigars, so you might check the den."

"Ewww."

"That's exactly why I'm in here rather than in there."

"Wise woman. What is it about men and their cigars anyway?"

"I have no idea," she says, "but they do remind me of my grandpa." The wistful expression on her face is a poignant reminder of the family she left behind as a young girl. "If you find my husband, tell him I was looking bored and lonely."

Laughing, I squeeze her shoulder. "I'll give him the message." I leave the kitchen and head down the short flight of stairs that leads to the den on the lower level where Hayden and I have been staying. I'm about to knock on the partially closed door when their voices stop me.

"So you already bought a ring?" Flynn asks.

"Yeah, Hugh hooked me up."

I raise one hand to my heart and another to cover my mouth to contain my shriek of excitement.

"So when're you going to pop the question?"

"I don't think I'm going to, actually."

Like a balloon stuck by a pin, I'm deflated, and tears fill my eyes.

"Why not?" Flynn sounds almost as disappointed as I feel. "I thought you were crazy about her."

"I am. I'm out of my mind over her."

"Then what's the problem?"

"Simon hates me. He made it clear he'll never approve of us together, and he's too important to Addie to pretend like that doesn't matter. Somehow, he even knows about the kink."

"Fuck. He came right out and said that?"

"He said word on the street is I need to tie up a woman to get off, and I could tell the thought of me with his daughter thoroughly disgusts him."

"Yikes. What does she say?"

"That she'll work it out with him, but we both know if she marries me, her relationship with him will be permanently fucked. She's said she can live with that, but what if she can't? What if she hates me someday for forcing her to choose between us? I don't know, Flynn. I just don't know. I'm fucking losing my shit over this."

The sob that's been trying to get out breaks free of the hand I've placed over my mouth. It's loud, and they go quiet. I know they heard me. I have to get out of here. I have to get out of here now. I push through the door that leads to the pool deck and run out into the rain that's coming down in sheets. It's a cold rain that soaks through the light dress I'm wearing in a matter of seconds. I reach the end of the pool deck and take the stairs that lead to a path we hiked the other day.

I hear him and Flynn calling my name, but I keep running. I can't do this anymore. All the determination I felt only ten minutes ago has deserted me in the face of his statements to Flynn. Either he wants me or he doesn't, but I can no longer love him enough for both of us. He's gaining on me, so I run faster, blinded by the rain and the wind and darkness. I should be scared, but I'm too numb to feel anything other than a fierce need to flee.

"Addison!" He's still quite a ways behind me, and just as I decide to cut right onto a different trail, my foot catches on a root and I pitch forward into the darkness, screaming as I claw for something to hold on to while sliding precariously downward, propelled by mud. My hand finds a narrow branch and I cling to it. I have no idea what's below me or how far the fall would be. Maybe this is it. I'm going to die out here, and whereas the thought of that would've terrified me an hour ago, now...

"Addie!" He's much closer now, and I don't want to die. I don't want this to be the end, even if my heart is shattered.

"Hayden!"

"Sweetheart, where are you? Keep talking to me."

"Down here."

"Oh my God. Don't move. Hold on as tight as you can. I'm going to get you." In the darkness, I can barely make him out about three feet above me. He's flat on his stomach, reaching down for me. "Give me your hand."

"I can't let go."

"Baby, you have to trust me. I won't let anything happen to you. I swear. Give me your hand."

The ground that's holding me shifts precariously, sending a jolt of adrenaline crashing through me that gives me the courage to reach for him, to put my trust in him. His grip on my wrist is tight enough to shatter my bones, but he doesn't let go. Flynn is there, too, pulling on Hayden as he pulls on me.

It takes both of them to drag me back up onto the trail and into his trembling arms.

"Oh my God." He holds me so tightly I'm afraid I'll truly break. "Addison. Oh my God."

Still on his knees next to us, Flynn's head is bowed as he pants from the exertion.

"Baby." Hayden sounds as shattered as I feel. "God, I love you so much. Don't ever run away from me again. Promise me. I love you." He's hugging me and kissing me and rocking me as the rain comes down even harder than it was before. "I need you to promise me."

"I promise. I'm sorry."

"No, no. You have nothing to be sorry about. I'm the one who fucked this up every which way. *You* are absolutely perfect, and I love you."

"Let's get you guys back to the house," Flynn says.

Hayden picks me up, and I wrap my arms and legs around him, burrowing my face into his neck, breathing in the scent of my love, the only man I'll ever love. Back at the house, he walks me directly into the lower-level shower, the warm water chasing the chill away. He holds me for minutes, or maybe hours, for all I know, before he sets me down to help me out of my sopping clothes while I do the same for him.

Then he lifts me back into his arms, and I squirm against him, needing the connection I can only get with him. He brings me down on his hard cock, entering me slowly, carefully, gently, as if I'm the most precious thing in his world, and for once, I finally believe that maybe I am.

"I love you more than my own life, Addison. If anything ever happened to you, I'd die, too."

"I'm okay. I'm right here."

"There was nothing below you but a sheer drop to the rocks, baby. You have no idea how close you came, how close we came…" A huge tremble runs through him, and for a second, I worry he might drop me. But of course he doesn't. He presses my back against the tile and pushes into me so deep, deeper than he's ever been before.

"I don't care what you thought you heard or what drove you into that storm, but you're going to marry me, you hear me?"

"Is that your romantic way of proposing?"

"Fuck romance, this is our life I'm talking about—your life with me. You *are* my life, Addison. You have to marry me. Say yes. Say you will."

"Yes, Hayden, I will." Because, really, what does it matter how or when he asks? The only thing I care about is that I get to spend my life with him.

Without breaking our intimate connection, he carries me from the shower, wrapping a towel around my shoulders as he sits me on the vanity to finish what we started. There's no sign of my fierce dominant lover tonight. No, this is all about love, and I feel his love for me in every touch, every kiss and every deep stroke of his magnificent cock.

I come in slow rolling waves that make me shudder from the powerful sensations that have me clinging to him as he comes, too, pulsing inside me and filling me with his heat. It's the single most powerful moment of my entire life, and judging from the way he looks at me, his life, too.

"Did we just get engaged while having sex in the shower?" I ask him when I can speak again.

"Not quite."

"What does that mean?"

After withdrawing from me, he wraps the towel around my shoulders and picks me up again to carry me into the bedroom we've been sharing. Closing the door behind him, he deposits me on the bed, gets rid of the towel and pulls the covers up and over me, which is when I realize I'm still shivering. "Don't move. I'll be right back."

Hayden disappears into the big walk-in closet where we've stashed our stuff and returns a minute later carrying a small velvet box.

As he kneels next to the bed, I sit up, trembling now for entirely different reasons.

He takes hold of my hand and bends his head to kiss the back of it. Then he looks up at me, his heart in his eyes. "When I was a little kid, I was desperately afraid of thunder and lightning. I can still remember the sheer terror of feeling like the world was going to explode at any moment, and no one would be able to find me. Other than when my mom had her issues, I've never felt that same kind of bone-deep fear again until tonight, when I realized there's something else I'm far more afraid of than I ever was of thunder and lightning—and that's losing you. I love you so much, Addison. If I have a million years, I'll never be able to show you how much."

Tears run freely down my face. "You already have, Hayden. You've shown me so many times. I've always known that you loved me. Always."

"Marry me? Have that house on the coast and the tribe of blue-eyed little kids who hopefully have their mother's disposition and travel with me and do everything with me?"

"Yes. God, yes."

He slides the incredible ring on my finger. "Now," he says, "we're officially engaged."

I throw myself into his arms, and we end up on the floor next to the bed, kissing wildly as the storm rages on outside. The only thought I have as he kisses me with a desperation he's never shown me before is that finally, finally, *finally*, he's all mine.

*Hayden*

Addie sits on my lap the next morning at breakfast, feeding me grapes and strawberries and bites of omelet while our friends keep up a running commentary on how disgusting we are and if this is what our marriage is going to be like, they want nothing to do with it.

"They're just jealous, sweetheart," I say to her as I accept another grape—and a kiss—from her.

Natalie made a big fuss about our engagement, insisting on celebratory mimosas while exclaiming over Addie's gorgeous ring. I don't think my bride-to-be even took an actual look at it herself until this morning. She was too busy making love to me all night long to be worried about what her ring looks like. I do love that she was far more interested in me than she was in the ring, which just confirms what I already knew about how devoted to me she is.

All at once, she goes stiff in my arms. I'm about to ask what's wrong when I see her father standing at the far end of the dining room, watching the two of us intently, his expression unreadable. When she moves to get up, I stop her with my arm banded tightly around her waist.

She seems to understand what I want and relaxes against me ever so slightly. "Dad? What're you doing here?"

"I flew him in," Flynn says. "I called him last night after Addie's accident to tell him it's high time he experiences the two of you together so he can see what the rest of us already do."

"And what's that?" I ask my best friend. I can't believe he's done this enormous thing for us, but then again, I shouldn't be surprised. He's my best friend for a reason.

"That you guys are meant for each other."

Simon takes a step closer to where Addie and I are seated. "I heard you had a close call last night, honey."

"Yes," she says softly, her eyes full of tears. "But Hayden saved me."

"With a major assist from Flynn," I say, unwilling to take all the credit. I can see that Simon is undone to realize how close he came to losing his only child. He looks like he hasn't slept, and his hair is standing on end.

"I'm sorry," he says, blinking rapidly. "I'm so sorry."

She pats my hand, and I let her up to go to him.

He wraps his arms around her and holds her for a long time. By the time he lets her go, they're both in tears.

Flynn nudges my shoulder and nods in their direction, telling me to join them.

Since I have no fucking clue what I'm supposed to do right now, I take his suggestion and get up to go to them.

Addie slides her right arm around my waist and shows her father the ring on her left hand.

He leans in for an up-close look. "That's one heck of a ring, honey. I'm happy for you."

"Thank you, Daddy." She wipes her face and smiles up at me.

Simon extends his hand to me. "Thank you for saving my daughter's life."

I shake hands with my future father-in-law. "Don't thank me." I look down at her beautiful face. She's absolutely radiant this morning, and I intend to keep her that way forever. "By saving her life, I saved my own, too."

# EPILOGUE

*Addie*

On Hayden's thirty-fourth birthday, I take him by the hand to lead him. I can feel his resistance and how hard it is for him to cede control to me for even the short time I've asked to have it. Getting him to agree to the blindfold was an epic challenge, but I know he's going to love this.

"This isn't how it works, Addison," he says in the low sexy growl that makes my panties melt. "You don't get to control me." He's reminded me of that several times since we set out from his house in town.

"You can do it. I promise it'll be worth it."

"I hope you think the punishment you'll receive later is worth it, too."

"Mmm, I know I will."

He makes a sound that's a cross between a growl and a groan, and I love that this is getting to him. I've been plotting this night for weeks, and now that it's finally time, I'm nervous and anxious and incredibly aroused—and only from *thinking* about what we're going to do. I can't imagine what actually *doing* it will feel like.

Devon has been awesome in helping me to plan my surprise for Hayden, and as we enter through the main doors at Black Vice, he's there to greet us. He has promised not to stay and watch, which is essential to my being able to actually go through with this. No one I know will be here, or that's what I tell myself.

It won't matter. We'll both be disguised to protect our identities. That's the only way either of us could do it.

Devon remains silent as I lead Hayden into the elevator that takes us to the second floor, where the Black Vice playrooms are located. In the weeks since I first came here to experience the BDSM lifestyle, my own experience has quadrupled. Hayden is introducing me slowly but surely to every aspect of the scene, and I love it as much as he does.

Just when I think he's taken me as far as I can go, we go further, and our connection grows exponentially every time we venture into the playrooms at both his homes. I prefer the one in Malibu because I'm the only one who has ever been there, but I try not to dwell on the past when I'm at his home in town. He's so focused on me and my pleasure that there's no way he has time to think about anyone else.

My confidence in him and our relationship has grown right along with my sexual experience, and I've never been happier in my life. I always knew we'd be magic together, and now I know it for certain.

Since the first night we were together in his room in Malibu, I've thought about how he said public scenes are one of his favorite things. I'm fairly resolute in not wanting to participate at Club Quantum. I'm not so liberated, at least not yet, that I'm ready to perform in front of my closest friends and colleagues. Hayden says I may get there someday, but until that day comes, I've arrived at another plan to bring that element into our relationship in a way I'm comfortable with. At least I think I am. I won't know for sure until we actually do it.

We arrive at the room Devon has designated for us, and he holds the door for me, winking as I walk past him, leading Hayden. The door clicks shut behind us, and we're alone. We've got fifteen minutes to get our act together before Devon opens the room to spectators. Showtime. I reach up to remove the blindfold, and Hayden blinks furiously until he's able to focus on where we are.

"What the hell, Addison? What's all this?"

"This," I say, taking a deep breath, "is your birthday present." I reach behind me to unzip the black dress I'm wearing, letting it drop to the floor. Underneath I've worn the sexiest lingerie I could find, complete with a lace-up corset, sheer black thigh-high stockings, a garter belt and a thong that barely covers my freshly waxed mound. I've topped off my outfit with four-inch spike heels.

Upon seeing my getup, his eyes go wide and his mouth forms an O as all the oxygen leaves his body in one long exhale. "Where the hell are we right now?"

"Black Vice. Devon was gracious enough to lend us a room for your birthday present."

"Which is?"

"A public scene tonight and a one-year membership to Black Vice so we can do it again any time you want to." From my purse, I produce the membership card I got for him as well as a black face mask I bought so no one will recognize him. I have one for myself, too. Devon was willing to let me vouch for Hayden's health since I'm the only one he'll be with at the club. "I asked Devon for a few of your favorite things, but I left the rest up to him. Even I don't know everything that's here for us to use."

He takes the mask from me and examines it carefully. "You're serious."

"Very serious."

"You don't have to do this—"

I take a step toward him and cover his lips with mine. Thanks to the heels, I'm able to reach his mouth without having to stretch too much. "I *want* to do this. I want to do it for you. Happy birthday."

He looks at me with so much love in those blue eyes that are rarely as cold as they used to be before he had me to warm him up. "You already had a party for me. You didn't have to do this, too."

"This is our own not-so-private private party. Unless you don't want to…"

"Oh, I want to. You bet your sweet, sexy ass I want to."

There he is, my strong, confident Dom, who has shown me heights of pleasure I never knew possible until I seduced him. He wraps his arms around me, his hands cupping my ass cheeks and squeezing.

I reach up to unbutton his shirt. "You're overdressed for this party."

He nuzzles my neck, setting off a wildfire on the surface of my skin. "Before I forget to tell you, this is the best birthday I've ever had."

"I'm so glad to hear that. It's the first of many great birthdays you're going to have."

"I can't wait. I love you so much, Addison. Just when I think I've got you figured out, you surprise the living fuck out of me."

I smile widely. "Don't get too comfortable, my love."

He rubs his enormous erection against my pubic bone. "I'm very *un*comfortable at the moment, and you're going to be, too."

I give him a coy look. "Now that you have me here, whatever will you do with me?"

He makes a closer inspection of the room, noting the spanking bench I requested as well as the ropes that are coiled and ready for him. I had to do some research to find out his preferred brand, and judging by his smile, I got it right. I always want to get it right for him. I strip him down to boxer briefs and run my fingertips over the muscles on his chest and abdomen. His cock is so hard, the tip sticks out of the waistband of his underwear, but I make no move to touch him there, as much as I want to. This is his scene to direct as he sees fit, and I can't wait to see what he'll do.

"I see that you've seen to your own needs by requesting the spanking bench."

As he knows, I've become an utter slave to his "punishments." I'm addicted to the thrill of his hand landing on my ass, heating me from the outside. Blinking rapidly, I affect an innocent expression and pretend to have no idea what he means.

He laughs as he helps me into the mask and arranges me over the bench, adjusting it to my height and seeing to my comfort the way he always does. I'm no longer afraid that I can't handle what he wants. He's shown me I can handle anything as long as I'm with him. It never occurs to me that he'll cause me more pain than I can take or that I'll disappoint him.

In the weeks since our engagement, he's been more relaxed, quicker to laugh, unburdened and generally happier than I've ever seen him. If I had to guess, he's no longer concerned about disappointing me either.

"Comfortable?" he asks.

"Uh-huh."

The soft ding of a bell indicates that our room is no longer private.

"Do you know what that means?" I ask him.

"Yep. Do you?"

"Yes. Are there people watching?"

"A few."

I try not to think about how I must look to the spectators with my ass in the air and my legs spread. I'm about to ask him how many people are watching when his hand comes down hard on my right ass cheek. He gives the left side a similar smack before he moves around to the head of the bench. His bare cock nudges at my mouth, and I take him in, sucking and tonguing the head as he pushes deeper into my throat. He's taught me how to open my throat to let him in, but it's difficult to do at this angle.

Of course he knows that and settles for shallower thrusts as he fists handfuls of my hair. I almost forget people are watching, that they can see my ass reddened from his handprints. What do I care who's watching or what they can see when I've got my lips stretched around Hayden's magnificent cock?

Then he's gone again, and I hear him rustling around on the left side of the room, presumably where Devon has supplied us with a "variety of toys," as I requested.

"Your friend Devon was very creative in what he left for us."

"How so?"

"You'll have to wait and see." I feel his cool, slick fingers on my ass, and brace myself. He always plugs my ass when we scene together. Sometimes he also fucks me there. I've grown to love that almost as much as I love when he spanks me and clamps my nipples. I surprise myself every day with the cravings he inspires in me.

The plug is huge and doesn't feel all that different than he does when he fucks my ass. I grit my teeth, determined to take it no matter how difficult it may be. By the time the plug is fully seated, I'm sweating profusely. And then it begins to vibrate, and I cry out from sensations I'm experiencing for the first time.

Hayden tugs my cheeks apart and licks me from back to front, and I come hard the second his tongue connects with my clit. He spanks my ass, reminding me that my orgasm belongs to him. I've been working on better controlling my reactions, but I'm not there yet. He says it can take forever for all he cares, but that's because he loves punishing me so much.

He pushes his huge cock into my pussy, making me scream as he works his way in, one inch at a time.

That we're doing this for an audience is secondary to what we're doing to each other. After a while, I forget all about the people watching because I'm so focused on him and what he's making me feel that there's no room for any other thoughts in my head. He fucks me hard, and I come again. He withdraws the plug in a slow, agonizing battle that has me on the verge of yet another orgasm. Then he pushes his cock into my ass as he pinches my clit, and I come, shrieking from the incredible pleasure.

I can't believe we're doing this, of all things, in front of an audience, but knowing people are watching makes it that much hotter than it usually is. His cock is deep inside my ass when he reaches around to cup my breasts, lifting me so my back is to his chest as he pounds into me.

I'm coming almost constantly, and he hasn't even gotten to his ropes yet.

With him throbbing deep inside my most private place, I'm thrilled that my surprise is such a hit, and I'm so thankful to have the rest of my life to spend with this extraordinary man who makes me feel more than I ever thought I could.

"Love you so much, baby," he whispers gruffly in my ear. Ever since the night in Mexico when he said it for the first time, he can't say it enough. "Thank you for this. Thank you for everything."

He pinches my nipples and thrusts into me, taking me to the place I can only go with him. The only word I can think of to describe it is rapture. Utter and complete rapture.

\*\*\*

Keep reading for a look at *Ravenous*, Quantum Book 5...

# Ravenous

## Quantum Series, Book 5

# Chapter 1

*Ellie*

While everyone celebrates Hayden and Addie's engagement, I slip out a side door, needing some air after watching the emotional reunion between Addie and her dad and his acceptance, finally, of Hayden. I'm so happy for both of them. I think they're great together, and Hayden needs someone like Addie to keep him grounded and sane. Not to mention after the shameful way he was raised, he deserves to be someone's true love.

As I walk out to the far end of the pool deck and look down on the sea below, I can't help but wonder whether I deserve the same. Watching my brother fall madly in love with Natalie, and now Hayden and Addie, who've gone from an unexpected kiss at the Oscars a few weeks ago to engaged, I've begun to question whether I'm ever going to get my turn. Both my sisters have been married for years to great guys I would've hand-chosen for them. For the longest time, Flynn and I were the Godfrey family holdouts, and now he's gone over to the dark side, too.

Though I suppose it's not really the dark side if the perpetually happy, silly grin on his face is any indication of his true feelings about love and marriage. Natalie is the ideal woman for him, and I'm thrilled for them. I used to worry he would never find anyone real or genuine in the fishbowl in which he lives. But Natalie is as real as it gets, and I adore her. My whole family does. Everyone is happy.

That leaves me as the lone holdout in the Godfrey family. At Flynn's wedding, I heard my mother tell someone she's proud of me for focusing on my career. My sisters both have successful careers—Aimee owns a dance studio, and Annie is an attorney—*and* they have beautiful families, too. They make it look easy, when I know it's anything but.

Annie and Hugh have been together since high school, and Aimee met Trent in college. Flynn was married briefly in his early twenties to "Valerie the Hag," as my sisters and I called her back when she nearly ruined our beloved "baby" brother's life with her shenanigans.

I've never even come close to getting married. Truth be told, I've never come close to being in love.

Guys are a mystery to me. No matter how great one of them may seem, there's always a downside. I've dated guys who were handsome and charming and said all the right things, only to find out they were saying all the right things to a lot of women—at the same time. Then you have social guy's alter ego, who is no less frustrating. You know the type—you have to pull every thought out of his head because God forbid he should share anything voluntarily.

I've dated the bad boys, the ones who make a woman's motor run on full steam, before their "badness" evolves into regular old bad behavior that's an instant turnoff. Then you've got your run-of-the-mill commitment-phobes, the ones who tell you from the outset they aren't looking to settle down—ever. Why should they when they can have a different woman every night of the week?

Recently, I had the misfortune of getting mixed up with a whole new type right when I thought I'd seen it all. You know what that guy was after, other than the obvious? An introduction to my famous brother. Yeah, being used to get to my brother was a real blast, and frankly, he turned me off on dating in general. I'd rather be by myself forever than be used to get to my famous family members.

Or so I tell myself… Then I'll see my adorable nieces and nephews, my ovaries melting from the craving for a child of my own, and I'm reminded that I'm not getting any younger. Soon I'll be thirty-six, which isn't ancient by anyone's standards, but my eggs are definitely on a timer.

Now there's a cheerful thought.

Between you and me, I'm thinking about having a baby on my own. Why not? It's the twenty-first century, after all, and I have friends who've done it. One of my college friends had twins by herself and then met a single dad two years later. They're married now and delighted with their combined family.

Not that I think having a baby would improve my luck on the dating front, but I'm sick of waiting for something that probably isn't going to happen, and I don't want to wake up someday, after that timer has gone off, and realize I missed my opportunity to be a mother.

I've gone so far as to look into what would be involved and have a doctor willing to work with me to make it happen. I'm due to see him again when I get home from Mexico, and the thought of actually doing it makes my skin tingle with excitement and fear and a million other emotions. I haven't told anyone, even my sisters, who usually know everything, but I suppose I'll have to cue in my parents before I actually go through with it.

I giggle at the thought of showing up at my parents' Beverly Hills home, thirty-six, single and pregnant.

"What's so funny, love?" a voice asks from behind me. And not just any voice, but the panty-melting voice with the British accent that makes me swoon every time I'm around him. I once talked him into reading *The Night Before Christmas* to my family just so I could listen to the way he said the familiar words. My only regret is that I didn't think to record it.

I turn to face Jasper, my brother's close friend and business partner, who has also become my good friend during my tenure as a production manager at Quantum. Oh Jasper… tall, blond, muscular in a lanky sort of way, handsome as sin, talented as all get-out and a manwhore of the highest order. He's the proverbial pot of honey when it comes to women, attracting them as effortlessly as he breathes. Speaking of a man who will never settle for just one when he could have them all, Jasper Autry fits that bill to a T.

"I was just thinking about something funny that happened at home," I say in response to his question, because I can't very well tell him I was thinking about egg timers and ovulation cycles.

"Care to share the joke?"

"It was one of those had-to-be-there things with the kids."

"Ah, I see." He hands me one of the two mimosas he brought outside with him.

"Thank you."

"You're welcome." His golden-brown eyes are always full of mischief, as if he's got a huge secret he's dying to tell me, or at least that's how it seems to me. Now is no different. Those amazing eyes are alight with glee. "How about our boy Hayden and our lovely Addie? Gotta say I never thought I'd see him so domesticated."

"He's happy," I say more sharply than I intended. "Nothing wrong with that."

Jasper's brow lifts in response to my tone. He's not used to women speaking sharply to him. He's far more accustomed to them dropping their panties at his feet than talking back to him. "Nothing wrong indeed."

"Sorry. I just mean it's nice to see. That's all."

"Believe it or not, I agree, even if my mates are falling like dominoes these days."

"You might not want to drink the water."

"Drinking the water is never a good idea in Mexico."

I crack up laughing, which doesn't surprise me. He makes me laugh frequently. His endlessly witty take on life is one of many things I enjoy about him.

"I couldn't help but notice you looked awfully pensive out here staring at the deep blue sea all by your lonesome. What's on your mind, love?"

God, I want to tell him. I want to tell *someone*, and why not Jasper, my good friend who I trust to keep my confidences confidential? He's not in my family. He's not one of my girlfriends who would try to talk me out of it, certain that my Mr. Right is just around the next corner waiting to be found. In fact, he might be the perfect person to test this idea on.

"If I tell you, do you promise not to breathe a word of it to anyone, especially Flynn?"

"Of course I won't tell anyone. Let's not forget you could fairly ruin me with the secrets you've kept for me over the years."

"This is very true."

He takes me by the arm and leads me to one of the double lounge chairs on the pool deck. "Step into my office. My initial consultation is free of charge, but only for the best of friends."

"You are far too charming for your own good."

"My mother says the same thing. I say I'm just charming *enough* for my own good."

Rolling my eyes at his outrageousness, I curl up on the lounge and take a deep drink from the glass, seeking some much-needed liquid courage.

"Now tell me this deep dark secret before I expire from curiosity."

With the moment of truth upon me, I blow out a deep breath, hoping to calm nerves that are going bat-shit crazy. "I'm thinking about… No, wait, that's not true. I'm not thinking about it anymore. I'm actually going to do it."

His brows lift, and I swear he stops breathing.

"I'm going to have a baby."

"You…" His gaze falls to my flat abdomen. "Like… Are you already… Oh. Well. Okay, then."

I can't help but laugh at his stuttering commentary. "No, I'm not pregnant at the moment, but I hope to be. Soon."

"Forgive me for asking the obvious, but I can't help but notice you seem to be stubbornly single. So who's the lucky guy who gets to father this child of yours?"

"Don't know yet. That's part of what has to be decided when I get back to LA. I've got thousands of men to choose from, and I have to decide whether I want looks over brains or maybe I'll get lucky and find both in one donor."

He closes his eyes and sighs. "Ellie…" Opening his eyes, he says, "For the love of God and all that's holy, you do *not* need to resort to a sperm bank to find a father for your child."

A flash of anger hits me. "When you're a single woman who wants to have a baby, you *do* need to 'resort' to a sperm bank."

"You, love, could have any man you want."

"That's not true. It's different for women. We can't run around the way you guys do without getting a nasty reputation, especially when our parents and brother are household names. It's not as easy as you think."

"I hadn't really looked at it from that point of view. I can see how that might pose a bit of a challenge. And P.S. we don't 'run around,' as you say."

"What would you call it?" I ask in the drollest tone I own.

A charming smile lights up his gorgeous face. "Having fun?"

"I've tried that route. Hasn't been all that fun. I'm done waiting for lightning to strike. I want a baby, and I'm running out of time to make that happen. I'm doing this." At some point during the getaway to Mexico, my plan moved from *maybe* to *definitely*.

"And you're sure you want to do it this way?"

"I'm sure that this is the only way to do it in light of my perpetually single status."

"It's not the only way."

I'm almost afraid to look at him, and when I do, the calculating look he gives me makes my skin heat with awareness of him. "What do you mean?"

"You could ask an old friend who is both handsome *and* smart, not to mention incredibly charming, to provide the start-up 'capital' you require to get your project off the ground."

I'm flabbergasted by what he's suggesting, but I can't show him that. I can't take the chance he might be joking. "If only I knew someone who fit that bill."

"You do. You know just the guy."

My heart is beating so hard and so fast, I fear I might hyperventilate. "And this guy would be willing to provide his 'capital' for such a project?"

"Under the right conditions."

After a long pause, I say, "What conditions?"

"It happens the old-fashioned way. No laboratories, turkey basters or test tubes, just hot, sweaty, no-holds-barred *capital infusion*."

My body ignites at the images that scorch my brain in the scope of five seconds. Holy shit.

Have I gone blind, deaf and dumb, or is Jasper Autry telling me he wants to sleep with me—and make a baby with me? "Are you for real right now?"

"My darling Ellie, I have never been more 'for real' in my entire life than I'm being right now." He leans in closer to me, so close that I stop breathing. "Say yes."

I swallow hard. "Are there other conditions?"

"Only a few."

"I'm listening."

"When you're with me, you're with *only* me."

"Same goes."

Nodding, he says, "Same goes. And we do this my way or not at all."

"What does that mean?" I ask, my voice squeaking.

"I'm in charge in bed."

I'm suddenly so turned on that I'm concerned there'll be a wet spot on the lounge chair when I get up. "What if I'm not into that?"

"Then there's no deal."

I take a moment to process what he's saying. He's dominant in bed. Oh. My. God. Clearing my throat, I say, "What about custody of the output of your input?"

Smiling, he says, "All yours with liberal visitation for the capital contributor."

"Would he or she know that you're the contributor?"

"If that's what you want."

"And you'd be amenable to legally binding documents that spell out these things in advance?"

With his finger on my chin, he forces me to look directly into his eyes. "I'd be amenable to anything that gets the supremely sexy and endlessly untouchable Ellie Godfrey into my bed."

Now imagine that sentence said in the sexiest fucking British accent you've *ever* heard. I know, *right*?! What the hell else can I say to that but, "Okay."

"Okay, what?"

"We have a deal."

He gifts me with the sexy smile that made a cinematographer into a worldwide celebrity. "Suddenly, I can't wait to go home."

\*\*\*

Watch for more on Ellie and Jasper's story, *Ravenous*, Quantum Series book 5, coming later in 2016. Make sure you're on my email newsletter mailing list and following the Quantum Reader Group to be kept informed of release dates for future Quantum books!

# Acknowledgments

A very special thank-you to the readers who decided to give M.S. Force a chance last year with the initial Quantum Trilogy and begged me to write Hayden and Addie's story. I hope you loved their story as much as I loved writing it. If you did, consider leaving a review at the retailer of your choice and/or on Goodreads to help other readers discover the series. You can join the Rapturous Reader Group at www.facebook.com/groups/Rapturous4/ to talk about the book with spoilers allowed. Also join the Quantum Reader Group at www.facebook.com/groups/QuantumReaders/ to be among the first to hear news about the series.

I love writing the Quantum Series and have many more stories in mind for the cast. I'm looking forward to writing Ellie and Jasper's story, *Ravenous*, in 2016. Stay up-to-date on the plans for future books by joining my mailing list at marieforce.com on the left side where it asks for your name and email address.

Thank you to Team HTJB for all you do to keep me sane: Julie Cupp, CMP, Lisa Cafferty, CPA, Holly Sullivan, Isabel Sullivan, Nikki Colquhoun, Cheryl Serra, Courtney Lopes and Ashley Lopez. Special thanks to my husband, Dan, for his daily support of my writing career and to our kids, Emily and Jake, who make me laugh. Love to my longtime beta readers Anne Woodall, Kara Conrad and Ronlyn Howe and to Holly, who is always my very first reader. Thank you to my copy editor Linda Ingmanson and my proofreader Joyce Lamb for your hard work on my books.

My readers gave me an absolutely incredible 2015, and I'm looking forward to a fantastic 2016. Thank you for your support of my books. I love you all!

xoxo

Marie

# OTHER TITLES BY MARIE FORCE

*Other Titles by M.S. Force*

**The Quantum Series**

Book 1: Virtuous

Book 2: Valorous

Book 3: Victorious

Book 4: Rapturous

*Contemporary Romances Available from Marie Force*

**The Gansett Island Series**

McCarthys of Gansett Island Boxed Set, Books 1-3

McCarthys of Gansett Island Boxed Set, Books 4-6

McCarthys of Gansett Island Boxed Set, Books 7-9

Book 1: Maid for Love

Book 2: Fool for Love

Book 3: Ready for Love

Book 4: Falling for Love

Book 5: Hoping for Love

Book 6: Season for Love

Book 7: Longing for Love

Book 8: Waiting for Love

Book 9: Time for Love
Book 10: Meant for Love
Book 10.5: Chance for Love,
*A Gansett Island Novella*
Book 11: Gansett After Dark
Book 12: Kisses After Dark
Book 13: Love After Dark
Book 14: Celebration After Dark
Book 15: Desire After Dark

*The Treading Water Series*
10th Anniversary Treading Water Boxed Set
Book 1: Treading Water
Book 2: Marking Time
Book 3: Starting Over
Book 4: Coming Home

*The Green Mountain Series*
Book 1: All You Need Is Love
Book 2: I Want to Hold Your Hand
Book 3: I Saw Her Standing There
Book 4: And I Love Her
Novella: *You'll Be Mine*
Book 5: It's Only Love
Book 6: Ain't She Sweet

*Single Titles*
The Singles Titles Boxed Set
Georgia on My Mind
True North
The Fall

Everyone Loves a Hero

Love at First Flight

Line of Scrimmage

*Romantic Suspense Novels Available from Marie Force*
*The Fatal Series*

One Night With You, *A Fatal Series Prequel Novella*

Book 1: Fatal Affair

Book 2: Fatal Justice

Book 3: Fatal Consequences

Book 3.5: Fatal Destiny, *the Wedding Novella*

Book 4: Fatal Flaw

Book 5: Fatal Deception

Book 6: Fatal Mistake

Book 7: Fatal Jeopardy

Book 8: Fatal Scandal

Book 9: Fatal Frenzy

*Single Title*

The Wreck

# ABOUT THE AUTHOR

M.S. Force is the erotic alter-ego of *New York Times* bestselling author Marie Force. The initial Quantum Trilogy was M.S. Force's first foray into erotic romance, but it won't be the last! All three of the first Quantum books were *New York Times* bestsellers, and the Quantum Trilogy becomes the Quantum Series with *Rapturous*, book 4, Hayden and Addie's story, out on January 19, 2016.

With more than 4 million books sold, Marie Force, is the *New York Times, USA Today* and *Wall Street Journal* bestselling, award-winning author of 40 contemporary romances. Her *New York Times* bestselling self-published Gansett Island Series has sold 2.2 million e-books since *Maid for Love* was released in 2011. She is also the author of the *New York Times* bestselling Fatal Series from Harlequin, as well as the *New York Times* bestselling Green Mountain Series from Berkley, among other books and series, including the new Quantum Series, written as M.S. Force.

Her goals in life are simple—to finish raising two happy, healthy, productive young adults, to keep writing books for as long as she possibly can and to never be on a flight that makes the news.

Join Marie's mailing list for news about new books and upcoming appearances in your area. Follow her on Twitter @marieforce and on Facebook. Join one of Marie's many reader groups. Contact Marie at *marie@marieforce.com*. Subscribe to her new blog to hear the latest and greatest news, including giveaways and other great prizes. Go to the blog at http://blog.marieforce.com and enter your email address on the upper right-hand side.

CPSIA information can be obtained at www.ICGtesting.com
Printed in the USA
BVOW11s1113281215

431155BV00001B/1/P